299 Days III: The Community

by

Glen Tate

Book Three in the ten book 299 Days series.

Dystopian Fiction & Survival Nonfiction

www.PrepperPress.com

299 Days III: The Community

ISBN 978-0615720968

Printed in the United States of America.

Prepper Press Trade Paperback Edition: November 2012

Prepper Press is a division of Kennebec Publishing, LLC

- To the real "Morrells" and "Colsons," who are the best neighbors a guy could have.

299 Days: The Community, the third book in the *299 Days* series, reunites Grant Matson with his family after his wife, children, and in-laws accept that the only way to survive the Collapse is to flee the comfort of their suburban lives and join him at his isolated cabin in the woods. With riots becoming more violent, power outages more widespread, and the military crumbling, Grant and others throughout Washington State realize they must organize if they want to endure.

From the secure confines of the relocated state capitol building, to a rural self-sustaining farm, to the developing community of Pierce Point, *299 Days: The Community* explores the mental, emotional, and physical changes everyone must make to adapt to a collapsed society.

The years of preparing and training position Grant to lead Pierce Point as he begins to navigate complex interpersonal dynamics and unpredictable situations to help build a new community that can withstand the threats closing in on them.

Will people join forces or stand alone? Can communities successfully organize themselves in times of chaos? Will what is left of government help those who cannot help themselves? And if so, at what cost?

This ten-book series follows Grant Matson and others as they navigate through a partial collapse of society. Set in Washington State, this series depicts the conflicting worlds of preppers, those who don't understand them, and those who fear and resent them.

For more about this series, free chapters, and to be notified about future releases, please visit **www.299days.com**.

Books from the 299 Days series published as of this printing:

Book One – *299 Days: The Preparation*

Book Two – *299 Days: The Collapse*

Book Three – *299 Days: The Community*

Book Four – *299 Days: The Stronghold*

Book Five – *299 Days: The Visitors*

Book Six – *299 Days: The 17th Irregulars*

Book Seven – *299 Days: The Change of Seasons*

Book Eight – *299 Days: The War*

About the Author:

Glen Tate has a front row seat to the corruption in government and writes the *299 Days* series from his first-hand observations of why a collapse is coming and predictions on how it will unfold. Much like the main character in the series, Grant Matson, the author grew up in a rural and remote part of Washington State. He is now a forty-something resident of Olympia, Washington, and is a very active prepper. "Glen" keeps his real identity a secret so he won't lose his job because, in his line of work, being a prepper and questioning the motives of the government is not appreciated.

Chapter 70

Car Wheels on a Gravel Road

(May 7)

Off in the distance, Grant heard the unmistakable sound of car wheels on a gravel road. There was a low rumble with the crackle of the tires on the crushed gravel. Then he heard a radio squawk. It was one of those little Motorolas Grant used in the Cedars. Paul had it on his belt during watch.

It was John. "We have visitors. Lots of them. Come quick." They jumped up and headed toward the guard shack. Chip had an AR and Paul had a shotgun. Mark had his revolver and Tammy was unarmed. As usual, Grant had his pistol. His AR was in the cabin.

He was scared to death. "Visitors … lots of them," sounded like a motorcycle gang. It was only about 100 yards to the guard shack. Grant had never run so fast; the adrenaline was pumping.

They ran out onto the road, exposing themselves. Grant and Chip quickly found some cover. Paul, just stood in the middle of the road, panting. Mark and Tammy stood by him, helping their son.

John had his 30-30 with a scope aimed down the road. The sound of the cars on the gravel road got louder. They were moving slowly. Was that a good sign or a bad sign? Were they slowly advancing, like professionals?

Then he saw it. The most beautiful sight ever: Pow's white Hummer. And, oh goodness, Drew and Eileen's car. Then, Lisa's Tahoe! Wait. It must be a car that looked like hers. It couldn't be hers. But, it had to be because that was Drew and Eileen's car!

It was hers! He recognized the license plate. No way!

Grant was elated. He ran up to John yelling, "Don't shoot. They're friendlies!" John lowered his rifle and Grant ran down the gravel road toward Pow's Hummer, holstering his pistol as he went, which was hard to do when running. Pow flashed his headlights. It was them!

Grant ran up to Pow's Hummer, looked in to make sure it was him and kept going right past the other vehicles to Lisa's Tahoe.

He saw her in there. The kids, too! Grant tried to open her door. It was locked. Of course. They had driven through a war zone to get there. She unlocked the door. He ripped the door open and screamed, "Thank God you're here! Thank God!"

Grant started hugging Lisa. He looked her straight in the eye and said, "There's the hug I meant to give you the other night."

She started bawling. The kids were screaming, "Daddy!" They were getting out of the Tahoe and jumping around with Grant and Lisa. Pow got out and watched. He felt a tear roll down his cheek. The other guys on the Team were taking it all in; Grant reunited with this family, all the great cabins, and the beautiful scenery. Pow had told them this place was great. He wasn't kidding.

The next hour or so was a blur to Grant. Drew and Eileen were crying, too. Grant was showing all the cool stuff at the cabin that would allow them to make it. Make it as a family. Things like the guard shack and telling them about fishing, Mary Anne's canning, the nightly BBQs, the neighbors, and introducing the Team to the neighbors. It reminded Grant of his bachelor party, which had all of his friends from the various phases of his life. Grant was the one guy all the guests had in common. They didn't all know each other, but they all knew Grant. He was the common thread and all his friends were in one place. It felt great.

Then something strange happened. Something Grant never saw coming. He was pissed at Lisa. She was pissed at him. Once the initial elation wore off, they were mad at each other. It made no sense, except that both of them had been mad at each other for days. Intensely mad. The maddest they'd ever been in their whole lives.

Grant was mad at Lisa for not coming out to the cabin earlier, for not being thrilled about getting the cabin, and for not understanding, let alone approving, of his prepping for what had happened. He had been right the whole time and she had been fighting him the whole time.

Lisa was mad at Grant for abandoning the family and leaving them in danger. Just taking off for politics. For being part of the WAB troublemakers instead of living a normal life. For not being a normal lawyer living in a normal subdivision and enjoying normal things, like golf. No, Grant had to be a terrorist and live out in the woods somewhere. He had been so worthless around the house for so many years and now he was Mr. "Let's Go Live Out in a Cabin"?

So, after about the first hour, things got tense between Grant and Lisa. They both kept telling themselves that they were together and safe and that's all that mattered, but they both couldn't help wanting to say to each other, "this worked out despite all the stupid

2

shit you did."

It was like an old wound. Like scar tissue. There had been wounds from the past. They were healing, but the scar tissue was there and the injury was still tender. Grant and Lisa felt themselves falling into their old debating routines with each other; Grant being pissed that Lisa didn't support his prepping and Lisa being pissed that Grant had caused so much trouble for the family.

The hug. This is just like the hug. Don't make the same mistake again, Grant told himself. "In marriage, it's better to be happy than to be right," Grant remembered his Grandpa telling him. The scars needed to heal for good. No more of that. Grant and Lisa didn't have the time or the luxury of bickering about who was right. They had to pull through as a family right now. Bickering and being "right" could get them killed. At a minimum, it would make them miserable out in the boonies with nothing to do but argue. No. That was done.

"Honey, I'm sorry for all that's happened," Grant said when no one was around. "We need to get along out here and I'm willing to do whatever it takes to make that happen." He held his arms out for a hug.

Lisa was reluctant. She knew that hugging him meant the argument was over. She wanted to tell him what an asshole he was. She wanted to tell him how much harder life would be out here without all her stuff, but she was tired. She was sick of all the fighting. She'd had the most stressful day of her life today and wanted to have a husband again. Maybe not the "normal" suburban husband she had before all this. But her husband. He wasn't so bad, after all. He had prepared a safe place for them with all they needed. Maybe not all they wanted, but all they needed. He was kinda cute, too. He was the love of her life, even though she still had no idea why.

She hugged him. It was warm. It was soft. It felt like home. Not a house kind of home. But the comfort of being with the ones you love. She still wouldn't say she was sorry; he would figure out she was because she was hugging him. That's all he would get. After all he'd put her through, an out loud "sorry" was not going to happen. He'd put up with it. He always had.

Grant felt like things were complete. His family was supposed to be here. They would be able to be a family again. They could walk the beach, have campfires and do all the things he thought they would be doing when he first got the cabin. Before Lisa decided that she would hate the place. Before the economy tanked. Before the country collapsed. When no one would listen to him. Chalk it up to a horrible couple of years. Maybe the worst they'd ever have. She kissed him. That was the "sorry" she couldn't say out loud. Grant knew it and Lisa knew that he knew it.

Things were different now. They would be a family. Everything else was details. That hug lasted a long time. Okay, work time. Grant realized that the Team needed to unload their stuff and settle in. He found Mark and asked him for the key to the yellow cabin. Grant gathered the Team. He walked them the few yards to the yellow cabin and said, very dramatically, "Gentlemen, here are your new quarters." He unlocked the door and they went into a very nice cabin. The guys were blown away. There were three beds and a nice couch; sleeping arrangements for each one of them. A nice kitchen, a great view, an amazing place.

"Wow, it's even better on the inside than on the outside when you showed it to me," Pow said.

"Whaddya think, guys?" Grant asked the Team, knowing the answer.

"Unreal, man," said Wes.

"Fabulous," said Bobby.

"I don't know what to say," said Scotty.

Pow just nodded.

Mark, Paul, Chip, and John offered to help unload the guys' stuff.

"What the hell? Did you bring an armory with you?" Mark asked when he saw all their gear.

The guys just nodded.

"Well, good," Eileen said. She had changed during that trip. She could feel her farm girl roots coming back to her. She knew how much safer they were at Pierce Point than back in the city. This didn't seem weird anymore. It felt like a blessing.

Chapter 71

A Partial Breakdown with Patches of Normalcy

(May 7)

How could so much be going so wrong all at once? Jeanie Thompson asked herself.

The power was going out for a few hours at a time every few days. Camp Murray, where the seat of Washington State government had been relocated after the state capitol had all the rioting and protests, still had a constant source of power. But the rest of the state didn't.

The FBI told Jeanie and the other people at Camp Murray that it was Chinese hackers attacking the software that ran the electrical grid; the program that routed power. If extra electricity was sent to the wrong place by the hacker, it would overload the system and could cause a cascading failure. It would fry the system, which would take days to repair *if* parts could be flown in and weeks with all the highway traffic jams. To thwart the surges, the Feds had to shut down the power for a while until the software was secure again. So, technically, the Feds were the ones turning off the power. Wait till *that* news gets out, Jeanie thought. People will be pissed. At the Feds.

The Feds, to their credit, had detected that the hackers had been repeatedly sending the extra power into California and various military bases in the West. The hackers had been doing the same to the East Coast and DC. Those seemed to be the two regions with the outages.

No reliable electrical source meant that the internet wasn't working. Oh, how reliant America had become on the internet. Government and most businesses couldn't function without it.

Everyone was sent home. Jeanie, the communications director for the State Auditor, didn't even want to think about the economic damage this was doing. No one was working and nothing was getting done. Maybe this was one reason why the stores were running out of everything. Their inventory was restocked via the internet.

The Feds were doing all they could to get gasoline out to the cities. They had commandeered all the gas trucks. They had a plan in place for this and, for once, the plan worked pretty well. Now the Feds controlled all the fuel in the country. They put the refineries on full production and started running truckloads of fuel. They drove them with police and military escorts.

At first, people moved over to accommodate the emergency vehicles. They weren't anymore, though. People were getting meaner and tougher. The roads were packed. The police and military escorts were needed because that fuel was worth its weight in gold. When a fuel truck would get bogged down in traffic, angry, violent motorists who ran out of gas would demand gas from the trucks. The police were shooting people who couldn't be subdued.

However—and this part really amazed Jeanie—there were some supplies getting through. Trucks were taking the back streets and some residents were helping them get through. Trips by semi were taking days instead of hours, but things were getting through. The fact that the food, gas, medicine, and other necessities were worth ten times what they were a few days ago helped. The market was an amazing thing. Everything was for sale, at the right price.

This meant that gangs were sprouting up. Not street gangs, although they were running wild without any police. White-collar gangs were taking advantage of the fact that the tanker of gasoline stalled in traffic in their neighborhood was now worth a million dollars. It was like stealing stalled armored cars full of cash with the keys in the ignition. In the cities, Russian and Asian gangs were the muscle behind the white collar gangs and were turning into the black market suppliers of everything. In the rural areas, which were much better off, local cops and related "good ol' boys" were taking things like semis of food and gas for "safekeeping." Gangs took many forms after the Collapse. The idea that a "gang" was the Crips or Bloods was so ... pre-Collapse.

Back in Washington State, the government was in a full chaotic panic. The police had been out fighting protests and looting, along with waves of crime for days. They were exhausted. Many cops were just leaving their posts and going home. Most would see if their families were okay, get some sleep and then try to go back out. But each day, fewer and fewer were reporting back for duty. With all the budget cuts of the past year, there weren't as many cops to start with. Many had decided that the lifelong employment and retirement they had been promised was another politician's lie and they had already been looking for something else.

The National Guard was in the same boat. Many guardsmen had been called up a few weeks prior for the "training," which was actually just preparation for the civil unrest that the Pentagon knew was coming. The Feds had done something a few years back that had never happened before: they stationed combat troops in the United States whose mission was to fight in the states. The military, of course, had about a million troops in the U.S., but they were assigned to commands whose mission was to fight overseas like Central Command, which covered the central part of the world, including the Middle East. A few years back, they created North Command to fight in North America. That action went largely unnoticed. NorthCom, as it became known, swung into action when the Collapse started. It strongly defended Washington, D.C. and coordinated federal combat troops to help state National Guard units.

But, fewer and fewer National Guardsmen were reporting for duty. Many were cops or others who were working their other jobs to the point of exhaustion. Others didn't want to leave their families during the crisis. Some tried to report for duty but got caught in the traffic jams.

Jeanie could see that the state government really had no idea what it was doing. She was talking to media all day long, giving the state spin. Things will be okay, we'll all pull through, people are helping their neighbors, terrorists are taking advantage of the disruptions, don't be a hoarder, and listen to the government for further information.

Even though Jeanie was in Chaos Central at the state's command post, she could see legitimate signs that not everyone was in a crisis. Oddly, most people were staying home from work, watching TV news, helping their neighbors, and eating the several days of food they normally had on hand in their pantries and refrigerators. It was not a complete breakdown of society. Things were bad, worse than anyone had ever seen in modern America, but not the end of the world. It was a partial breakdown with patches of normalcy.

Chapter 72

Closing the Parts Store

(May 7)

Steve Briggs was running out of inventory at his auto parts store. He hadn't seen a shipment in days. He was in the very isolated town of Forks, on the extreme northwest tip of Washington State, so he got his supplies in batches from a distribution company. The truck usually came on Tuesdays and Fridays. He hadn't seen one in a week.

The internet was out, so he had to phone in orders to the distributor's Seattle office. That seemed to take forever; he really missed the internet. The Seattle office seemed really shorthanded. The people he normally dealt with weren't at work. He was on hold a lot. Each day, the Seattle office told him that they couldn't get various parts from their California suppliers. He would have to make do with what he had in stock.

With the internet out, how could he process credit card orders? That's how most of his business was conducted. He could accept cash, but he paid his suppliers via credit that went through the internet. He couldn't just hand his distributor a bag of cash once the parts came.

He started wondering, if he and everyone else had to start paying for things in cash, would there be enough cash to do this? People didn't carry too much cash around anymore. They paid big bills, like a new clutch or car battery, with a debit or credit card. He did the same, like the year's worth of truck insurance he just paid for. So if everyone needed a lot more cash, where would it come from? The bank didn't have much. They kept some in tills, but a few days ago people started coming in and trying to get their money out of the bank. Besides, the bank had closed yesterday with the national bank holiday. So people only had the cash they had on hand. For some people, that was maybe $100. How would anyone buy things?

Then there were the prices. Everything was going up. It seemed like a 10% increase just from the week before. Now that everything seemed to being coming apart, prices went crazy. It wasn't "inflation" in the sense of "this costs a dollar more than last week"; it was "I hear they have these, but they're $100 now."

Steve would have to pass these increases on to his customers, which would be hard. The unemployment rate in Forks was…who knew? It was always high, but it recently seemed way higher than usual. Many people in town had government jobs of some kind, with the game department or the environmental agency. Some teachers had been laid off. Two of the police officers had been laid off, too. About the only government jobs that were untouched were at the government utility that supplied power and water in town.

But no one was going hungry. Almost everyone had deer meat in the freezer. Plenty of fish, too. If an older person didn't have any, neighbors and relatives would share, like they always had. Lots of people had gardens and canned. The one grocery store in town was already getting low on things, but that wasn't terribly unusual. Since it was an hour to the next town of any size, if a semi took an extra day to get there, people would notice it on the shelves.

Steve was most concerned about the older people on prescription medications. The little drug store in town, run by his neighbor, Jerry, was running low. Jerry said that some people really needed particular medicines and he was going to go into Port Angeles to get some.

Given all that was on TV about the looting in the cities, Steve was also worried about crime. There wasn't any increase in crime in Forks; at least so far there hadn't been. There never were enough police to do the job, even during normal times. People relied on each other. They knew everyone in town.

Some folks in town were concerned about the few Mexicans who lived in Forks. Not Steve. He knew them because they came into the parts store. They were mostly hard workers; family men. Just like Americans used to be.

Another reason Steve wasn't worried about crime in Forks, population 3,000, was that everyone had guns, though no one was carrying them. On the news, they had pictures of people carrying guns at neighborhood checkpoints. There was none of that in Forks.

The power outages weren't that big a deal. They were inconvenient, but not the end of the world. They had a generator at the small hospital and the old folks' home. The internet being down was hard on the businesses like Steve's and a few white-collar businesses, like the accountant and real estate office that couldn't do any work.

School was cancelled because everyone was glued to the TV, and parents wanted to be around their kids. Steve was glad school was cancelled. He liked having the kids home.

Steve was beginning to get concerned because the gas station

9

hadn't had a shipment in several days. He knew the underground tanks were big and could last for a while, but if he couldn't get parts, he knew that fuel supplies would be scarce because they both got to Forks the same way: semis. He wondered how long this would go on before things got back to normal. Then again, he had known this was coming. A country boy can survive.

Chapter 73

This Ain't Paddy Cakes Anymore

(May 7)

Tom Foster's home was near the historic district of downtown Olympia, within walking distance from the WAB offices. His family had been shut in their house for two days as the protests raged. They were nothing like the usual little protests they saw in the state capitol. These were more like mobs. It reminded him of the WTO riots in Seattle in 1999, but worse. Riot police, the smell of tear gas, broken glass everywhere, constant sirens. He'd been awake for most of those two days. He'd doze off for a few minutes and then wake up when he heard more sirens or yelling. He was starting to lose his grip on reality. He couldn't tell what was real and what might be a dream from when he dozed off.

His family was handling it well. His wife, Joyce, was scared, but not saying so. Even before all of this, she had been afraid that some loony leftist would attack her husband. They got death threats every so often.

Tom's son, Derek, was fifteen years old. He was a good kid and looked exactly like his dad. Derek was looking forward to defending his house against the people who seemed to hate his dad. He had even started carrying a bat around lately and would love to use it.

Tom had his gun; a 9mm Sig Sauer handgun. He was so glad he'd gotten that. It seemed crazy at the time, but now he understood why he needed it. He could not have slept at all if he hadn't had it.

They had enough food for a few days. They basically watched the place to see if anyone tried to break in. It wasn't random crime they were afraid of, although that was a concern. They were afraid that someone in the crowd of angry leftists would realize that evil Tom Foster of the Washington Association of Business "hate group," a group representing small businesses, was sitting right there. Mobs of union thugs had been "visiting" the homes of people they didn't like. Tom had not heard of any mobs attacking the families, but there wasn't a lot of specific news anymore. The news focused only on giant events like the Olympia protests and looting in Seattle. The national news constantly reported on the terrorists' strikes, the regional power outages and the Southern and mountain West states "opting out" of the federal government. Besides, even if the media found out that homes of "right wingers" had been attacked by the mobs, they probably wouldn't report it. It didn't fit into the media's general theme of "concerned public employees and vulnerable citizens expressing their anger at budget cuts."

Two days after the big protests started, Tom decided to finally venture out of his house. It was early morning and things were pretty quiet. Even union thugs had to take a rest, and protesting was probably some of the hardest work these government employees had done in a while. He tucked his gun into his pants and left while Joyce and Derek were asleep.

Things were okay for a few blocks around his house. The destruction seemed pretty contained to the offices downtown. WAB's beautiful brick office building was eight blocks from his house. As he got closer to his office, he became more and more reluctant to see what had happened. He knew the protestors would hit WAB's offices, but he could not believe what he saw two blocks from the office.

There was smoke rising up from the direction of WAB's offices. Oh, God. They didn't. Did they?

Tom started to run toward the office, but he could only jog because the gun in his belt would come out. So he jogged, holding his gun in his belt. He wondered if any of his employees were still in there. He had sent them all home, but maybe some came, anyway. He prayed not.

Tom got closer and could see all the windows smashed and swastikas spray-painted on the beautiful brick walls of the historic building. Were the swastikas to say that WAB were Nazis or were the protestors admitting they were fascist thugs? Tom knew that the protestors were too stupid to understand that they were the actual fascists. He concluded that they spray-painted the swastikas to make people think the occupants of the building were Nazis.

As Tom got closer, he was actually a bit relieved. The fire was pretty small. It was a brick office building, so the structure wasn't burning. It looked like papers and other combustibles inside the building were burning. That beautiful building now looked like a charred hull of its former greatness. It looked like a black eye on a beautiful woman.

Tom ran in and checked to see if anyone was in there. He pulled his gun out when he went through the front door. He remembered what Grant had told him about checking to make sure the safety was off when he wanted to use the gun. He found himself pointing the gun like he'd seen in the movies.

Tom ran through the office to see if anyone, friend or foe, was in there. It was empty. Thank God. He looked around at all the destruction. It was weirdly quiet in the office. The only sound was the soft crackle of small fires, and papers blowing around. No voices. No hum of office machines running. No phones ringing. Just soft crackling.

Now that he knew no one was in the building, Tom went to his office. He saw the pictures of his family on his desk had been smashed, which pissed him off. This wasn't just political anymore. It was personal. These assholes were trying to kill him and his family. He was going to try to kill them back.

Tom had always shied away from the "Patriot" and "Don't Tread On Me" side of the conservative movement. Every time he saw the Don't Tread on Me flag, he had become uncomfortable because it seemed to imply people couldn't wait to hang "Loyalists," like during the Revolutionary War. It was a little too … dramatic and violent. Not that he thought Patriots and those with a "Don't Tread On Me" flag were violent; he had been to Tea Party rallies and knew they weren't. It's just that there was an implied message that liberty must be restored by "any means necessary." That scared him. Not because he was afraid of a fight—he fought the government all day, every day—but because he didn't want to become a hater. He was concerned about people like Eric Benson, a young WAB lawyer, who seemed to have turned into haters and actually enjoyed the "we'll do what we have to do" part of the liberty movement. Tom knew how good people could ruin their lives with hatred.

His thinking around this changed quickly, though, when he saw his beloved WAB offices on fire. Now he understood the violence. "They're trying to kill me" kept running through his mind as he looked around his office, burning and trashed.

Violence? Why hold back on violence? It had already happened to him. He didn't start it. "This ain't paddy cakes anymore," he muttered to himself. This is a game for keeps. They wanted to kill him and his family. It's on.

In an instant, Tom's entire outlook changed. At his core, he was a "Patriot" and would protect his family "by any means necessary." He would try not to be a hater, but that seemed like a luxury in these times. Protecting his family and trying to restore liberty were more important than the ill effects of hating people. In fact, Tom thought, hating people might be necessary to have the strength and mental clarity to do the things that needed to be done. That was it: hate is a tool. A necessary tool.

Tom had to get out of the WAB building. He couldn't take all the destruction. He jogged back to his house, holding his gun in his belt. That gun felt different on the way back. On the way there, it had seemed so foreign and weird. A gun? Him? Carrying a gun?

Now, after seeing the destruction of the WAB building and realizing how much these people really hated him, that gun didn't feel weird anymore. It felt like a tool. A tool as necessary as hate.

After a block or two, Tom knew what he needed to do. It was time to get Ben and Brian's families, the senior WAB staff who would be targeted by the protestors or government or whomever, to the Prosser farm.

Tom snuck up on his house. He'd seen on TV too many times when people just walked into their house, only to have a bad guy waiting for them. He carefully entered the house.

His wife was in the kitchen crying. That sound always gets a guy's attention. He goes into problem-solving mode, to do what it takes to make that crying stop.

"What's wrong, honey?" Tom asked Joyce.

"They say you're a terrorist," she choked out through the tears. "A terrorist!"

What? Tom couldn't even understand what she was saying. He wasn't a terrorist.

Joyce pointed to her laptop on the kitchen counter. On the screen was a list titled "Persons of Interest." Under the "F"s was "Foster, Tom…Wash. Assn of Business."

Tom wasn't surprised. The political attacks had been increasing for months leading up to this. Before he saw the burned out WAB offices, this terrorist-list thing would have surprised him. Not now. It seemed mild compared to what he'd just seen.

"This is just a list of Persons of Interest. That's not a terrorist list," he said. He wanted to reassure his wife.

Joyce screamed, "Read the top of the list!" He did. It explained that the people on this list were "Persons of interest to the police for possible illegal activities, including domestic terrorism."

Huh? "Domestic terrorism"? That was like the environmental terrorists or the white supremacists or whatever. Not a business association. He kept reading. Sure enough he was on the same list as people described as "Red Brigades," "Skin Heads," "Animal Liberation Front," but also "Tea Party," "various 'Patriot groups," and "tax activists."

Tom looked for his name again. He couldn't believe he was on this list. Oh God. So were Ben and Brian. "Wash. Assn of Business" was by their names, too. Grant, too.

"We need to get the hell out of here," Tom said as he grabbed Joyce by the wrist. "Right now. We're going to the Prosser farm. They burned the office and trashed it. They're trying to kill us. Get Derek and let's go."

Joyce cried louder. Her grandfather had lived through the Holocaust and this seemed a lot like the story he told about leaving Holland.

Chapter 74

Mailroom Guy to the Rescue

(May 7)

The Prosser Farm was owned by the WAB mailroom guy, Jeff Prosser. It was between Olympia and Frederickson, a couple of roads off of Highway 101, and was hard to find, even with directions. There was a steep hill to climb before the road dipped down to Jeff's farm and his neighbors, all of whom were relatives. The farmhouse was down a long road and surrounded by a state forest. It was the perfect hideout.

Tom called Ben and Brian. Voice service was working, although it hadn't been the night before. He told them about the POI list and that they needed to go to the Prossers' like they had talked about two days before. They would meet at Tom's house. It was a central location. A little too close to the capitol where the protesting had been going on, but it was the plan and he didn't want to change things up. He wanted to get the hell out of there.

Joyce, Derek, and Tom were packing as quickly as they could. They threw clothes, computers, and medicines into their car. Joyce made sure their family photo albums were packed. She thought about her grandfather. Was she being dramatic? She hadn't slept in two days; maybe that was it. No, her husband was on a list of "terrorists" and his office had been burned only a few blocks away. How could it get any more dramatic?

It took about an hour to pack. Tom kept looking at the clock and out the doors and windows. He was sure a group of thugs with torches were coming. He had his gun in his belt. Would he be able to shoot someone trying to attack his family? Hell, yes. He'd shoot all of them. And like it. He had thought the Campaign Finance Commission suit against WAB was an attack on him. That seemed like child's play compared to this. He had never fought for his family; he had never had to, though. He was making up for lost time. He was so ready to kill those bastards. He just wanted his family to make it first.

Brian's family was the first to arrive. They came in Brian's car and Karen's minivan. The Trentons arrived soon after in one vehicle, Ben's Expedition. Brian's kids were fourteen and twelve, and Ben's were seven and four. Their kids had grown up together. They viewed Derek like an older brother.

It seemed so normal to have the Jenkins and Trentons pulling up to the Fosters. They did it every Super Bowl and Fourth of July, going to one of their houses or Grant Matson's house. Except, this time, it was eight in the morning and there was smoke in the distance. And they were all "terrorists."

They were all trying to calm each other and downplay what was happening. This was for the kids' benefit, so they would think that they were going out to a party, like the Super Bowl or Fourth of July, except at the Prosser farm this time.

Ben told the kids about all the horses and cows out there and how much fun they would have at the farm. The older kids knew something was up; they'd been watching the news the past few days. School had been closed. There had to be a reason for that and the sirens the past few days were surely related.

Ben was almost in a trance, watching his seven year old and four year old playing. He marveled at how innocent they were. They had no idea that the country they were born into was over. They would probably never know what liberty was.

"Unless the good guys win," Ben heard himself say. Right then and there, Ben decided that he would do whatever it took to give his country back to his kids. He would do it for them. He had been hoping that things would just work themselves out politically, but the past few days proved that would likely never happen.

Derek was doing a great job of keeping the kids calm. He knew exactly what was going on. When the kids would ask why they were going to a farm and when they could come back home, he would change the subject.

Ben, Tom, and Brian got together in the garage. "Did everyone bring their guns?" Tom asked, revealing the pistol tucked in his belt. Ben and Brian nodded. "On you?" Ben nodded. Brian didn't.

"Karen doesn't know I have that," Brian said. "It's in my suitcase."

"Not good enough," Ben said. "It needs to be on you," he said, pointing to the right cargo pocket on his shorts. "Your wife being pissed at you about a gun is the least of your concerns right now."

Brian was embarrassed. "You're right. I'll get it." To redeem himself with the guys, he said, "I brought my shotgun and all the shells I have." Brian's dad had given it to him in high school for duck hunting.

Some of the kids came into the garage, breaking up the meeting. The guys went into the house to round everyone up and didn't talk too much about what was happening. They didn't want to alarm their wives and children, and had decided to not tell the wives about the POI thing, although they knew it was only a matter of time before Joyce told them. The guys went over the route out to the Prossers', which was about ten miles away.

"Do the Prossers know we're coming now?" Joyce asked Tom. Nope. Tom grabbed his cell phone and said, "Thanks."

Tom started to dial Jeff's number. Then he dropped the phone. Duh. Calling Jeff's phone would lead the authorities right to the farm.

"They'll be expecting us," Tom said. He picked up his phone and tried to act like he accidently dropped it so Joyce wouldn't get more concerned about the police trying to find them.

Tom had a mischievous idea. He dialed the office numbers of some government officials he hated. Now, if the cops pulled up Tom's phone records, the people he hated would be "terrorists," too. Ha! The cops would be thrown off his trail, trying to figure out if those asshole government officials were "terrorists." Tom didn't feel an ounce of guilt.

"Let's go," said Tom. They all piled into their vehicles, and left Tom's neighborhood through back streets so they wouldn't have to go near downtown. Tom was especially trying to avoid the area around the WAB offices so none of them would see the burned out building. That would be too much for them. It was too much for Tom, too.

The drive to the Prosser farm was anti-climactic. There was hardly any traffic. No cop cars. There were a few other cars packed to the gills with families bugging out to somewhere.

Tom led them there very efficiently, signaling plenty of time in advance in case someone didn't remember how to get there. He stopped at yellow lights so he wouldn't leave half the convoy stranded behind. Before they left, he had told them to run a red light rather than split up the group. It didn't take long to go the ten miles to the farm and the kids were doing just fine.

Jeff Prosser was waiting at the gate with his 30-30. He knew Tom and the others would be coming; he just wasn't sure exactly when. And he figured that if they weren't coming, he still needed to be guarding the place. Things were crazy; he couldn't just sit around his house. He had to do something, and guarding the gate with his 30-30 seemed like the right thing to do.

Jeff saw some cars coming down the road; they were

recognizable. He had a huge smile on his face. This was actually happening. He was helping his friends hide out. The mailroom guy to the rescue!

Jeff waved to them and opened the gate, which was at the entrance to Prosser Road. The Prosser family had owned this land for over a hundred years. Prosser Road led to a half dozen houses, including Jeff and Molly Prosser's farm. The other houses were owned by relatives of the Prossers. They were a tight community.

The Prosser farmhouse was on a slight hill with a barn and two more outbuildings. There was a fence all around the property. There were a few other farmhouses around. This place was extremely defensible.

Each car slowly passed by him. The third car was Karen's. She was upset that Jeff was standing there with a gun; she feared that would scare the kids. But the kids weren't scared at all. They were relieved that they recognized the guy with the gun.

Molly heard and saw the cars coming. Since there weren't any gun shots, it must be their guests. Wow. That was an unusual thought. She wondered if she'd ever thought such a thing. Nope.

Molly tried to mentally prepare herself to have three families of houseguests coming for the next … who knew how long. She was glad to have them there. Her farmhouse was modest compared to the other families' suburban homes. She had always been bothered by this. Not that she was jealous—she loved her farmhouse just the way it was—but she couldn't help wondering if she'd measure up to the other wives. After Jeff told her they might be coming, she spent the entire day and into the night getting things ready for her guests. She got out sheets and blankets and figured which rooms would have kids and which would have couples. She got lots of food out of storage; she got the "store bought" food out first because that's what the other families would be used to. She was ready to feed her guests. The families probably had been up all night and were stressed; nothing would be better than something to eat before they unpacked at their new quarters.

Molly went toward the front door and caught a glimpse of herself in the entryway mirror. She saw that she was wearing her best casual outfit. She was trying to impress. She laughed to herself and realized she would impress them by having a safe place for them to stay until this was all over. That mattered a whole lot more than clothes.

The families came into the house carload by carload. They were all relieved to get to the farm safely. The kids started running around with nervous energy. They wanted to see the horses and cows. Molly showed each family their rooms. There were enough rooms for everyone, but just barely. The couples had a room to themselves and then all the kids split two rooms, one for boys and one for girls. Molly was proud that her farmhouse could become a comfortable place for three additional families to stay.

"Who's hungry?" she asked. The kids all said they were. The grownups were busy unpacking. "Come on in here and I'll make you a farm breakfast."

After everything was unpacked, Jeff motioned the guys to come into the barn to talk. "Is everyone armed?" he asked. They all nodded.

"We each have a Sig 9mm, and Brian has a shotgun and some shells," Ben said.

"How much 9mm do you have?" Jeff asked.

"I got," Tom said, "I dunno, ten or twelve boxes of shells from that gun store Grant always went to." At fifty rounds per box, that was a decent amount of ammo. Especially since they didn't plan on shooting much, or really at all.

"I have some rifles and shotguns. You guys know how to use them?" Jeff asked.

Brian nodded. Ben and Tom halfway nodded. Jeff made a mental note that he'd need to show them how to use them.

"Hey, Jeff, we'll need to park our cars out of sight," Tom said.

"Why?" Jeff asked.

Tom explained the POI list.

"Oh, that's why," Jeff said, trying to downplay the significance. Jeff knew he was doing them a favor by letting them stay out there, but now he was harboring fugitives. They weren't fugitives, Jeff corrected himself. They were his friends who needed help. Besides, Jeff had decided long ago that he was going to do something for the war.

Yes, a war. Jeff knew this was coming. Despite being "just" the mailroom guy, he had a very high IQ. He paid attention. He had quietly watched the government get nastier and nastier and he knew it was coming to a head. Now was that time. Jeff didn't plan on joining some military unit. He would make his contribution right there at the farm, however he could.

Tom could sense that Jeff was trying to process the whole "terrorist" thing. "If the POI listing is a problem," Tom said, "we can go. We don't want to put you in a bad spot."

"Go?" Jeff said. "Hell, no. You're my friends. You're in trouble.

I can help. Besides, we get about one stranger a year down this road. They are usually lost. The other houses around here are family. They're more conservative than you guys. You'll be fine out here," Jeff said, hoping it was true. Oh well. Jeff knew he'd die someday. Might as well be helping his friends.

He was proud to tell them the next part. "We have enough food out here for several weeks for all of us; maybe a couple of months. And we can grow enough for next year. Easy. We can everything from our garden and butcher our own meat. We have milk cows. We have all kinds of food stored out here. I figured something like this was coming long ago, so we've been preparing for a while. We've been getting extra of things we knew we'd eat, like canned foods. Got 'em on sale, even. Worked out pretty well." That was an understatement.

Then Jeff got a really big smile. He pointed to what looked like a gas station pump out by the house. "See that? It's my diesel tank. I have almost 500 gallons in an underground tank. It's for my equipment, but my truck runs on diesel, too." He was beaming. "We don't have to worry about the gas stations being out of gas."

This place was perfect. It was almost like it was meant to be a sanctuary for them.

Chapter 75

Don't Come Back Here

(May 7)

Nancy Ringman had gone insane. After she got in the fight with Lisa Matson, she went over to Sherrie Spencer's and started screaming about how Lisa had attacked her. Nancy was yelling about Grant being a terrorist and "POI."

She went from house to house telling people that they needed to come to the neighborhood meeting that night to hear about how she would be organizing a safety committee to protect them against terrorists like Grant. Most people just stared at her, but some believed her.

Ron Spencer was standing guard at the neighborhood entrance when Nancy came by. She was yelling at him about having a gun out. He'd had enough.

"What the hell is wrong with you?" he yelled at Nancy. "I heard you attacked Lisa Matson and now she has left."

Nancy started in about how Lisa had attacked her. Ron knew that wasn't true. Nancy started yelling, "It's you and your guns that are doing this. Things were fine until you and the others started all this macho stuff, like 'guarding' us. We don't need you. Things were fine without you."

Ron could see that there was no reasoning with her. He didn't want to be distracted with a crazy lady when he had to watch to see if criminals were attacking, so he waved her off.

Ron was on guard duty for another hour or two when Len came running up to him.

"The Matson house got vandalized," Len said, breathless. "Go see. I'll take guard duty."

Ron ran the two blocks to the Matson house. He rounded the corner and saw "POI" spray painted in big letters on the garage door. The front door was open. He went in, with his shotgun ready for quick use in case the vandal was still in there.

He couldn't believe it. The house was trashed. Everything was destroyed. It looked like a bomb went off in the place. He had been in that house so many times and now it was destroyed.

It was ugly in there. He wanted to leave. Before he did, he searched each room to see if the vandal, who he suspected was Nancy, was still in there. She was nuts and might try to attack him, too. The house was empty.

Now that he knew Nancy wasn't there to attack him, he had time to think. Lisa needed to know what happened. He pulled out his cell phone and took pictures of the destruction. He sent them to Lisa's cell phone. The message said, "Don't come back here."

He ran out of the house. He had to go arrest Nancy.

Chapter 76

You May Leave, Colonel

(May 7)

NorthCom was trying to keep control of the military units in the U.S. Most were just scrambling to keep up with the relief efforts. They didn't have time to think about politics right then.

Oath Keepers kicked into action. Its thousands of members refused to comply with unconstitutional orders. One of those orders was the order to arrest "terrorists," including U.S. citizens on U.S. soil, who had been designated as terrorists by the President (but in reality were just names on a list compiled by military and law enforcement and civilian politicians). They were to be held indefinitely and without trial. Without trial. In military custody; not the civilian court system. That had been authorized by the 2011 National Defense Authorization Act.

Major Bill Owens, a military lawyer in the Texas Guard, was one of the thousands of Oath Keepers. There was a meeting of San Antonio-area Texas Guard senior officers, which included Bill. NorthCom briefed them on what was happening and what was about to happen. The NorthCom colonel said that they had activated their plan for combating "civil unrest," which included seizing civilian weapons, setting up checkpoints, and searches without warrants. The colonel asked if there were any questions. Bill felt a strange calmness and raised his hand.

"I'm JAG," Bill said, referring to the acronym of a military lawyer, "and have to ask how this is possibly legal, sir." The colonel seemed annoyed. Who was this major to be questioning him like that?

"The President signed an Executive Order under his war powers," the colonel responded. "Surely," the colonel strained to see Bill's rank insignia, "Major, you understand the President's broad war powers."

"Yes, sir," Bill said. "But he is still subject to the Constitution, which includes the Second and Fourth Amendments. The Treason clause requires a civilian trial for making war on the United States, so the NDAA power for the President to detain 'terrorists' in military custody is unconstitutional, sir."

Silence.

Bill continued, "These measures you at NorthCom describe, sir, would be unlawful orders and none of us need to follow them. In fact, it would actually be illegal to follow them."

The colonel knew this was coming. They had been dealing with these Oath Keepers assholes in every unit. This major was about to lose his commission.

"You're done talking, Major," the colonel barked. "You're wrong. Our legal staff at the Pentagon has researched this. It's entirely legal. The NDAA and Insurrection Act allows this. And you will obey a direct order, Major."

More silence.

Bill stood up. He could not believe how calm he was.

"No, sir," Bill said. "I will not obey an illegal order." Bill stood at attention. He now realized the meaning of the phrase "stand up for your rights." He was literally doing it.

More silence. The colonel was trying to stare him down.

The Texas Guard commander, a brigadier general, spoke up.

"Major Owens is one of my best legal advisors and I think he's right," the Texas Guard general said. "My men will not follow these orders. They are illegal. Is there anything else NorthCom wishes to tell us, Colonel?"

The general had already spoken extensively with the Texas Governor, who was the Guard's general commander. The general had told the Governor that none of the guard units would follow this federal nonsense. The Texas Governor had watched the Feds botch the Mexican refugee fiasco and he wasn't about to let them screw up more.

"You may leave, Colonel," the Texas Guard general said.

Everyone in the room realized that, at that moment, they were witnessing the beginning of the Second Texas Republic.

Chapter 77

Time to Tuck

(May 7)

It was getting dark and Grant was wide awake. He'd slept most of the day, and was elated by the arrival of his family and the Team. There was no way he could sleep now. Besides, he had guard duty.

Chip came up to him with a cup of coffee. Grant reached for it, assuming it was for him. Chip shook his head. "Not for you. For me." That seemed strange.

"Okay, but how can you sleep when you're drinking coffee at night?" Grant asked.

"I'm not going to sleep," Chip said. "I'm going to pull guard duty. You need to settle your family in." Chip smiled. He knew that Grant's real family had arrived. Chip would be part of this family, too; just an extended member of it.

Grant started to tear up. Why? It was nice and everything for Chip to take his guard shift, but why tear up? Everything was just so emotional at that moment. Grant collected his composure and said, "Thanks, man. I mean, really, thanks."

Chip just smiled wider and nodded. He grabbed his AR and did a press check of his 1911. "Gotta go." He walked a few steps and then turned to Grant, "I'm proud of you, man. You left your family when you had to. You weren't some pussy just crying in the corner of your suburban home when the shit hit the fan. You were a man. And it's working out well for you." Chip turned and kept walking to the guard shack.

Grant got choked up. He had to admit it: he was proud of the stand he'd taken. But his mind shifted to thinking of all they had to do out there to make sure they made it.

Where to start? Grant thought. He needed to get people settled in. He started, of course, with his own family. He found Lisa and said, "I'm thinking that you and I get the downstairs bedroom that has a door." It had a comfy queen size bed. Grant had got it at a garage sale for $100 and it was like new. He remembered when he got it thinking that he might need to sleep on this for several years out there so he better get a good one.

Grant continued, "The kids can share a bed in the loft." Lisa nodded. "Then I'm thinking your parents could share the other bed in the loft. It will be comforting to the kids to have grandma and grandpa around."

Lisa thought about how weird it was to have kids sleeping together and the grandparents also sleeping in the same room. She started to say something, but realized that this one cabin was all they had. There was no big house with separate bedrooms and no second house where the grandparents lived. This was how people slept in the past. It would have to do. It might actually be a good thing to have everyone under one roof. Family was a good thing, especially in a crisis.

"I guess so," Lisa said. "I mean it's just for a few days until this thing blows over."

Grant nodded. A few days? He was playing along, knowing this could go on forever. "Yeah, just a few days," he said, a little ashamed of himself for misleading her, although she had to be eased gently into the new reality, as did the kids and grandparents. Grant remembered that he'd spent the last few years mentally preparing for a Collapse. It was going to take a while for everyone else to catch up with him.

"We have a full bathroom, a shower and everything, so that's taken care of," Grant said. "The only thing we don't have out here is a washer and dryer, but I talked to the Morrells yesterday and they said we can use theirs." Lisa smiled. Grant had thought of everything. She had to admit it.

Grant motioned for her to follow him upstairs to the loft. He pointed to the big dresser. "This will hold a lot of clothes. Besides, they only brought enough for a week or two so there's not much to put away." Grant purchased the dresser when he got the bed at the garage sale. They matched. Only $50. Kind of a 70's look to them, but they were solid, like furniture used to be built when things were still built in America. Way back then.

He opened a drawer and there were some of Manda's clothes in there. "I had her bring some of her old stuff out a few months ago. We brought out some of Cole's clothes, too. I saw this …" he stopped. He was about to say he saw this coming, but he was determined not to gloat, so he pretended to switch topics. "I saw this dresser at a garage sale when I got the bed. Just $50."

Lisa made a mental note. They would have far fewer changes of clothes out there. But, then again, that meant doing fewer loads of laundry. That would be one of the big changes to living out at the cabin that she and everyone else would have to adapt to: wearing the same clothes all the time. Tee shirts and shorts or jeans, at least in the summer. No dress up clothes; those seemed like a waste. Besides, no one brought dress up clothes. Dress up for what? Work in an office? No one was going to work anymore, at least not out there. Dress up for a fancy dinner at a restaurant? Not happening. Lisa realized that she dressed up for other people, to fit in with them when they were similarly dressed up, but there was no one around now who was dressing up. She could live in tee shirts and shorts or sweat pants when it got cooler. It would take some getting used to, but it would be fine.

Lisa realized the same would be true for makeup. She didn't bring any. At first she felt naked without it. Then she thought about it. She put on makeup to go to work or the mall. That wouldn't be a problem anymore. At least, until things got back to normal. She wasn't around her girlfriends who all wore makeup. She didn't need to impress anyone out there. So, after her first impulse, which was to feel naked without makeup, she actually got comfortable with the idea. She didn't have to spend all that time on makeup. What a relief. Maybe this vacation out at the cabin wouldn't be so bad after all. "Vacation" was what she was calling it in her head. She was viewing this as a vacation.

On every vacation they had ever been on, Grant would bring in the heavy luggage and Lisa would put it in the dressers and closets of whatever hotel they were in. She wanted to organize the stuff. Grant would get one dresser drawer for his stuff and she and the kids would get the rest of them. Grant and Lisa smoothly transitioned into their vacation roles. "I'll bring in all the stuff," Grant said. "It's all in your Tahoe, right?"

"Yep," Lisa said. "Thanks."

Things were feeling a little "normal."

While Grant was out at her Tahoe, he saw Drew and Eileen chatting with John and Mary Anne. They were about the same ages. It was nice to see them making friends so quickly. Not that he was surprised; it was just nice.

When Grant came up to them, Mary Anne and Eileen were talking about canning. "Oh, I haven't canned in years," Eileen said. "But I'd love to get back into it." Grant remembered that Eileen and Drew grew up in little tiny farm towns in Eastern Washington. They would get snowed in for weeks at a time. They had some skills to dust off and use out there.

Grant said, "Excuse me." He motioned to Drew and Eileen.

"When you're ready, I can show you where you will be staying and where to put your stuff." They broke off the conversation and followed Grant back into the cabin.

As they were walking toward the cabin Grant said, "It'll be a little cozy, but…"

"We'll probably be up in the loft," Drew said. "Fine with me. I snore a little, but not too bad."

"I think it will be great to be so close to the kids," Eileen said.

When they got upstairs to the loft and saw their bed, a nice queen size, next to the kids' bed, Eileen said, "This is how we did it back on the farm. A few kids per bed and grandma. Six kids, but not six bedrooms like everyone has now." Grant nodded.

That's right, Grant thought, things were getting back to what was historically normal. It was not "normal" anywhere else in the world or throughout history for everyone to have their own room and several bathrooms in each house. It was nice, but not normal by world standards. People didn't burst into flames back in the day when kids shared beds and grandparents lived in the same house. In fact, it made most families closer. It would take a little adjustment, but Grant thought this coziness just might be a good thing. Hey, he thought, they had free babysitting built right in with the grandparents there. And they had people with skills, like canning, right there, too.

Grant showed them their dresser drawers. "I'll go out to your car and get your things," he said to Eileen, knowing that she would account for about 75% of the luggage. Sure enough. Drew packed light. He was happy to bring just casual clothes. He had worn a suit for years and couldn't stand them. This would be like a fishing resort vacation, except with the family instead of his business buddies.

Drew still had his pistol on him although it was concealed. Out in his car, he had a shotgun and a few boxes of ammo. He also had a .357/.38 Marlin lever action carbine and a few boxes of ammo, which would be nice for him to have. He had a Ruger 10/22 carbine and an old Browning Buckmark .22 pistol. Perfect. He had one suitcase of clothes. That was it.

Eileen had filled the car with her suitcases. That was fine. She had brought some dress up clothes. She was looking at the cabin as a more "normal" vacation where she might have people over and want to dress up or maybe go out to a nice dinner. She could think that if she wanted. There was no harm in having those things as long as she didn't get upset when she had no occasion to wear them. She brought a lot of makeup. That was fine. Maybe Lisa could borrow it if she really wanted to have some.

Lisa came up to Grant and whispered, "Uh, I don't have any feminine supplies. How long do you think we'll be out here?"

"Long enough to need them, maybe," Grant said. That was an understatement. But he didn't want to say that he assumed they could be out here for a few years.

Grant had meant to go to Costco and get several hundred … feminine supplies. He didn't even like saying "tampon." He almost got some of … those things one time, when he and Manda were at Costco. He was about to give her a bunch of cash and have her go in and get several hundred for her and her mom, but he chickened out. He just couldn't acknowledge that she and her mom … needed those. It was totally irrational, but he was raised that men just didn't talk about that topic. At all. Ever.

Grant felt like an idiot. Mr. Prepper didn't have a very important and totally foreseeable item. He was kicking himself for not just manning up and buying several cases of … those things.

"In the morning I need to go to the store and get some," Lisa said.

What? She thought she would just waltz into town and get some like this was some item on her shopping list? Did she have any idea how dangerous things were out there?

Normally, Grant would volunteer to go on an armed escort run into the looting city and get the supplies, but not these supplies. There was something about a guy buying feminine supplies that was, well, impossible. He thought about it: he was really willing to risk his wife dying on a trip into town just so he didn't have to buy tampons? What was wrong with him? Talk about "normalcy bias" — he was suffering from it. Not for long.

"I'll go into town with some of the guys for backup," Grant said. "We'll make a big list of things like this and hit the store in the morning."

Lisa smiled. She remembered how, just a few years ago, Grant would joke that the most humiliating thing that could happen to a man was buying tampons. But, now Grant was being a good husband and doing it. He wasn't so bad, Lisa thought.

"Thanks, dear," she said. "Are you sure you can handle this?" she said with a wink. "I mean you're walking around with a machine gun, but I'm not sure you can handle buying tampons." It felt good to be joking around again. So good.

Grant started laughing so hard that it turned to tears. Happy tears. He quickly got control of his emotions. He was having a lot of these emotional spells lately. But so much had happened. He hugged Lisa again.

"You will be well taken care of," he whispered to her. He wasn't gloating, but he wanted her to remember that he had promised to take care of her months ago. She kept hugging him, too. She appreciated that her husband had gone to all this trouble to take care of them, even if it meant her being mad at him if she caught him And she appreciated that he wasn't gloating.

After a while, he let her go and said, "I gotta get the Team all set up in their cabin."

She said sternly, "There is something you need to do first." She smiled and said, "Cole needs to be tucked."

More of the happy tears. Oh, God, how Grant had wanted to tuck that boy in. For days.

"Hey, Cole," Grant called out. "Time for tucking." Grant climbed up to the loft and went over to the bed where the kids would be sleeping.

"Oh, yes, Dad," Cole said with a huge smile.

Grant tucked in Cole. The lights were still on and people were moving around the loft putting their things away, so Cole wouldn't be sleeping for a while, but that wasn't the point. Tucking was about Dad being there. Grant hugged Cole so hard that he was afraid he would squish him.

"Good night, lil' buddy," Grant said.

"Good night, Dad," Cole said with a big smile.

This is what you are supposed to be doing. I put you and them here. You're safe, but you all have jobs to do.

Grant hadn't heard the outside thought in a long time. But it was crystal clear. Grant said out loud, "Thank you."

Chapter 78

The Third Amendment

(May 7)

Grant was so happy that he was tearing up again. He needed to stop that, especially in front of the Team. He was the oldest one and couldn't have them thinking he was a sobbing old man, so he got back into his persona as Grant, the member of the Team.

He walked over to the yellow cabin. It was fully dark now. There was some moonlight, but it was still hard to see. He didn't want to twist his ankle when he had so much to do. He got out his Surefire E1B flashlight from his 5.11 pants and noticed his pistol. There it was on his belt in the holster. It had been on the whole time he was talking to Lisa and the grandparents. No one had said anything like, "Get that dangerous thing away from me." It was now perfectly appropriate to wear a side arm, when just a few days ago, he hid his guns from them.

"Things have changed," Grant said out loud to himself as he walked down the gravel road to the yellow cabin. He listened to his Romeos, that he called "hillbilly slippers," softly crunch on the gravel. He would never forget the sound of car wheels on a gravel road. Never. It was the sweetest sound of his life.

The guys' trucks were all parked near the yellow cabin, which was right next to the guard shack. What a great place to house four extremely well-armed and well-trained men. He wondered about the owner of the cabin, that guy from California. Would he be pissed that they sort of took over his property? Oh well. He was probably stuck in California and couldn't use it, anyway. Besides, if he did make it to Pierce Point, they would give his place back and pay him some kind of rent.

The Third Amendment. Grant thought about the little-known Third Amendment to the Constitution. It said that troops would not be quartered, which meant housed, in private homes without the owner's permission, in most cases. The British had forcibly quartered troops during the Revolutionary War and the colonists hated it. Grant and the Team would honor the Constitution out there, Grant thought. Even the inconvenient Third Amendment. That's how they would do things out there.

32

As Grant walked up, Bobby and Wes were unloading a final load of things from their trucks. They were happy to see him.

"Awesome place, man," Bobby said. He was grinning so widely he couldn't contain himself.

"My pleasure," Grant said. "Well, it's not exactly mine, but I'm guessing it's okay to borrow it."

Bobby and Wes nodded. Grant pointed down the road the opposite direction from his cabin. "There are lots of empty cabins here. If the guy who owns the yellow cabin comes back, it shouldn't be hard to find one for the neighborhood's security force. I would think most people in the neighborhood would kind of welcome it, to be honest. You know, having armed men whom they can trust nearby. Kind of a bonus, nowadays."

Grant grabbed a duffle bag from Wes's truck bed and brought it in with them.

Pow and Scotty were inside putting their stuff in dressers.

"Bobby's got the couch," Pow said. "He's the shortest and can fit on it without a problem." Bobby shrugged.

"Like when I'm at your momma's house and you have to sleep on the couch," Bobby said. Momma jokes. Some things never change.

Scotty opened the refrigerator, which was empty. "We gotta do something about this," he said.

"Yep," Grant said. "Way ahead of you. Make up a list. In the morning we'll go into town and get a last batch of whatever is still on the shelves. I have some 'feminine products' to get." They all laughed at him. Grant was actually proud that they were laughing at him. He was taking care of his family, which was the highest honor a man could have.

"But, seriously," Grant said, "I am not letting my family know that this is probably the last set of supplies we can get in town. They haven't been in the stores like you have and don't know how bad it is. I am trying to make them believe things are as 'normal' as possible. I'm selling this to them as a few days of a 'vacation.' I need you guys to play along."

"No prob," Pow said, understanding how hard it must be for Grant to try to keep his family calm during all that was going on. "Hey, you're the landlord so what you say goes."

That was reassuring to Grant. A house with four extremely well-armed men, who couldn't be dislodged from the place without a professional SWAT team, were saying, "Hey, you're the landlord." Grant would never trust well-armed strangers with the location of his cabin. He realized how important it was to know — really know — the people invited out to a bug out location. Grant was thankful for the "coincidence" that he had been training with these guys for a couple of years and had gotten to know them extremely well.

He thought about the outside thoughts and all the things that had fallen into place to make this whole set up possible. He knew, with absolute certainty, that everything was happening for a reason and they had a job to do. Absolute certainty.

"Can one of you guys help Chip with guard duty tonight?" Grant asked. "We really should have two guys out there. Besides, I don't want Chip to be lonely."

Scotty raised his hand. "No biggie. I can't sleep now, anyway. I'll grab one of you tonight to replace me if I get tired." They all nodded. That's how the Team did things. It was amazing.

"So, Scotty, to answer your question about the fridge," Grant said. "We'll be making a milk run tomorrow morning, but we should have a nice big breakfast first. I have some grub at my place. Can you guys keep a secret?" Grant paused for effect. "A couple months of food, at least a couple months for my family, but you can share it, too."

Wes said, "We know. Pow told us." Pow looked a little guilty.

"I know it was a secret, Grant, but I figured it was okay to tell the guys," Pow said shrugging.

"Of course," Grant said, realizing that he had been taking the secrecy about the contents of the "spider shed" a little too seriously now that the Collapse had hit and he was among friends out there.

"It's other people I worry about," Grant said, which was true. Random people knowing that they had food would guarantee some break-in attempts. Maybe even an armed mob. But not with the Team and the Morrells and Colsons.

"So we'll have some pancakes in the morning," Grant said. He had been looking forward to big breakfasts with the Team and his family. "What time sounds good to you guys? Sun comes up at about 5:00. We all need to sleep. What about 7:00?"

Grant noticed that, despite feeling like they were in military mode, he was using the civilian times instead of "0500" or "0700." That made sense. They were civilians. This reminded Grant that one of the things he liked so much about the Team was that none of them were mall ninjas or military wannabes. They were just sheepdogs with guns. They didn't have to try to be anything they weren't. They were comfortable in their own skin, but not cocky. It was the perfect combination.

Grant realized that they might be hungry now. They had been on the move since about dinner time and it was now about 11:00 pm. "You guys need some dinner or a late night snack?"

"I do," said Wes. The others didn't disagree.

"We had some deer steaks BBQ'd right before you guys came," Grant said. "I bet Tammy," he pointed up the road to the Colsons', "put them in the fridge. I'll go see. You guys should come with me so they can see you."

Scotty had an MRE in his hand. "I'm fine" he said. "I'll take this and go hang out with Chip." Grant hated to see an MRE used when other food was available, but he wasn't going to tell people what to eat. Besides, showing alarm at the use of an MRE would imply impending starvation. He didn't want to have people worrying about that. It was just one MRE and they had a bunch of them out there.

All of them, except Scotty, left the yellow cabin. They had pistols on their belts, of course. Wes pointed at his AR propped up on the couch, motioned to it and asked, "should we bring these?"

Grant shook his head and said, "I don't think we should carry ARs all the time around the cabins. At least for now. Probably later. But for now I don't want the neighbors to feel like this is Afghanistan. I don't want them wondering if we'll turn on them. So let's downplay the firepower. For now. Pistols for sure, though. What do you guys think?"

"With Chip and Scotty guarding the entrance, we'll be okay without ARs," Pow said.

"Let's go get our eats on, gentlemen," Grant said. This felt so good. Hangin' out with the Team. At the cabin.

Grant wanted to say hi to Chip. They walked out to the guard shack. "Hey, man, thanks for taking guard duty," Grant said. "Scotty will be joining you in a minute. Don't hesitate to get me if you need me."

Chip said, "Sure. I talked to John and Mary Anne and they'll put me up in their guest bedroom."

In all the activity, Grant had totally forgotten about Chip's accommodations. He felt bad about that. "Oh, cool, I figured they would," Grant said, as he realized he'd made the assumption they would do that.

"It'll be good to have us spread out a little in the cabins," Bobby said.

"We're going to see if the Colsons have any leftover deer steaks for the boys," Grant said to Chip.

"They're fantastic, guys," Chip said as he rubbed his stomach. Chip was a thin guy.

Grant didn't want Chip to feel abandoned. He asked, "Chip, you need some more coffee?"

"Nope, I'm fine," he said.

"All right, then," Grant said. "We're off to get some grub." Right then, Grant's stomach growled. He remembered that he hadn't eaten dinner, either and all of a sudden he was really hungry.

They went to the Colsons and were consciously talking in their normal voices as they approached so the Colsons wouldn't think strangers were sneaking up on their house.

Tammy answered the door and was glad to see them. The Morrells were at the table.

"You guys hungry?" Tammy asked. It reminded her of when Paul had his friends over growing up. She had loved feeding the boys.

"Got any deer steaks?" Grant asked. "I tried to eat one earlier tonight, but these jackasses decided to show up. With my family or whatever. Interrupted my damned dinner." Everyone was laughing and smiling.

Tammy opened the refrigerator and got a platter covered with foil. "Eat up, boys."

They did. It was amazing how much food hungry men could eat.

After a while, Grant said, "Hey, I'm having a pancake breakfast tomorrow morning. Come over at about 7:00." Everyone said they'd be over.

They didn't talk about guard duty, food supplies, looting, inflation, the collapse of America, or anything like that. They just ate. It was a group of people who had known each other for a couple of hours, yet they were eating like they had grown up together. It was an amazing time.

Grant wanted his family to come over, but he knew Lisa would be trying to get Cole and Manda to sleep. There will be plenty of chances to have the whole neighborhood together for dinner in the coming … days? Weeks? Months? Who really cared. They were there and they were safe. They were way better off than most of the country.

Chapter 79

Pancakes

(May 8)

Morning came way too fast. After deer steaks at the Colsons', which went past midnight, Grant quietly snuck over to his cabin and collapsed into bed. He was so tired that he didn't even remember his head hitting the pillow. He had slept most of the previous day, but the emotions of the arrival of his family and the Team had wiped him out.

Grant woke up with Lisa next to him. Wow. That felt great. He honestly thought that would never happen again.

He looked at his watch. It was 6:30. He had some pancakes to start cooking. He got up and got the pancake mix out of the storage shed; a five pound vacuum sealed bag. He would have to tell the Colsons and Morrells that he had the food because they would see the vacuum sealed bag and realize something was up.

Oh well, it was fine for them to know. Keeping the food storage a secret made sense before the Collapse and before he fully trusted them. Besides, they had shared their deer steaks the night before and would be sharing many other things until this was over. They were in this together. They would only get through it by sharing. The cabin neighborhood of the Matsons, the Team, Morrells, and Colsons were now a gang. Not the motorcycle kind of gang, but a group taking care of each other.

Grant's favorite smell in the morning was pancakes and the enticing scent called to the others, as well. Slowly, people started stirring in the cabin. It was magic. They were all together and Grant was getting them up with pancakes. The sun was shining into the cabin through the evergreen trees. The water was still and beautiful.

Grant wanted to make sure Cole, who needed the same routine because of his mild autism, was okay with his new surroundings. He had been to the cabin plenty of times, but never with his grandparents sleeping in the other bed in the room. Grant went up to the loft. Cole was awake, talking to his sister.

"I'm happy that we're all here," Cole said. That melted Grant's heart. Cole really, really needed that tucking in last night.

"Me too, little buddy," Grant said. "I have some pancakes for you, pal. We have syrup, too." Grant didn't tell Cole that the syrup was a different brand; whatever they had at the Dollar Store. He was curious if Cole's need for routine would allow him to eat a different syrup.

"Sounds delicious, Dad," Cole said. Grant had never heard Cole say the word "delicious" before.

The new syrup would be a test for Cole. He was a growing thirteen-year old boy and constantly hungry. Grant figured Cole's hunger would override his need for routine.

He needed to invite the Morrells, Colsons, and the Team over, and went to get his hillbilly slippers on. He felt naked, though. His pistol. He forgot his pistol. He quietly went into the bedroom where Lisa was sleeping to get his gun belt off the nightstand. She was stirring.

"Whatcha doing?" she asked, half awake.

"I need to invite the neighbors over for breakfast," Grant whispered. "We have some things to talk about."

"Could you not leave that gun on the nightstand right by our heads?" she asked politely.

Okay, Grant thought, decades of thinking guns spontaneously combust had rooted itself pretty deep in her. She was fine with him wearing a gun and carrying an AR, so this wasn't too bad. He had to pick his battles.

"Sure, honey," Grant said. "By the way, your dad and I talked to Cole about guns again. We told him that it's only okay for him or any other kid he's around to touch a gun if a grownup is there and gives permission. I asked him to repeat it back to me and he did."

"Good," she said. "You know, I see kids in the ER with accidental gun shots." That was a fair point.

"That won't happen here," Grant said. "Your parents or Manda are constantly with him. My guns will only be on me or under the bed." Grant would put his AR under the bed. Probably his shotgun, too. At least at first, until Lisa got comfortable with his AR and shotgun being propped up on the wall by the bed.

Under the bed was not an ideal quick-reaction spot, but he was trying to ease his wife into this whole situation. He was trying to convince her that this was just a week-long vacation while the government got everything back in order. Grant realized he could try to win an argument or he could have his wife on board with the most important decision they would make in their lives. It was an easy choice.

"I understand your concerns," Grant said. "I will be ultra-careful. The good news is that with the guard shack and the Team, I don't need to have guns out too much in the house. We are safe here. Very safe."

Lisa nodded. She would rather not have any guns around, but she, too, was more interested in a harmonious stay out at the cabin than trying to win an argument. Besides, with all that had happened in the past few days, her opinion of guns had changed a little bit.

Grant grabbed his pistol belt. He hid it from her. Not that she didn't know it was there, but he thought "out of sight, out of mind." That's why he kept his tactical vest with magazine pouches in a suit bag in the closet. That thing would definitely scare Lisa so he kept it out of sight. For now.

When Grant was in the kitchen, he put his pistol belt on. Ahhh. He had missed the weight of the pistol and his mag holders with four full magazines. He felt naked without it. With his pistol on, he felt like things were back to normal. A new normal.

He went outside. It was gorgeous out; about seventy degrees, with a slight breeze from the water. He went to the Morrells. Chip was making them coffee. Grant told them to come over in a while.

Grant went to the Colsons. Paul volunteered to pull guard duty while the rest of them ate. Paul didn't like people to see him eat. He was so heavy that he thought people would look at him funny for eating a meal, like he should only be eating carrots and celery or something. He usually ate alone.

Grant went over to the yellow cabin. The Team was sound asleep. They probably stayed up late telling and retelling war stories from the trip out and from their various milk runs.

He went to the guard shack and saw Scotty. God, he looked impressive. Standing in a tactical vest with his AR across his chest. He looked like a military contractor. The average criminal would see him and run away to an easier target. That was the point. Grant hoped they would get through this whole Collapse without ever firing a shot. He knew that was unlikely, but it would sure be great if it happened.

"There's hot, tasty pancakes at my cabin, Scotty," Grant said.

"Awesome," Scotty said. "I'm starving." He looked down the road. "Nothing at all last night. Some dogs started barking around 2:30. Could have been a rabbit they were hearing. It could have been…" He didn't need to say.

Dogs were great burglar alarms. The Colsons had two little dogs who yapped when someone was coming up to their house. It was annoying at first, but reassuring now.

"Paul's coming to relieve you, then it's pancake time," Grant said with a smile.

Scotty nodded. He was watching the road the whole time they were talking. In most settings it would be impolite to not look at someone during a conversation, but guarding their families was more important.

This felt so right. Like it was meant to be. Grant was getting that feeling a lot lately.

As he headed back to his cabin, Grant realized that he had a choice to make. He could continue with the story to his family that this was just a week or so of vacation and then everything would turn out fine or, he could use this first meeting to set the tone for the whole stay out there. First impressions were everything. The breakfast meeting would be the first time the whole group was together.

This was an easy choice. He needed all these people to realize that they were in a survival situation. The most important thing — the very most important thing — in a survival situation is the will to live. Everyone needed to understand the dangers and then decide whether they'd do what it takes to make it through it.

Grant had eased his family into the "vacation" thing as much as possible. Now it was time to take the easing process up one level, from vacation to permanent stay.

Surprisingly, Lisa had already come to this conclusion. Not from Grant's brilliant managing of the situation, but from reality.

While Grant was out rounding up people for pancakes, Lisa checked her cell phone. There were the pictures of her trashed house and Ron's message, "Don't come back."

It is real now, she thought. It wasn't some big misunderstanding that would lead to a few days at the cabin because Grant overreacted and she was humoring him. This was real. She couldn't go back. Some lunatic, probably Nancy Ringman, had decided to go after her family. All the "politics" that Lisa hated weren't just a game anymore. The government, or at least some psycho in the neighborhood, hated Grant for some reason. He was on some terrorist list and their house had been destroyed. There was no going back there. Not until things fundamentally changed and the Nancy Ringmans of the world were no longer able to do things like this.

Lisa felt violated. Someone had come into their beautiful home and destroyed it. Their home. Lisa had worked so hard to make it just the way she wanted it and then this happened. She kept looking at the pictures on her phone. It was ugly; both the trashed house and the reason it happened. There was something dark and almost demonic about the whole thing.

Well, at least this solved the problem of whether she and the kids really needed to be out at the cabin, she thought. Okay, then. This cabin thing sucked, but at least she wasn't in the house when the destruction happened. She and the kids were in a safe place. She took a deep breath. This was where they needed to be for a while. She would make the best of it. People were stirring and coming over. It was time for breakfast.

Pretty soon, the cabin was full of people eating and talking. Perfect, Grant thought. When he came in, they seemed to unconsciously realize that he was the leader. It was his place and he was the common thread connecting all of them. He knew he needed to lead. He'd been doing it his whole life and he felt very comfortable leading out there at Pierce Point.

"Thanks for coming over this morning," Grant said. "I wanted to go over a few business items while we're all here. I guess it's no secret that things are kinda going downhill back in the city. Things will be rocky for a while. We will have to count on ourselves for food and security. I hope this is temporary; it probably will be. But we can't count on things just getting back to normal. Therefore, I propose that we treat our mutual survival as our jobs. Just like our former work jobs. We should put the time and energy we normally put into our old jobs into getting food and taking care of things here on Over Road. If things get better, this will have been a great big adventure we'll tell our grandkids about." Grant smiled. He wanted to be positive. "Is everyone okay with what I'm talking about here?"

Most people slowly nodded, including Lisa. He didn't know about the text and pictures of their trashed house. Lisa wouldn't tell Grant about that. It would be one more thing for him to worry about and she didn't want to worry him.

Grant had to get buy-in from the group on the big picture. It was time to go into the details. He had been thinking about them for quite some time.

"Good," he started, "sounds like we're all on the same page. Now that we have a full picture of how many of us are out here, we can start talking about splitting up duties like guard duty and food. If it's all right with you guys, I'd like to put Pow in charge of the guard duty." Everyone nodded.

"Chip," Grant continued, "I consider you part of the Team, so you'll be doing that kind of stuff, too." Chip grinned. He got enjoyment from being treated like one of the young guys. The guys on the Team nodded, too. They liked Chip. Everyone liked Chip.

"John, Mark, Paul, and I already know the drill," Grant said. "Could one or more of you guys get with Pow and the Team and go over the guard duty details?" John and Mark nodded. Grant wanted to make the three of them feel like they had something to add to the Team. He wanted them to be integrated to the largest extent possible, even though they weren't tactically trained or as well armed as the Team.

"John knows how to fix things," Grant said. "I'm sure others do, too, but I'd like John to be in charge of things like that."

Grant remembered Paul and his welding and machine shop skills. "Of course Paul knows welding and other heavy machining. John and Paul can be the fix-it crew." John gave everyone the thumbs up sign.

"Speaking of Paul," Grant said. "He's on guard duty right now. With he and John doing all the repairs, those two probably shouldn't be in the guard rotation," Grant said, looking at Pow. Besides, Grant didn't say it, but John was a little old and Paul was, well, totally out of shape. They wouldn't be the best for guard duty.

"We're doing well on food," Grant continued. "The Colsons have plenty of steaks." He didn't want to say "deer" because the kids wouldn't eat them. "So I'd like Tammy to be in charge of the nightly group dinners." She nodded. "Mark and John can work on getting plenty more dinner material out in the forest and the beach." More nodding.

"If my 'job' is hunting and fishing, I'm good with that," Mark said with a big grin.

Grant looked at John and said, "Yes, John, that would be hunting and fixing things for you. Double duty. But Mark will be the lead on hunting and fishing if that's okay with you."

"Hunting, fishing, and fixing things is what I'm doing during my retirement anyway," John said. He gave the thumbs up again.

"Mary Anne is a gardener and canner," Grant said. "So is Eileen. I bet you two can team up to make sure we have lots of good stuff." Both ladies smiled. They were glad to be part of this. It wasn't all about guns. There were roles for everyone. People can't eat guns.

Grant continued, "It's not like we need to start gathering food and preserving it right now. I have plenty of stored food and can share. Most of you do, too. But Mary Anne and Eileen should start thinking about what to grow and preserve now and then we can do it in the summer and fall, if things go that long, which would surprise me." That was a lie; Grant fully expected this to go a full year; and probably several years.

Mary Anne said, "Like the apple trees. We can get all the apples in the summer and can them."

"Exactly," Grant said. "We're at the planning stages now. Thank goodness this thing hit in the spring. Maybe you can find out if you need some canning supplies. We'll figure out how to get some in time for canning later. That kind of thing." Grant had been thinking about canning apples since he came to the cabin and saw the wild apple trees. Now it was time to get those wheels in motion.

"Drew, I need someone to keep track of all the stuff we have," Grant said. "An inventory. Who has a generator, who needs prescription medication, that kind of thing. This is more important than it might seem." Drew was glad that there was a role for a retired accountant.

"We'll continue to have breakfasts here for a while," Grant said. "We have quite a bit of pancake mix. But at some point, we'll be switching over to other things." Grant knew that the pancake mix would be running out in a week or two. Breakfast for about fifteen every day would exhaust even the best cache of food. He didn't want to say that because it could cause panic, but he wanted to introduce the idea that he couldn't keep doing breakfast for fifteen every day. "We have lots of biscuit mix," he added. Introduce the idea that things will run out, but remind them that there were substitutes. He wanted to balance lowering their expectations while also instilling hope.

"Lisa is in charge of medical things, of course," Grant said. What Lisa didn't know was that Grant already had a plan for her to be the Pierce Point doctor. In fact, being able to offer an ER doctor to the residents was a key part of his plan to build up Pierce Point as a solid defensible and sustainable community. But, he needed to ease her into that.

"Knowing Lisa like I do," he smiled at her, "she will be helping with absolutely everything when she's not doing medical things. So I guess her second job out here is 'being Lisa.'" She smiled at him. She was glad that Grant appreciated all she did in addition to her doctor job.

"I'd like each of you to talk to her about any medical conditions you have," Grant said. Everyone nodded.

"Manda," Grant said, "you have a duty, too, and a very

important one. You will be taking care of Cole. He doesn't need full time attention, but you need to be around him. You will be helping with lots of miscellaneous things. So will Cole, but you're in charge of him, okay?"

"Of course, Dad," Manda said.

Grant looked to see if Paul's five-year old daughter, Missy, was there. She was. "Tammy, do you think Paul would mind if Manda looked after Missy, too? I think Missy and Cole could become friends." What Grant didn't say is that Missy, at age five, had roughly the same language skills as Cole, at age thirteen.

"Sure," Tammy said. "With Paul doing his job out here and me at the power company, Missy could use some looking after, especially now that there are…" she almost said, "criminals roaming around" but she didn't. "There are more things going on," she said.

"Tammy," Grant said, "is a special case. In addition to the dinners at her place, she has a traditional job. At least I think you do, right?"

"As far as I know," Tammy said, "I'm still working at the power company."

"Well, go to your job," Grant said. "Lord knows we need the power to stay on. Could you still coordinate the dinners? You can ask any of us, including me, to help you with that."

"Sure," Tammy said. Working her normal job and cooking for everyone was typical for her.

Grant said, "That's a good point, too. I'm sure we'll all pitch in with whatever we need to. I, for one, don't have any specific duties. I'll just make sure all the other stuff gets done, but I'll be working on these things from dawn until dusk. Is everyone all right with me having that role?" Grant figured the Morrells and Colsons would be fine with him running things since he brought the Team to protect them. The Team would be fine with it because Grant brought them to Pierce Point. His family would be fine with it because they were his family.

More general nodding of heads.

"We don't have a washing machine at my cabin," Grant said. "Could we do laundry at the Morrells' or Colsons'?"

"We have fewer people using our machine so we could do it," Mary Anne said. Tammy nodded.

"The Team's cabin has a washer and dryer so you guys can do your own laundry," Grant said. "Don't be lazy bachelors."

That brought up a good point. People feeling like others weren't doing enough. It wasn't a problem now, but it could be over time. Especially with so many people who didn't really know each other.

"If anyone has a concern about their duties or other people's, let me know," Grant said. "No, seriously, let me know. Even if you think I'm not pulling my weight. We'll all be helping everyone and I'd like it to be as smooth as possible."

Grant realized he was making it sound like they were in a work camp. So he said, "Hey, we won't be working all the time. We are out here in a beautiful place and our day jobs, except Tammy's, have been put on hold. This is a vacation in a sense. We have to do things we normally didn't have to, like hunt, can food, and guard our neighborhood. But we can still have lots of fun. I think this might actually be relaxing once we get into the swing of it."

Grant looked at Lisa. She wasn't fully going for it. She was expressionless again. Not that she disagreed with Grant, she was just waiting to see if this really would be a "vacation."

Grant continued, "Beach walks, campfires, playing board games, getting to know each other. This could be decent."

Grant had to close this by tying everything together. "This beats the heck out of what most people in town are having to go through." More nodding.

He even saw a slight nod from Lisa.

Chapter 80

My Husband Got Himself in a Little Trouble

(May 8)

The first meeting of the Over Road People, as Grant was calling the group out at the cabin, went well. He had a plan and the group agreed with his approach. He was very proud that things seemed to be going well. So far.

At first, he was surprised that these strangers were working so well together and seemed to understand that things had fundamentally changed. He thought about it and realized there were two reasons why this was true. First, the new arrivals, like Lisa, had seen with their own eyes how things had broken down; riding in an armed convoy tends to prove to a person that things aren't like they used to be. Second, most of the people there, like the Colsons, Morrells, and the Team, were preppers. They weren't surprised that everything they'd been planning for was coming true.

After the business of the meeting was done, Grant patted his tummy, which was flat because he was in the best shape of his life and said, "I'm hungry." Manda brought him a big plate of pancakes, which smelled delicious.

Everyone was talking with each other. There was a friendly buzz in the air. They were still getting to know each other, as the introductions the night before were rather brief.

After he ate, Grant said to Lisa, "So I'll go into town and get the 'feminine products' and other things."

Lisa looked scared. She shook her head. She knew something he didn't know.

"You don't want me to get those things?" Grant asked. He was relieved.

"No, honey," she said. "We need to talk." She motioned for him to come into the bedroom.

This seemed pretty serious. Grant followed.

She whispered, "Grant, you can't go into town." She was searching for the words. She might as well just tell him.

"Um, you're on a list of 'terrorists,'" she said. "It's called the 'Persons of Interest' list. 'POI' for short. It's one step down from a wanted list. They say they just want to talk to you. Nancy Ringman told me you were on it. I looked it up myself; it is true. It says you work for the Washington Association of Business and something about 'Rebel Radio,' whatever that is."

Oh, shit. At first, Grant thought Lisa was kidding, but he hadn't told her about Rebel Radio so she must have got that from looking on the internet.

Grant was initially stunned, but then he wasn't. He knew that it was only a matter of time before this corrupt government of bullies did this. It's what collapsing governments always did.

Grant didn't know what to say. He thought he was in trouble when he killed those looters, but this was worse. He assumed he had to lay low because the cops would find out he was WAB and perhaps not give him the benefit of the doubt on his self-defense. His court cases for WAB had taught him that "conservatives" often don't get a fair shake in the current so-called "justice" system.

Grant didn't know what to say. He was on a terrorist watch list. What is there to say?

"I'm sorry, honey," he said finally. "I'm sorry I'm causing you and the kids trouble like this." It was quiet for a while in the bedroom. Outside, people were talking and having a great time.

"I wish it hadn't happened, but it's not your fault," Lisa said finally. Whoa. That surprised Grant.

"I can see what's going on," Lisa said. "People like Nancy Ringman." Lisa proceeded to tell Grant the story about how Nancy had thrown Cole to the ground.

Grant was not mad. Sure, he didn't like what Nancy had done, but he knew that he couldn't just march over to her house and punch her in the mouth. Besides, she was far away. She couldn't hurt them out there.

Lisa finished the story by saying, "Now I get what they're all about. They're crazy. They hate anyone who crosses them. So it's not your fault."

She added, "You know, when Cole screamed, 'Why are you hurting us?' it got me thinking. Why are they hurting us? They're crazy and desperate. It's not your fault."

Wow. Thank God that's what she thought.

"The government can't even keep the power on all the time or the internet up. They can't put out fires or stop protestors and looters. I don't think they can start finding the people on their list." Grant was half serious, half trying to calm Lisa.

"Yeah," Lisa said. "That's probably right. Anyway, you can't go into town. Not until things calm down and we can clear all of this up."

That was a surprisingly positive way to look at this. Maybe she wasn't suffering from as much normalcy bias as Grant had thought. Or maybe the Nancy Ringman thing had changed her. Either way, Grant was glad that Lisa was back on his side.

"Okay, I won't go into town," Grant said. Then he thought of a new problem. "How do we tell your parents this? They'll probably be disappointed that their daughter married a terrorist." They both started laughing and couldn't stop. It was a release from all the emotion.

"I'll have to tell them," Lisa said. "Should we tell everyone out here?"

"Good question," Grant said. "I'll have to think about that. I trust all of them, but I don't want to freak them out," he said. "Oh, wait. They'll probably read it on the internet, anyway. Crap. We should probably just tell them." This sucked. Then Grant had an idea.

He pointed out toward everyone in the next room, "If they're all with me and I'm on some watch list, then that makes them accessories. Harboring a fugitive. They're in this with me. That should give them an incentive not to report me."

Lisa was impressed. She never thought lawyers were terribly useful. She loved Grant, but she saved lives and he just argued about the meaning of words. However, this harboring a fugitive concept was a useful idea.

"Good idea," she said. "I'll tell them. I'm all nice and everything and you're a terrorist, so I can break it to them more softly than you. What do you think?"

God, it felt great to have her on his side again.

"Sounds good," he said. Grant paused, "Who else is on the list? Anyone else from WAB?"

Lisa nodded. "All of you. Tom, Brian, and Ben."

Grant hadn't thought of them in a few days. He'd been so busy worrying about his own family. Were the WAB families okay? Maybe they needed to come out there.

"I should call them," Grant said, and then instantly realized how stupid that was.

"No way," said Lisa. "That's what they'll be waiting for. Assuming there are any police or FBI or whatever available to monitor these things. Probably not, but it's not worth the risk. For either you or who you're calling."

Grant thought about Manda's phone. He could use that one.

But he didn't know a fake phone the WAB guys might be using. He just had their numbers. And a call to one of their numbers could be fatal.

Grant realized that he had no way of contacting them. None. They were totally on their own. He felt guilty. He should have seen this coming and he should have made plans for them to bug out to his cabin. He planned on doing that, but things blew up so quickly. There were too many things to plan and not enough time. Then again, months ago he wouldn't have approached his co-workers with this idea because they would have thought he was crazy. It was kind of their fault, Grant realized, because his friends had treated him as a little crazy for being a "survivalist" so Grant hadn't pushed it with them. And now they probably wished he had.

Lisa and Grant were silent as they thought about their friends getting arrested and … worse.

Grant needed to use humor to lighten up the mood. "Well, I'll just tell Pow to go buy you some tampons." They broke into that uncontrollable emotional-release laughter.

They came out of the bedroom with tears in their eyes. Everyone looked at them, not wanting to ask what had just happened.

Lisa smiled and said, "My husband here has gotten himself in a little trouble. We need your help." She proceeded to explain about the POI list and how everyone in the cabin were now accessories.

Lisa was trying to gauge the reaction of her parents. Would they be devastated that their son-in-law was a "terrorist"? Or would they realize what was really going on?

She did a great job with the announcement, and reminded them, "It's not like the police can just send a car out to go get people. There are no police right now. There's no way they can actually get Grant. Besides, he's just a 'person of interest.' He's not actually wanted."

She paused. "Don't tell a soul about this. Not one. We don't need the attention. Seriously. Please do not tell anyone. Since this list is just symbolic and no one can do anything to actually get these people, put it out of your mind. It didn't happen."

Chip added, "We need Grant so we can make it through this. He's pretty involved in what we're all doing out here. We can't do anything to put him out of commission." Chip was concerned that his stash of guns was in the basement of someone who was on a watch list. That would increase the odds of attention they didn't want.

Eileen was concerned. She wanted to know more about the list. She asked who else was on the list, and found out all the conservative politicians that she had voted for were on the list. It was clear that the list was entirely political. She couldn't really get her mind past the fact that her son-in-law was wanted, but at least it wasn't a real crime.

The Team thought Grant being a POI was cool. They knew that the guns they owned either had been outlawed by some executive order or would be soon. They had cast their lot with the outlaws. Now it was official.

The Morrells were excited about it. They hated the government and this made Grant a hero.

The Colsons were fine with it. They didn't like the government, but Mark and Tammy worried a little that a POI would generate some interest from the authorities about their little community. But they also realized that the government had its hands full right now. Besides, Grant was a lawyer and it was just a "persons of interest" list so, if the authorities restored order, Grant would probably talk his way out of any trouble. It's not like he was an actual terrorist.

It was time for some humor. Grant needed to show everyone that he wasn't worried about being labeled a "terrorist."

"Hey, Pow," Grant said, "since I can't go into town, the Team should. Guess what's on the shopping list?" Grant motioned for Pow to come over. Grant whispered to him that tampons were on the shopping list.

"No way!" Pow said. "I will do anything for you, brother, but..." He looked at Lisa and said, "Okay, man. Even that. You owe me." No one else got the joke, but it still helped lighten the mood.

Next, they talked about how to go into town and get supplies. They decided that one person from each family would come to make sure they got the right things. One member of the Team would drive them and be armed. Concealed pistols on each guy and ARs in the trucks. Each family member would go armed, except Lisa, who still couldn't stand the idea of having a gun. Actually, the reason she didn't want to have a gun was that she didn't know how to use one. She didn't want to look stupid, so she maintained the "guns are bad" thing that she had believed her whole life up until yesterday.

They were coming up with prioritized shopping lists. There was so much to get. It was kind of frightening how much they needed for the next ... while. No one would put a timeframe on their stay out here. Everyone kept thinking it would be a while, though they had no idea how long it would be.

As scary as it was not knowing how long they'd have to be out there, it was reassuring that they could go to the store, at least in armed groups and still get things. Probably. Depending on what was on the shelves.

The Over Road People hadn't initially appreciated how far ahead of the rest of the population they were, but they were starting to appreciate it now. They knew the real situation that America was in. Many people out there—despite the riots, looting, terrorism, power and internet going off sporadically and the government issuing all kinds of emergency decrees—still didn't understand that they needed to stock up. The Over Road People understood that, when they went into town that morning, they would probably get the last of the stuff on the shelves and at the gas pumps.

They started to round up cash. They only had a few hundred dollars between them. The ATMs were out of order. No one carried huge quantities of cash anymore and prices would probably be outrageous. They quickly realized they would have trouble buying anything with the cash they had. A sense of doom came over the group. Everything had been going so well until now.

Drew got up and motioned for Grant to come with him outside.

Chapter 81

The Fredrickson Milk Run

(May 8)

Drew took Grant out to his car.

"What's going on?" Grant asked.

He put his finger up to his lips to signal that Grant shouldn't talk.

When Drew was at his car and where no one could see him, he unlocked his car and pulled something from under the driver's seat.

Drew was holding a large mailing envelope. He smiled and handed it to Grant.

"Go ahead and look inside," Drew said, still smiling.

Grant opened it. It was full of $100 bills. He couldn't believe it. Drew kept smiling.

"I had a little account," Drew said, "on the side for a big trip I was planning on taking Eileen on." He paused and looked out toward Fredrickson. "No use trying to take a trip now. I pulled this out of the bank about a week ago, when it was obvious that the banks would be closed soon. I didn't tell Eileen. Do you think she'll be mad?" Grant could relate.

"Yes, for about five minutes," Grant said. "Then she'll be glad and, if she's like Lisa, she'll never tell you she's glad. She'll just be nice to you like nothing happened, like she had never been wrong." The two men laughed because they knew it was true. Eileen and Lisa were so similar.

"Where should I keep this?" Drew asked.

"We have some other high-value items," Grant said with a wink. "I can't say right now what they are, but you'll see in a while. I could keep your envelope with them." Drew would never trust someone with tens of thousands of dollars of cash, but Grant was his son-in-law and had basically sent an armed team to rescue him. Besides, what good is cash if you don't have guards and a safe place to stay?

Drew pointed to the envelope of cash and said, "Don't lose this."

Grant realized the politics of the situation. "Drew, this is very generous of you," he said. "I want you to get the credit with everyone for this. You can hand out the money. A few hundred bucks a carload. I will put the rest of the money in the safe place first so they don't see it."

Drew nodded and smiled. He wasn't looking for "points" with the Over Road People; he was just trying to get them supplies they'd all need.

Grant knew that Drew, who was a little older than the others and didn't have traditional survival skills to offer the group, needed to have a role everyone would appreciate. Handing out $100 bills, especially in a crisis, was a good way to make friends.

"Sure," Drew said. He started thinking about the insane inflation that would be roaring that morning. "I think with all the crazy prices, $500 a carload ought to work. I'll take another $1,000 in case we need more. I have my gun and there's all your guys with their guns, and there's John who's got a gun, too. We'll be fine carrying around all that cash." Grant nodded. Drew counted out a number of $100 bills and gave the envelope with the remaining cash to Grant.

"Don't watch where I'm going," Grant said, only half kidding. After Drew had gone back inside, Grant walked around the cabin a few times and then quickly disappeared into the basement and came right out, double checking to make sure the basement door was locked.

When Grant was done, he found Drew in the cabin chatting. He hadn't handed out the cash yet. Grant motioned for him to come over. One by one, Drew handed out $500 to each driver. Eileen looked at Drew as if to say, "What?" Drew put his finger up to his lips to tell her not to say anything.

As Drew handed out money to each carload, Grant would say, "This is one of Drew's contributions to the effort." Everyone's eyes were wide. It wasn't every day they were given a handful of $100 bills. They all thanked Drew. He was very proud that an old accountant was able to contribute to the effort.

"Now the hard part," Grant said to Drew. "You have to go tell Eileen where the money came from." Drew nodded and went to find Eileen.

She didn't take it well at first, but, just as they predicted, she was okay with it after it sunk in. "I told her they were loans," Drew said to Grant. "And I told her that I'm crazy. She seemed to accept that," he said with a smile.

People gathered by the truck they'd be taking into town. The Team had a dog tag chain visible around their necks. They had their "badges" under their shirts. Those could really come in handy.

Everyone got in the trucks and headed out. They would be going into Fredrickson, the town a few miles from the cabin. The town had a couple of big stores, but was much smaller than Olympia.

Pow took Lisa. They would focus on getting medical supplies. And ... feminine products. They would be going to the drug store first.

Bobby took Mary Anne. She would focus on canning and preserving supplies. She would also buy bulk food and gas. Everyone was trying to get gas and gas cans. Grant had two five-gallons cans at the cabin with gas, including Stabil, which was the additive that allowed gas to be stored for years without deteriorating. But that wasn't enough. They would need more. Lots more.

Wes took John and Drew. They would focus on bulk food first and building supplies second. Specifically, they were going to get pancake mix, biscuit mix, oatmeal, and any other items that were cheap and easy to store (and cook) that could be the breakfast anchor at Grant's cabin. Let the grasshoppers clean out the Doritos; the Over Road crew would get the oatmeal.

Scotty took Mark. They would focus on hunting and fishing supplies. They would also get household items, like matches and Stabil gas preservative. Grant had printed out a list several months ago from the Survival Podcast forum and put it in the storage shed. It was called "The 100 Things to Disappear First in a Crisis." It was invaluable.

Given the danger of the grocery store, Wes wanted to bring a rifle with him, but couldn't walk around with it. He asked Grant, "Hey, man, you got that AK underfolder out here? It could go under a baggy shirt."

Grant smiled. "Sure 'nuff, brother." He got his AK with the wire stock that folded under the gun so it was much shorter than a fixed-stock rifle. Grant called the underfolder the "checkpoint" gun because it was small enough to be hidden in a car and get past a checkpoint. When he started using that phrase it was a joke, but it was serious now.

Grant also got a big buttoned-front camouflage hunting shirt sized for his formerly heavy self. He handed Wes three extra 30-round loaded magazines. Wes put the underfolder on with the sling and threw the hunting shirt over it. Perfect. The AK was undetectable.

Drew just watched. He'd never seen an AK-47 and now a guy he'd known for a few hours was wearing one concealed and Drew was getting in a truck with him. Drew had his revolver and a pocketful of shells.

This all seemed normal. Not normal in the sense of it being

common, just normal in the sense that there was such a good reason to do it.

Mark brought his shotgun, which was a nice duck hunting gun. Scotty had a tactical shotgun that would work better. Scotty pulled Grant off to the side, explained that Mark was bringing a duck gun and asked, "Shouldn't I let Mark use my Benelli?" That was his high-end tactical shotgun that looked like a SWAT gun. "It's shorter and holds more rounds."

Grant said, "Nah, I don't want to overwhelm these guys with our tactical stuff. We need to integrate with them and they'll integrate with us, eventually. It's just day two out here. Besides, I bet Mark has shot that thing hundreds of times. He's probably really good with it. And, in a pinch, he could carry that around town and everyone would just think he's a good ole' boy hunter, not a threat like they'd think if they saw your tricked out Benelli." Scotty nodded.

Grant had another idea. He wanted to get Mark into the effort instead of just riding along with the Team. He turned to Scotty and Mark and said, "Hey, how about if you two go in Mark's truck instead of Scotty's? It would make sense for the neighbors to see a familiar truck instead of all these strangers' trucks driven by strange men." Mark liked that idea.

Mark said, "I can take the lead, so the Pierce Point people can see me. I can wave like everything is normal. And I know how to get to Frederickson and," he motioned toward Scotty, "you guys don't."

Scotty was realizing that there was a little politics involved in everything. "Good idea," he said.

Mark was relieved that he was having a part in all this. He liked the young men on the Team and was very glad they were there, but he didn't want them running everything. Mark lived here. He knew the area, the people in Pierce Point, and the hunting and fishing. He was a country boy and a former Marine. He knew how to take care of himself. Grant could tell that Mark's pride was a factor. Mark wasn't a jerk about it, but he had skills. Grant wanted them to be utilized. All the tactical stuff of the Team was fine, but a local country boy is just as important an asset. In fact, if Grant had to choose, he'd take all Marks over all Team members, when it came to generalized skills to make it through this. But Grant was lucky to have both local country boys like Mark and John—and the Team. This combination was the best of both worlds.

The Team would use their CBs to keep in contact with one another while they were on the road. Scotty quickly detached the magnetic antenna on his truck and put it on Mark's truck, which was a black Chevy four-door Silverado. They were good to go.

Grant and Chip would stay behind for guard duty. Paul was the backup guard. Chip probably could have gone into town and he wanted to, but he realized that they would need at least three guys to repel anything that could come. There probably wasn't enough, but it would have to do.

At 9:30 a.m., the trucks rumbled out of their little compound with Mark in the lead. Mark's diesel truck made that distinctive pinging sound.

Once they got past the guard shack and onto the paved road, they were all on high alert. Not only for cops or bad guys, but also to see what life was like in a quickly collapsing America.

It looked like everyone in Pierce Point was home on this Tuesday morning. No one was going to work, which made sense. Other than for essential services, like Tammy at the power company, there wasn't much point in people going to work with the internet down, gas in short supply, and everyone worried about their family's safety. School had been cancelled days ago, so parents needed to stay home.

Families were outside talking to their neighbors with their kids running around. No one was visibly armed. It looked like a block party with everyone out and talking to each other, except there was no party atmosphere. It reminded Grant a little of 9/11. Back then, neighbors were out talking to each other; sometimes for the first time ever.

Many nice people waved to Mark and the strange collection of trucks and people with him. They went by the Pierce Point Store, a little country store the size of a convenience store with a gas pump. There was a sign on the pump saying, "Out." The store was locked up; presumably with emptied shelves.

There were several cars in the parking lot, with people talking at one another from their windows. They waved at Mark and looked at the rest of the convoy of strangers. Some in the parking lot had been noticing quite a few strangers. They figured that people with cabins were coming out and bringing their friends. That was fine with the Pierce Point full-time residents. The "cabin people," as the "full timers" called them, were usually nice and spent their money there. The cabins at Pierce Point weren't so fancy that most of the cabin people were stuck up.

The three mile drive through Pierce Point was quiet. They noticed one guy going to his mailbox with a gun on his belt, which seemed odd. Not the gun, but the fact that anyone would be expecting the mail to be delivered. Mail service had been suspended days ago. It was probably this guy's normal routine to check the mail in the morning.

As they came down the hill toward the turn onto the Frederickson road, there were a few pickups of men with rifles and shotguns guarding the bridge. There was a beater car parked sideways blocking the bridge and acting as a gate. This was the bridge over a little river that Pow had noticed when he came to see the cabin months ago. It was a natural choke point. A volunteer fire station was situated on the Pierce Point side of the bridge, where most of the trucks were parked. Nearly 100 yards of road and the turn off toward Frederickson was on the other side of the bridge. The 100 yards of road allowed those turning off the Frederickson road a chance to slow down and park before they were cleared to cross the bridge. It was an ideal checkpoint. Beyond ideal: absolutely perfect.

Mark recognized the lead guy at the checkpoint. It was Rich Gentry, a former county sheriff's deputy. Mark had always liked Rich, who had quit the force a few months ago because of all the corruption. Rich was a very respected guy in the community.

The convoy slowed down and Mark waved at Rich and his handful of men. One of them signaled for Mark to stop, so he did. Scotty grabbed the CB. Mark mouthed, "They're okay" about Rich and his guards, and Scotty said into the radio, "Mark says these guys are okay."

Rich came up to Mark's window. He was in his mid-thirties and in good shape. He was part Indian and had relatives on one of the nearby Indian reservations.

Rich said, "Howdy, Mark. How are things?"

"Okay, given the circumstances," Mark said. "Glad to see we have a guard set up. Been any trouble?"

"Not so far," Rich said. "but there will be. Some druggies will try to get in here, including our local druggies." Rich meant the Richardsons, a family of meth addicts and their shitbag friends. Pierce Point had been putting up with them and their petty theft for a while, but that had been when there was law around. Most people wanted to shoot the Richardson trash, but that wasn't possible with the police there to apprehend "vigilantes." However, things were different now.

Rich continued, "We're also making sure people coming in have some business in here. We wave in the full timers and we ask the cabin people where their cabin is or the cabin they're coming out to. So

57

far, everyone has checked out."

Rich, a curious cop by habit and training, looked at the other trucks full of strangers. "Who are these guys?" he asked Mark.

Mark trusted Rich, but didn't want to go spilling the beans at the drop of a hat. "Friends of mine," Mark answered. "They're friends of Grant Matson, the cabin guy who has a place by me. They're solid. Some young guys from the city who need a safe place. They're clean cut 'yes sir, yes ma'am' kind of guys. We're taking Grant's family into town to get some supplies. We're carrying concealed, of course." Mark didn't think it necessary to mention Wes's hidden AK or all the ARs in the trucks.

Mark pointed to his shotgun that was in the cab of the truck. Rich nodded. Scotty had thrown a jacket over his AR, which was between his legs. Scotty was glad that Mark had a "duck" gun in the cab of his truck instead of a tricked out SWAT shotgun. The duck gun looked much less threatening to the law, or whatever Rich was right now.

Rich said, "We hear things are pretty rough in town. Not full-on violent, just very tense. In fact, I'm surprised the stores are open, but they are. Most, anyway. Even some of the gas stations. My former colleagues," Rich meant the sheriff's department, "are pretty much gone. They've been working nonstop for several days. Most are back with their families. The single guys are sitting in grocery stores and trying to stop fights. There's no law anymore." Rich wanted to say more, but didn't.

"There's no law anymore" rang in Mark and Scotty's ears. It sounded so weird for someone to say that.

Mark nodded. They needed to get going. "We'll see you in a few hours."

Rich said, "Beware of the Mexican gangs. They've always kept to themselves, but I'm hearing that they are starting to get aggressive now." Frederickson, like many towns in the West, had a sizable Mexican population. The vast majority were hardworking families, but in every group there were always a few bad apples. The Mexican gangs were tolerated by the law-abiding Mexican populations and the cops tolerated them too, making lots of "donut money" on the side for looking the other way. This is why Rich and all the decent cops had left the force.

"Will do," Mark said. He looked at Scotty, who nodded. Mark waved and Rich gave the signal to move the car. A man jumped in and drove a few feet forward, opening up the bridge for traffic. The Over

Road trucks drove past, each driver making sure to make eye contact with the guards and wave. Rich was writing down their license plate numbers on a clipboard.

Chapter 82

Drug Store and Gas

(May 8)

There was more traffic on the road to Frederickson than there had been on the previous day; quite a bit more traffic coming from Frederickson toward the other little communities on the water, like Pierce Point. There were at least a dozen of these communities, all with varying mixtures of full timers and cabin people. It seemed that quite a few cabin people had the same idea as the Matsons and they were bringing out their friends and relatives.

As they went toward the outskirts of Frederickson, Mark motioned for Scotty to give him the CB. He said into the CB, "Pow, you're the only truck who doesn't have a local riding who can tell the driver where the store is. Follow me and I'll get you to the drugstore."

"Roger that," Pow replied. That was a little "military" for Mark's taste, but he was sure glad those boys were along for the ride. This ride into town was the most danger Mark had been in since the Marine Corps. He was glad to have well-armed back up.

They were going by a gas station at the time, so Mark said, "Meet back at this gas station at noon." That gave them two hours to get their stuff. He handed the CB back to Scotty.

"Bring your handheld CB with you," Scotty said. They were small enough to fit in a big pocket.

Pow got on the CB and said, "Don't hold them in your hands when you're walking around. People will want to steal them and you can't draw with your hands full." That alarmed Lisa, but she was getting used to these kinds of conversations.

Wes, John, and Drew were the first to peel off. They headed toward the big grocery store in town. Next, Bobby and Mary Anne went to the farm supply store. Pow followed Mark to the drugstore. The CBs were quiet.

Mark got Pow to the drugstore and said on the CB, "There it is."

"Thanks," Pow said. "We got it from here."

Mark and Scotty headed out to the big store with sporting goods and hardware. It was like a mini Wal-Mart, but locally owned.

Pow got out of the Hummer, looked around and then opened Lisa's door. He looked like a Secret Service agent, except he didn't have a suit and earpiece.

The place looked okay. They went in. At the entrance was a rent-a-cop with a gun on his belt. Pow had never seen one with a gun; most rent-a-cops just had radios. There was a sign by the rent-a-cop that said, "No Prescriptions." Pow greeted him and kept walking.

The drug store was crowded. People were acting semi-normally, filling up their carts. Some seemed a little tense, but it was a lot more normal in there than Pow expected. It seemed about right to Lisa, who hadn't had had the same experience Pow had in the drugstore with Mrs. Nguyen.

Lisa went to the first aid aisles. The store still had most things. The junk food and sexual products aisles were pretty bare, but they still had first aid supplies. The grasshoppers had priorities.

Lisa started putting bandages, gauze, rubbing alcohol, burn cream, and similar items in her cart. She was just grabbing all they had. She had no idea what it would cost, but she had $500 and was going to use it. Maybe for the last time.

She went to the over-the-counter medicine aisle and got all the anti-diarrheal medications and electrolytes she could. Lisa remembered a doctor friend of hers who went to help after the Haitian earthquake. Her friend told her that when essential services are gone, most of the deaths are from the diarrhea that comes from water-borne illnesses. Of course, this could be completely preventable with a few cents worth of anti-diarrheals and electrolytes.

Lisa got all the pain relievers she could. Pow kept an eye on her and the other people in the aisle. He would periodically check around corners to make sure no one was lurking. It was probably overkill, but he didn't want to return to Grant and explain why his wife had been killed. Besides, Pow was really good and he wanted to use his skills.

When Lisa had a full cart, Pow got out the list the guys had made. He got shaving supplies, deodorant, shampoo, toothbrushes, and toothpaste.

While he was doing that, Lisa went over to the feminine aisle. She saw Pow and asked, "could you get another cart?" He brought one to her and she filled the second cart with feminine products. She couldn't imagine being without those and they might not be able to go to the store for a while.

Lisa and Pow checked and rechecked their lists. For the first time, they looked at the prices. They hadn't seemed to have gone up yet. The store's pricing computers were probably hard to change for thousands of products, so the prices remained the same.

"Got everything?" Lisa asked Pow.

"Yep. You?" he asked.

"Yep," she said.

They headed to the checkout. There was a line, but not an abnormally long one. Pow couldn't look at the tampons in the cart. He swore that if anyone gave him shit about it, he'd shoot them. He just might. He laughed at himself for being so stupid.

The bill came to $217.

"Plus the 50% surcharge" the checker said.

"The what?" Lisa asked.

"The surcharge," the checker said. She'd been explaining this all morning and some of the people were getting angry. The rent-a-cop perked up.

"We can't change all the prices in the computer fast enough," the checker said, "so we have a surcharge at final check out."

Even with a 50% surcharge, this was still a bargain. Lisa motioned for Pow to shield her from view, which got the rent-a-cop, fearing she was pulling a gun, to stand. Pow motioned to him that things were cool and said, "She's just counting the money."

Lisa, using Pow as a shield, hid the bills she was counting out; there was no need for someone to see the wad of cash and try to rob her. She rolled up the four $100 bills in her hand and handed them to the clerk, whose eyes got big. She'd been seeing lots of cash this morning, but four $100 bills was still a lot of money.

Without thinking, the clerk said out loud, for everyone to hear, "Out of $400." Lisa and Pow cringed. "Shut up!" they wanted to say to her. They got their change.

Pow was in full ready mode. People knew they had some money and they had two carts to wheel out to the car. This was the prime time to be attacked. They wheeled the carts slowly to the Hummer. Pow walked around the car once to make sure no one was lurking. Again, overkill. But this was not the time to be worried about whether people think you're overdoing it. This was the time to come back home alive and with your stuff.

They loaded the items into the Hummer and Lisa looked at her list. "How about some gas?" she asked. Pow looked at his gas gauge. He was at a half tank. He had a big tank, but his Hummer wasn't exactly fuel efficient.

"Sure," he said. Filling up would probably eat up the rest of the money. They found a gas station nearby. It had a line about eight cars long. People seemed calmer than they were in Olympia when Pow and Lisa left there yesterday. Still, Pow had his concealed Glock and an AR in the Hummer.

While they were waiting, Pow got out of the Hummer so he could see all angles better. He was scanning everyone, looking for sketchy people and any trouble. He felt like it would be more polite to stay in the Hummer and make small talk with Lisa, but he had a job to do. They'd have days or weeks or whatever to talk back at the cabin. Lisa was quiet, sitting in the passenger side trying not to make eye contact with people.

It was finally their turn at the pump. The handwritten sign said, "Pre Pay Inside. Cash." This created a dilemma. Would Pow go in and leave Lisa and the stuff, including the AR, there? Or would Lisa have to go in with the cash? Pow decided that they would both go in. He motioned for her to follow him. He made sure the Hummer was locked.

They went into the store where an Arabic man said, "Cash. $15 a gallon. What pump number?" Lisa got out the almost $200 she had and said, "Fill up on pump…"

Pow finished the sentence, "Three." Lisa put all that money on the counter. It looked weird paying that much for a half tank of gas.

They left quickly, because Pow wanted to be back with his AR. He thought about how gas was $10 a gallon yesterday and $15 today. This wasn't good. The gas station owner thought he was a brilliant businessman for selling gas at $15 a gallon.

Pow and Lisa filled up as quickly as they could. Their money got them about twelve gallons; enough to get Pow to almost full. They zoomed out of there. Pow felt so much better with that gas gauge needle near "F." He navigated his way back to the rendezvous. It was 11:10 a.m. They had a while to wait. He got on the CB and told the others where he was and that he could help them, if necessary. Except that he didn't know how to get where they were. He made a mental note that if they went into town again or anywhere else, they would need to have someone in each vehicle who knew their way around. There was no doubt that getting lost could get someone killed.

Chapter 83

Picking Up Chicks

(May 8)

Mary Anne and Bobby went to the farm supply store. She went there a few times a year. It was owned by a nice family.

The parking lot was full and there were plenty of people there, but everyone was polite. There were no armed guards. Bobby saw a few of the shoppers with revolvers tucked in their belts, only semi-concealed. The farm store seemed much safer than the grocery store and gas stations Bobby had been to in Olympia on the previous milk runs.

Mary Anne hoped the farm supply store would have canning supplies and seeds. Sure enough, they had some. Lots, in fact.

She started with the canning supplies. She had a Presto canner from Wal-Mart and it was okay but she knew she'd be canning large quantities this summer and fall. Lots of salmon, clams, and oysters and then fruits and vegetables.

She couldn't believe they still had pressure cookers. She got two of the All Americans, the twenty-one quart ones without a rubber gasket, so they would last a lifetime. They weren't cheap, but this was no time to save cash … which would probably be worthless pretty soon, anyway.

She had some canning jars at home, but not nearly enough, so she got three cases of quart jars and five cases of pint jars, which was about half of what they had in stock.

Mary Anne realized how important canning lids were so she got 200 of each size lid. She remembered that Mrs. Roth, an elderly lady in Pierce Point, had a bunch of canning supplies that she never used. She would go see Mrs. Roth later and ask to have the lids in exchange for some of the canned food they made.

"Do you have any more of these?" Mary Anne asked the clerk.

"There's a limit on items per person," she said. Mary Anne vaguely recognized her as one of the owners' daughters.

The clerk thought a while. No one was really buying the canning supplies. Most of the customers at the farm supply store already had canning supplies. She figured Mary Anne could have about half of what they had in stock. "You're okay with the stuff you have," she said.

On to the seeds. The best selection of seeds was available a few months earlier, but it was early May and they still had plenty to choose from.

"These are heirlooms, right?" Mary Anne asked the clerk.

"Most of them are," she said. "The non-heirlooms are marked on the packages as 'hybrid.'"

Mary Anne knew heirloom seeds were the kind to get, as they would produce fertile seeds in the next crop and the seeds would continue to produce with seeds for the next season, and then the next. Non-heirloom seeds were good for only one season. Hybrids were better than nothing, but not the sustainability Mary Anne wanted.

Mary Anne started putting lots of seeds in her cart. She would get "calorie crops," food that contained the maximum calories. There would be no fancy gourmet crops this year. The years of gourmet meals were over in America, at least for most people. She picked out lima beans and crowder-type shelling peas.

While not "calorie crops," she got plenty of tomatoes and onions. She even got lettuce, although it might not grow very well in Western Washington. It would probably do okay, it just wouldn't be a staple like the next thing on her list, which was potatoes.

They had seed potatoes. Russets and red Pontiacs. Mary Anne noted the irony of her Irish ancestors escaping a potato famine in Ireland 150 years ago and now that might be what would be feeding her and her neighbors.

She realized that she'd need seed for crops to grow in the cooler season and "root cellar crops" that would store well. She got cabbage, squash (which she hated, but others might like), and carrots. Lots and lots of carrot seed.

The clerk saw this and said, "There's a limit on seed purchases per person."

Mary Anne was a little embarrassed. Was she hoarding? She wanted all the seeds, but didn't want to be seen as a "hoarder."

"What's the limit?" she asked.

"We kind of decide it based on each customer," the clerk admitted. "Pick out what you'd like and then we'll see," she said. Normally a varying limit would be unfair, but Mary Anne trusted the store to be fair.

Mary Anne saw they had chainsaws. John had a large one and a small one, both Stihls. She knew the kind of oil to get for them. She bought a case of it. They could have all the gas in the world but without that oil to mix in it, the saws wouldn't work. She remembered the blade lengths of John's saws and got a spare chain for each one.

Mary Anne heard some chickens. That's what they needed. The store had a bunch of chicks and chickens. She got twenty chicks, a few hens, and a rooster. That would supply roughly an egg a day, and the rooster and hens would produce fryers once in a while. They didn't have a chicken coop, but John could build one. Chickens didn't eat much and sure produced tasty protein.

Mary Anne rounded out the shopping trip with chicken feed and fertilizer.

Bobby noticed that they were attracting attention with their cases of canning supplies and huge load of seeds. People were starting to look at them like hoarders. "This is probably enough," Bobby said to Mary Anne. "We should get going."

Mary Anne wanted to keep getting things; she might not get a chance to come back for a while or ever. But she looked around, noticed it was silent in the store and that everyone was looking at them. Yep, it was time to go.

"I think I have everything on my list," Mary Anne said.

They paid for their items. Prices hadn't gone up there. Mary Anne thought that if she had extra seeds she'd bring them back to the store, if she could get there and let them sell them to someone else. There was an honor system at the farm supply store. Besides, the family who owned the store had their own farm, and were largely self-sufficient. They didn't need to rip people off to survive, so they didn't.

Bobby loaded all the stuff into the back of his truck. The chicks were chirping. He'd never picked up a box of live, noisy things.

They had just over $150 left. The farm supply store had a gas pump. "Do you have any gas?" Mary Anne asked the clerk.

"Yep," another clerk said. "But, I'm sorry, it's $10 a gallon."

"That's okay," Mary Anne said. She remembered they had gas cans in the chainsaw section. "Could I get a couple of gas cans and fill them up?" The clerk looked at the other customers, who didn't seem to be objecting and then nodded. Mary Anne got two five-gallon gas cans, the new plastic ones she didn't like, and went out to the gas pump outside.

Between the gas cans and Bobby's truck, it was a little less than fifteen gallons. She gave the clerk all her cash. "Keep the change," she said. It was the least she could do for all the extra stuff they let her buy. "We'll be back when we can," Mary Anne said. "I'll try to bring some seeds back if I can." The clerk nodded. She hoped Mary Anne would.

Bobby looked at his watch. It was 11:20 a.m. Time to head back to the rendezvous point at the gas station. It was only a few minutes away, but Bobby expected traffic or even a roadblock. He didn't want to be late.

He got on the CB and thought he'd have some fun and tell them that they had "picked up some chicks," which was technically true, but then he decided that this wasn't a time for joking and causing confusion. Stay off the radio if you can, he remembered Ted saying. So Bobby simply said into the CB, "Bobby here. We're all set. Heading to the meeting place unless anyone needs any help." Everyone radioed in that they were okay.

Chapter 84

Grocery Store

(May 8)

Wes, John, and Drew were heading toward the big grocery store in town. It looked like they weren't the only ones with that idea. The parking lot was packed. There was a line to just get into the parking lot, so they got in the line, which wasn't moving.

Wes didn't want to idle his engine for an hour, waste gas, and then not be able to do any actual shopping, given that they needed to be back at the rendezvous point at noon.

Drew said, "We could just park a few blocks away and walk in. We'll have to haul our stuff, but at least we'll be in there." Wes pulled out of the line and looked for street parking nearby. He found some about two blocks away. He was glad he didn't have his AR in the truck because he would have to leave it in there when he went into the store. He had the AK underfolder concealed beneath his hunting shirt so he didn't need an AR.

"I've got the cash, so let's go," Drew said. They got out of the truck and walked toward the grocery store. The crowd got bigger as they approached the entrance. People were antsy and some were arguing. A fight broke out as they got to the entrance. Two women were pushing each other and arguing over something. Bystanders pulled them apart. This was going to be an interesting trip to the grocery store.

One police officer stood inside the store at the entrance. He was young and looked very tired. He seemed oblivious to the women fighting and appeared useless, but he was there to make people think things were still "normal." Wes walked right past him with an illegally concealed rifle. Those kinds of laws seemed so quaint right now.

They noticed large swaths of shelves were empty. There were still some things, especially things that wouldn't keep long. The junk food was wiped out, though. People thought they could get by long on chips and cookies?

John pulled out the list, "Beans and rice." He headed toward the aisle they were on. He knew where they would be because this was his usual grocery store. They were pushing their way, politely, through the crowds choking each aisle. The beans and rice in five pound bags were cleaned out. There were some one-pound bags left. John started grabbing as many as he could.

"Hey! There's a limit!" a voice yelled out.

They turned around and there was a store clerk.

"No more than five of any item," he said angrily. He looked tired. He'd been in arguments for the past twenty-four hours with customers.

"Oh, sorry," said John. He put back all but five of the packages of beans.

John looked at his list. "Flour and mixes." He headed over toward that aisle.

Same thing. Large packages of flour and biscuit mix were gone. A few one-pound packages were left. John started looking at his list. "Gentlemen, it looks like we're not getting the staples here. We'll get the other things, like syrup." They got pasta sauces, jams, and lots of canned food. They were careful to limit things to five of each.

While they were getting canned beans in the Mexican food aisle, a woman was arguing with the clerk. "I'm getting five of the low-fat refried beans and five of the regular beans," she yelled.

"They're the same item, refried beans," the clerk said.

"No, they're not. They're different!" she shouted.

"I'm going to have to ask you to leave," the clerk said. He held his hand up as some kind of signal. There was probably someone upstairs watching the aisles through the one-way glass to spot shoplifters. Pretty soon, some checkers came up to the woman.

"Okay, fine, I'll only get five cans of beans," she said, obviously frightened and embarrassed. This kind of confrontation would have been amazing a week ago but seemed pretty normal now.

John ran out of the items on his list that were still available. He started to put things in that he thought people would want and things that would store for a long time.

A clerk came up, looked in his cart at all the things and said, "You know we have a $200 limit, right?"

Oh crap. They probably had $350 worth of food in their two carts.

Drew said sternly, which was a little out of character for him, "No, we didn't. Was there some sign we missed?"

The clerk just glared at him and walked off.

"Let's get out of here with our $200 of stuff," John said. "I've got an idea."

"We split up into three sets of shoppers so we have three limits?" Wes asked.

"Won't work," the clerk standing next to them said. "We know you three are together." Next time, if there was a next time, they would come in separately.

In the checkout line, the checker said, "You know about the surcharge, right?"

"Nope," John said.

"Everything is double what the shelves say," the checker, who was nearly falling asleep, said.

"I'll remember that when this is over and I need to find a new grocery store," John said. The checker rolled her eyes. She'd heard that all morning.

They checked out and, once they got to the $200 limit, John said to the checker, "You guys can reshelf the rest." She looked up and said sarcastically, "Thanks."

"Stick your hand out," she said to all three of them.

"Why?" Drew asked.

She had an ink stamp. "We need to stamp your hand to show you've been in here today. Only one trip per day."

They stuck their hands out and got stamped with a red star. "How appropriate," Wes muttered. But then again, the grocery store was free enterprise. If they said one trip a day, then it was one trip a day. Wes couldn't resist asking. "Is this store policy or some government requirement?"

The clerk just stared at him and starting ringing up the next customer. She didn't care and was exhausted. Politics really didn't matter. Getting through her shift and getting back home with some food for her kids did.

John pushed the cart of food they picked out but couldn't buy off to the side. Wes and Drew hated to leave all that food in the cart for re-shelving, but John seemed to know what he was doing.

They left with one overflowing shopping cart, walking by the cop who looked like he would pass out soon.

How to get that cart of food out to the truck? Wes couldn't bring the truck up to the entrance because the parking lot was jammed. They'd have to make a few trips.

Wes grabbed a plastic bag in his left hand. "I'd take two bags, but," he pointed to his chest where the AK was, "I need to have one hand free." John and Drew understood.

"I'll stay behind with the goodies," John said. He had a

revolver so he'd be okay. Drew grabbed two plastic bags and followed Wes.

Wes took the lead in the walk out to the truck. This was where they were most likely to be robbed. A pair of shifty looking young men were watching them, paying particular attention to Drew, an older guy with his hands full. Wes sensed what was going on, lifted his hunting shirt partway to show his pistol (but not his AK), and shouted, "Someone else." The pair seemed to understand and moved along.

God, the situation was getting worse, Wes thought. The milk runs back in Pow's neighborhood just yesterday were nowhere as dangerous as this one. Things had really gone downhill in just twenty-four hours.

The long walk to the truck with two bags of heavy groceries was starting to wind Drew. He never did things like this in his retirement. Well, former retirement. Drew realized that he had a job now: surviving. Easy things like going to the grocery store were no longer easy. He'd have to work for things like food, but he was so glad he was with his family and could be there to help them. He started to ponder how much things had changed and wondered what life would be like in the next days or however long this went on. But his main goal was to get all the food into the truck and get out alive.

Wes was briskly walking without any trouble. He was scanning all around, especially to the rear. He knew that was the most likely avenue of attack. He could feel that he was walking much more confidently than the average person. He had an AK-47 and a pistol, which helped increase confidence. He knew that bad guys would sense who was confident and who was scared and they targeted the scared.

They got to the truck and Wes put his bag in the cab. He motioned for Drew to do the same. It was crowded, but it wouldn't make sense to leave the bags in the bed where anyone could steal them.

"Let's go try to get a little closer to John," Wes said. "You can go and lead him back to where we are. I'll follow you and keep my hands free," Wes said patting his AK. "I've got you covered, Drew." Drew had never had anyone say that to him. At least, not in reference to being covered in a gun sense.

They moved as close as they could, which was a block from the parking lot. Drew got out and went over to the store entrance to get John. Between the two of them, they got all the bags of groceries in their hands. They were glad to see Wes coming up behind them. They noticed how much more confidently Wes moved compared to everyone else in the parking lot.

They got to the truck. Wes motioned for them to put the new bags in the bed, as well as the ones from the cab.

John said, "I know where we can get some staples, but we might not be too welcome." He pointed a direction for Wes to drive. Off they went.

They went about six blocks to a rundown part of town. Wes looked around and didn't see a grocery store. "Where's the grocery store?"

John smiled.

Chapter 85

Trouble at the Tienda

(May 8)

John pointed to a Mexican tienda, a neighborhood store about the size of a convenience store.

"There?" Wes said. "Do they even sell to people like us?" Wes had a bad feeling about this.

John nodded, "Yeah, I buy stuff here all the time. The best tortillas in the world."

Drew motioned that he'd stay with the truck. He was tired and had the least shooting experience, by far.

John and Wes went in. For the first time in this whole ordeal, they were scared. When they walked in, everyone stopped talking. The other customers, all young Latino men, stared at them. The Latinos weren't gangsters, just young men.

John said, "Hi. You guys open?" The store owner just looked at him. John pointed over at the fifty-pound sacks of red beans and the twenty-five pound sacks of rice. "How much are those?"

"We're closed," said the store owner in a thick Mexican accent. He looked mean.

"We have cash," John said.

That seemed to insult the store owner. He raised up his hand and the young men started walking toward John and Wes.

Wes instantly drew his pistol with his right hand. With his left hand, he quickly undid the two buttons on his hunting shirt, just as he'd practiced a few times before they left. There was his AK. Out for the whole world to see. Which was the point.

This stopped the young men cold and they instinctively put their hands up. None of them were armed. John fumbled for his revolver and clumsily pointed it at the store owner.

It was silent for a few seconds.

Wes finally said, "I think it's time for us to go. Sorry to have troubled you, señor." Wes was sincere. He realized that the beans and rice in that store were for the store owner's family and friends. Maybe those young men were a gang, although they didn't look like gangsters. In the past few days, "gang" had come to mean a group of people connected in some way protecting themselves. Neck tattoos, baggy pants, and gold teeth were no longer a prerequisite. Hell, Wes and John were part of a "gang" now. Who were the well-armed ethnic outsiders in the tienda? John and Wes.

Everyone was still silent. Wes was walking backwards very slowly and deliberately, keeping his pistol on the young men. Everyone in the room could tell that Wes knew what he was doing. John was in shock and walking backwards, too. Wes felt enormous relief when he went out the door and back onto the street.

Wes covered the door as he yelled to John, "Let's get the hell out of here."

Drew had been scanning the area and saw Wes and John walking out of the store with their guns out. What was going on?

Wes and John jumped in the truck and took off.

"What happened?" Drew asked.

John looked down, obviously embarrassed. "We went to the wrong store."

"We need to be out of this part of town," Wes said. "They'll be looking for us. We didn't make any friends today."

Wes was pissed at John, but when he thought about it, he shouldn't have been. John had not foreseen that the Mexican store would only sell to Mexicans, but he should have realized it. Wes had a feeling not to go in there and should have listened to his gut. Having a pistol and an AK probably made him feel invincible, so he wasn't trusting his intuition. He wouldn't do that again. Wes felt like he was making mistakes. He knew what happened when mistakes were made in an environment like this.

They had failed. They didn't very much get anything on their list. They had to draw guns and now people were out probably trying to kill them. Great. At least they had some cash left over.

Wes got on the CB. "Limit of $200 on groceries. We have cash left over. We'll be staying out of the Mexican part of town. Anyone need us to go get something?"

Chapter 86

Hardware Store

(May 8)

"You could try the hardware store for some gas cans," John said. He pointed the direction to the hardware store.

Wes was silent. He was trying not to be pissed at John because they'd be working and living together and needed to be on good terms. Wes made a deliberate effort to lighten up and started to chat with John and Drew as they headed to the hardware store.

On the way, they saw some graffiti. "Don't Tread on Me" was in yellow spray-paint on the wall of city hall. Interesting.

They found the hardware store. Wes said, "I'll stay in the truck with the stuff." John and Drew went into the store.

Drew asked where the gas cans were. The clerk laughed and said, "We sold out two days ago." Drew and John decided to get all the miscellaneous things they could think of. Things were pretty picked over, but there were still some items. They got duct tape, rope, nails, screws, nuts and bolts. They found some Coleman fuel and some small propane canisters. There were a few packs of batteries left; they got an assortment of every kind they could think of. They didn't have a list, so they were just guessing what they might need.

John found some work gloves. He put as many pairs as he could into the cart. "You can never have enough gloves," he said to Drew. "These could save your hands and you'll need them."

They went to the checkout line, which was pretty long. They paid for their things. No surcharge there, probably because all the good stuff was gone. They had a little money left over, but not much. It was weird: money didn't have the same feel it used to. The things in the store were much more valuable than the money.

The hardware store was near the sporting goods store where Mark and Scotty were. They saw Mark's truck in the parking lot. John and Drew dropped off their hardware store items in the truck and told Wes they'd go over to the sporting goods store to see Mark and Scotty.

Wes was glad to be in the truck, with the AK and scanning for the Mexicans who might be looking for them. Then again, he thought, why would they want to find someone with an AK? All the Mexicans were doing was kicking some people out of their store; that's not the kind of thing to go hunting people down over. Oh well, even if no one was looking for them, Wes would continue to scan the area for threats. This town was on the brink of being a warzone. Wes could feel it. He was listening to his intuition this time. Bare shelves, no cops and plenty of sleep-deprived, scared, hungry people who had never run out of anything. This was going to be ugly. But not in Pierce Point. Hopefully.

John and Drew went over to the sporting goods store. It was one of the last local sporting goods stores around. The nearest Wal-Mart was one town away.

The camping and hunting sections of the sporting goods store was picked over. There were plenty of basketballs and golf clubs left, though.

Mark and Scotty had a cart full of fishing gear and crab pots,. Mark had plenty of these things, but he'd need more now that he'd be a full-time fisherman and hunter. They had also grabbed a few basketballs for stress relief.

John saw Mark and asked, "Do they have any .280 Winchester?" That was ammunition for a hunting rifle John had. It was an obscure caliber.

Mark smiled, "Yeah, three boxes of it. There's a one-box limit for the common calibers. But yours is an oddball caliber, so we could have all we wanted. From the dust, it looks like those boxes of .280 have been on the shelf for a couple years."

Scotty was excited about what he found. "Hey," he said excitedly, "I got ten boxes of .357 Sig. That's an oddball caliber, for sure." Bobby had an extra Glock 22 in .40. He switched to 9mm so he didn't use it much or keep much .40 ammo. But about a year ago, he got a replacement barrel for it in .357 Sig for a hundred bucks from Lonewolf Distributors. It took .40 magazines, which he had. Now, with the .357 Sig replacement barrel, he had a .357 Sig and ten boxes of ammo for his .40 Glock he no longer used. Pretty cool. Scotty had thought Bobby was crazy to get an extra barrel in some weird caliber, but now he saw why.

"We could only get one box of the normal stuff," Mark said. "30-06, 30-30, .270. Oh and shotgun shells. Forget about it. They're all gone." That made sense. Everyone and their dog had a 12 gauge, so those shells would fly off the shelves.

Mark and Scotty's cart had Coleman stoves and lanterns. Mark pointed to some little packages in the cart, "Best find of all is the water purification tabs. Pure gold."

They paid and left. It was 11:45 a.m. They headed back to the rendezvous point.

The two trucks and the Hummer gathered and those who still needed to, gassed up. They told each other what they got and what they didn't and heard the quick version of the Mexican tienda story. Lisa was horrified. She had no idea Wes was carrying an "assault rifle." They didn't have time to be chatting. They needed to get out of town and get back to the safety of Pierce Point.

As they were leaving, there was a disturbance between two gas station customers. They started punching each other. A customer nearby drew a handgun. That stopped the fight. Everyone was on edge. They guy drawing the handgun ran away, leaving his car there.

"Time to boogie," Pow said. "That guy'll be back for his car." They were glad to be on the road back to Pierce Point.

On the ride back, Lisa could not stop thinking about how different things were. Fights, "surcharges" at stores, limits on purchases, people with guns, money not being worth much. And chickens. Lisa hated chickens. They were noisy and stupid. Yet, somehow, she had gone from being a respected physician to an amateur chicken farmer in twenty-four hours.

Chapter 87

Words of the Day

(May 8)

Jeanie woke up in a military barracks. She hadn't slept in…she didn't even know how long. It felt great to have slept. The difference was amazing. Now, with a little sleep, things didn't seem so totally out of control.

She got ready for work. "Work"? Sitting in a military base and spinning the destruction of Washington State to the idiot media seemed like a strange job, but it was her job. She was safe on base, doing something important, and helping to calm down the crisis. Just yesterday, when she was sleep-deprived and terrified, the situation seemed hopeless. Now this mess seemed like a series of problems that could be tackled one by one. Besides, everyone around her seemed to be calm, so she shouldn't overreact to things.

The more she thought about it, the more she concluded they might actually get through this. They would laugh at how they thought all this was the end of the world. Things always seemed bad right at the beginning, but got better. They'd make it through. Things *would* get better. Especially now that she'd had a good night's sleep.

She missed her bathroom and her makeup. Oh well. Most of the women around her were military and had no makeup, so she would fit right in. She only had a few changes of clothing, but there was a note on her door that she could leave her clothes to be cleaned. They thought of everything here at Camp Murray.

Her roommate in the two-person barracks had already gotten up or was still awake. She was a National Guard JAG officer. They had met for a minute a few days ago or whenever that was. Time was blurred together.

Jeanie went to the cafeteria or, as the military people called it, the "DFAC," which stood for dining facility. The food was really good. She had expected slop like she'd seen in the movies. In the past few years, some of the stimulus money had gone toward remodeling the National Guard headquarters at Camp Murray. She noticed the plaque with the date of the work and the contractor's name. As a campaign person, she recognized the name of the company as one that had given lots of money to the Democrats. But who cared. The place looked really nice. It had kind of a "palace" feel. They were being very well taken care of.

During a breakfast of organic oatmeal and fresh organic fruit, Jeanie wondered about Jim, her boyfriend on Guard duty somewhere. She knew he'd be safe with all those soldiers around him. She also knew that, as a computer guy, he would be in a headquarters away from the fighting, if there was any. She texted him. A few minutes later, he texted back saying he was fine and he'd be back home in a few weeks once this was all cleaned up. For the first time in about a week, she was actually feeling hopeful.

She was also feeling like she wasn't a bad person to be working for the government during all of this. They were solving the problems that hit them like the "perfect storm." The electrical outages, internet problems, terrorism, spike in gas prices, the May Day drop of the dollar, the Mexican refugee problem, the Southern states talking like they were leaving the union and the nuclear exchange in the Mideast. All of this came at the same time. Even the best government would have a hard time coping with all this at once.

Things were bad, but not the end of the world. About 90% of the people were safe in their homes. They were listening to what the government told them to do. Sure, there was more crime than anyone had ever seen. Some people on medications were dying because the just-in-time inventory was screwed up with the internet outages and especially the traffic and gas shortages preventing the semi-trucks from rolling effortlessly up and down the interstates. McDonald's was out of french fries, but people would live. This was starting to feel like a national-scale Katrina, not Armageddon. Sure Katrina sucked and innocent people died, but in a year people were basically back to normal after some adjustments. That's surely what would happen here.

After breakfast, Jeanie went to the conference room where she was working. Someone told her a briefing would start in a few minutes. She logged onto the internet. They had a reasonably stable connection. She checked the local news. She needed to know what they were reporting because her job was to get information to the local news. It said there was some isolated looting in Seattle, some gas stations out of gas, Interstate 5 jammed and people were told to stay home, medically-dependent people flocking to hospitals that were overwhelmed. Lots and lots of "neighbor helping neighbor" stories. Plenty of scenes of National Guard and police helping people. Things might actually be okay.

People started coming into the conference room. Jason, the guy from the Governor's Office who had been briefing them, opened the day.

"Good morning," Jason said. "I hope most of you got to sleep last night. I know I sure feel better now that I have. Here's what's going on now. First, DC has authorized federal and state authorities — and that would include us — to seize critical infrastructure and supplies under the Insurrection Act. We need a nice word for this. Any PR people want to help me with that?"

Jeanie raised her hand and said, "Requisition? It has a military and temporary sense to it."

"Requisition it is," Jason said. He was impressed with Jeanie's smarts and she wasn't bad looking, either.

"So," Jason continued, "we're requisitioning gasoline, prescription medicine, trucks, food, and other things. Stress to people that this is temporary. Everything will be given back once the Crisis — oh, yeah, that's the term DC wants us to use, 'Crisis' — is over. So 'requisition,' 'temporary,' and 'Crisis' are the words of the day." The political people were accustomed to using key words that had been focus grouped and tested by polls, the "words of the day." They were sometimes called "talking points."

Jason continued, "First responders will keep records of the things they … requisition and there will be a claims process when this is over." He paused for a moment.

"Here's the part that people can't know," Jason said. "We don't have any money to pay people back with. You guys familiar with the Olympia situation know this. So brush off the questions about 'how will this be paid for.' Stress the need to get medicine to people and that kind of thing. Ask them, 'how much is a human life worth?'"

Everyone wrote down that talking point: "how much is a human life worth?"

"Second," Jason said, "thinking a little more long-term, we are going to start up some state farms. You know all that wheat and potato farmland in Eastern Washington? We're going to organize some farms to produce food and distribute it. The feds get some of it, but they have to transport it, which could be a problem if we had to try to solve that one on our own. We get most of it, and transporting it over to Seattle from eastern Washington will be less of a problem than transporting it to LA. We'll work with the large agribusinesses in the state. We'll offer employment to people to go over there and work on the farms and processing plants."

Jason didn't say it, but the political strategist in him loved the idea of the Governor solving a big problem like food production, getting all the credit, handing out jobs, and helping the agricultural companies that had been helping the Governor and her selected candidates with donations. It was perfect. This would be permanent. The state would be in a new and giant business—and people would be begging them to do it. Never let a good crisis go to waste, he thought.

"Here's something that's in the works," Jason said. "You can describe it to reporters off the record and on background. The official announcement will be coming in a while. We're coming up with a way for people to pay for their necessities. Let's face it: inflation is off the charts. Some stores aren't taking money anymore. ATMs are shut down and so are banks. People need a way to get things. We're working on expanding the EBT cards." Those were the "electronic benefits transfer" card, which were given to welfare recipients with their welfare money on it. They were accepted like debit cards at places that accepted regular debit cards.

"We will probably call the new cards 'Freedom Cards,'" Jason said. "We're already calling them 'FCards' for short."

Jason put his finger up in the air to emphasize this next point. "Don't call them 'ration cards,' but that's essentially what they will be. We can pre-load them with the amount we want people to have and we can track what people are getting." He didn't say it, but people like him and the people in the room who were crucial to the recovery would get more—lots more—loaded onto their FCard. He also didn't say it, but while they could theoretically track what people got, they didn't have enough data analysts to really know what everyone was doing. They did, however, have enough analysts to track what "problem people" were getting. They would be the ones visited by the Freedom Corps for "hoarding." He wouldn't tell them that right now. That was a different briefing for a different day.

"The difficulty right now," Jason said, "is that the internet is down sometimes. So electronic cards aren't working all the time, but as we fix the internet and electricity problem, we can start to bring the FCards online. But, first things first. We need to have products in stores for people to buy with the cards so we're working on that."

Jeanie wondered how the cards would be paid for. She raised her hand.

"Yes, Jeanie," Jason said. Jeanie was thrilled that he knew her name.

"I know we're supposed to dodge the question from reporters

about how we're paying for everything," Jeanie said, "but we should know these answers. So, how are we paying for the FCards?"

"Excellent question," Jason said, "and I have an excellent answer." He couldn't help being a little flirtatious with a beautiful and smart woman like Jeanie.

"We're 'securitizing' — another word for the day — financial accounts," Jason said. "That's not news yet, so don't mention it. But all those bank accounts, mutual funds, 401(k)s, and pensions people have? The federal government has taken them in for safekeeping; 'securitizing' them. They are now safe from the ups and downs of the market. So, like Social Security, the federal government will guarantee a return on them. But," Jason grinned his widest grin, "we have to take possession of the funds."

People in the conference room were stunned. Was this guy grinning about the federal government taking all the money everyone owned?

"So," Jason said with that same wide grin, "all those securitized funds are what will be drawn on for FCards."

It was brilliant and horrific, Jeanie thought. Americans had trillions of dollars just sitting in those accounts; money that was useless now that the banks were closed. And even with the out-of-control inflation, trillions of dollars was still a lot of money. It was enough to buy plenty of wheat and potatoes. People would never let the government take their bank accounts in normal times. But now, with no way to get their money out of those bank accounts, the Feds knew that people would be more than happy to use that money to eat. They had no choice.

And, Jeanie realized, now that the government had taken over all the accounts and no one had retirement money anymore, the government could start up a new system. Social Security on steroids. Even after the current Crisis was over and food was back in the stores and people weren't using FCards, their retirements will have been wiped out. Now people would be forever dependent — entirely dependent — on the federal government for their retirement. There goes the Republican Party, Jeanie thought. If there would even be elections any time soon.

Jason continued. "One bad thing out there is that most law enforcement and some Guardspersons," he used the politically correct term instead of "Guardsmen," "are going back to their families. They're worn out and overwhelmed. We don't have figures on it, but there is a pretty significant AWOL problem. So we've come up with a solution: the Freedom Corps." The news about Freedom Corps had leaked out a few days ago, but the people in the conference room likely had not heard about it, so Jason briefed them.

"It's a civilian law enforcement auxiliary," he continued. "It's loosely modeled on AmeriCorps and all that. The feds came up with it. So we'll be rolling out the Freedom Corps here. People are encouraged to join up and take care of their neighborhoods. They won't be armed by us—we don't have any extra weapons—but they are authorized to carry guns." He paused.

"Oh, that's the other thing," Jason said. "Guns. We've banned them. Private ownership is illegal. Now, we're not—I repeat—not — going to seize them. We don't have the person power to go get them, which is not for public consumption, but the part about guns being banned is. We can't have criminals and vigilantes out there. If the authorities, which now include the Freedom Corps, find someone with a gun, they can seize it. No one will be arrested unless there is some other reason to do it."

Jason was on a roll. "Here's another thing not for public consumption: there are no jails any more. They emptied out, first from budget cuts a few weeks ago and now because the guards either went home or were killed, so we have no place to put law breakers. Local law enforcement and some Guard units are creating makeshift detention facilities. They're using schools and that kind of thing, but we're going out of our way not to arrest people because we have no place to put them." He thought for a moment, "And we have nothing to feed them. Yet."

He waved his arms for emphasis, "Stress to people that the President has this authority in an emergency. It's part of his authority as Commander in Chief and it's authorized under the Insurrection Act and the NDAA."

"Also stress," Jason continued, "that all of this is temporary. As things go back to normal, we'll end all of this."

Jason pointed his finger up in the air to make a point. "That's the other thing: normal. Stress how things will get back to normal. Remind people of what normal is and will be. Tell people they'll be able to go back to their jobs, get groceries, even go out to eat. People need hope. Thinking that normal is just around the corner is what they need." Even though it's not true, he thought to himself.

Jason had been in meetings with the Governor in which she made it clear that most of these "temporary" measures would be permanent. The state needed to take over most of the economy to dig itself out of this financial hole. Besides, people were begging the state to take care of them. It was perfect.

Jeanie sat back and thought. She could spin this stuff. No problem. Most people would be glad their government was "doing something." She was troubled by it, though. This ration card — or Freedom Card or whatever — was the perfect way to control people. Pop off about the government and your card gets zeroed out with a few keyboard clicks. Support the government and magically your account balance goes up.

She thought about Grant and the other WAB guys who were on the POI list. Well, there weren't any jails or any cops, so they probably wouldn't be arrested. Given all the things on the government's plate right now, arresting political opponents couldn't possibly be a high priority. Besides, they were just "persons of interest;" they weren't actually wanted for a crime. They'd be fine, she told herself.

But the gun thing really disturbed her. She didn't personally own a gun, but she was a Republican political strategist. Banning guns would cause most conservatives and many independents to hate the government. This was a really big deal and these liberals didn't seem to understand that. She knew that in rural areas and good chunks of the suburbs, people would hear that guns — things they desperately needed right now — were illegal and some neighbor in a funny Freedom Corps helmet would be taking them. Oh, but don't worry, no one is going to jail ... because there are no jails. So you can't have a gun but there are no jails to put bad guys in. Only politicians could come up with this. But...

Hey, you're taken care of, Jeanie reminded herself. She knew her FCard would be loaded up. Well, actually, she'd be eating great food there at the Camp Murray DFAC. She had the best organic oatmeal served to her and machine gun nests protecting her. She was in her late twenties now. Maybe she had been too idealistic about politics, conservatism, and Republicans and all of that. She needed to take care of herself and her boyfriend. And the State of Washington was helping her do a very good job of that right now.

Jeanie started dialing the phone to start her daylong talks to reporters. She had some news to get out there. The State of Washington was taking bold actions to help people in this temporary situation and things would be back to normal pretty soon.

Chapter 88

The Big Meeting

(May 8)

The drive back to Pierce Point was quiet. The roads were packed. There were many cars and trucks loaded up and leaving the town, heading out into the sticks where people had cabins. It looked like the Friday before Memorial Day, Fourth of July, or Labor Day, except it was Tuesday and the people looked terrified instead of relaxed.

Still, the people on this road were a tiny fraction of a percent of the people back in Olympia and its surrounding towns. Only a very small number were bugging out. Most of the people were just sitting in their homes awaiting official instructions from the TV and internet. Almost none of them had ever experienced anything like this, so they had no idea what to expect. This was the first time stores had been out of things, the first time they had run out of cash and the first time police were practically nowhere to be found. Most people couldn't believe this would last long. Many thought it would be a few days off work or school, like a snow day that went on for a week or so.

As the convoy reached the turnoff to Pierce Point Road, they slowed down to make it through the gate. Paul's gate was up now and was a beautiful piece of work. It had a solid four-inch diameter metal pole with a solid anchor and lock. It was possible for a person to go under the gate, but it would take some effort and some time, which meant the guards would have plenty of opportunities to shoot anyone trying it. The metal pole gate would stop all vehicles.

Dang, Pow thought, this entrance to Pierce Point was made to be defended. The 100-yard stretch from the main road to Frederickson to the bridge gave entering vehicles time to slow down so they could be evaluated for entry. The two-lane bridge was just wide enough for a car parked sideways to block the entry. The volunteer fire station on the Pierce Point side of the bridge was perfect for stationing men. To top off the perfection of this defensible position, the road after the bridge went up a hill, with a beautiful tree line to pack full of snipers.

The road was the only practical way into Pierce Point. The rest of the development was surrounded by a small river in some places and by steep hills on the rest of the boundary. Intruders avoiding the bridge and the guards would have to go from the Frederickson road, across a small river, across some open ground that had houses flanking it with fantastic fields of fire and up the side of the hill. It was too steep for vehicles; intruders would have to be on foot. Then the intruders would have to go up Pierce Point Road for about a half a mile; a road with a tree line that was perfect for ambushes. A well-trained and equipped military unit could make it into Pierce Point, but no one short of that could.

Rich Gentry was making full use of the terrain he had been given. He had a half dozen well-armed and organized men. His hardest task was administrative: keeping track of who lived there and who their guests were.

As Mark's convoy approached, Rich went up to greet them. He recognized Mark's truck and the others in his group, but he checked them out in person, just to be sure.

"Hey, Mark, how were things in town?" Rich asked, knowing that all the other guards and everyone else would be interested in the answer. Rumors were flying like crazy. Who had gas and what things cost was a topic of constant conversation.

"Slippin' a little," Mark said. He described the surcharge and $200 limit at the grocery store and that gas was now $15 a gallon. He described the limits on ammunition. He didn't mention the Mexican grocery thing since, technically, brandishing a rifle like that was illegal. Why tell an ex-cop that your friend just committed a crime?

"You have any additional riders from when you left?" Rich asked.

"Nope," Mark said, glad that Rich was thinking of things like that.

"There's a meeting tonight at 7:00 at the old Grange hall," Rich said. The Grange was a farmers' association that saw its heyday in the 1950s. They had buildings for meetings throughout much of rural America, especially in the West. Most of them were pretty rundown, since few Granges still met. They had a cinderblock building painted white in the middle of Pierce Point. The tiny Pierce Point Church rented it on Sundays, which is how the Grange paid the utilities. The building was run down, but always had a fresh coat of paint on it and was clean. A few elderly farm families took great pride in their Grange hall.

"I'm not a homeowners' association kind of guy," Mark said. "What's the meeting about?" As if he didn't know.

"Security," Rich said. "We want to get some guards and patrol volunteers together. You and," Rich pointed to the trucks driven by the Team, "your young friends are welcome. Bring John, too."

Rich noticed the CBs they had. Those would be extremely handy to have. Rich was initially surprised that the authorities were allowing CBs to operate. There were probably all kinds of protests being planned with CBs and every other means of communication.

Rich, who was an active Oath Keeper, knew that CBs would eventually be used by the Patriots. Why wouldn't the government jam the CBs? Then Rich realized that the truckers needed CBs and the authorities needed the truckers. CBs meant supplies got to where they needed to be and preventing the unrest that came from the population not having supplies was more important to the government than preventing people from communicating for anti-government purposes.

"See you at 7:00," Mark said. He was glad that an old Marine like him could help out. He was really glad the Team was out there. He thought how much better they were squared away than the people in Frederickson, let alone what Olympia must be like. He didn't even want to think about Seattle.

Rich waved them through, but he still looked into the trucks as they went by. He noticed the chicks and chickens Mary Anne had. Someone thought this little crisis was going to last for a while, he thought.

They pulled up to the Over Road guard shack. Paul was there with a shotgun and Chip had an AR. They waved them in. Everyone parked at the Matsons and started unloading the goods. They were telling everyone the stories and describing what they got. The chicks and chickens got the most attention. John started planning to build a coop.

Grant was disappointed that they only got $200 worth of groceries and no staples, although the jam and syrup would come in handy for the biscuit and pancake mix they had. Calories were calories. That was funny, Grant thought. He was thinking of food as calories now.

There was a smell; a BBQ. Chip had started it up around noon. Paul got some frozen salmon out and they were ready to cook it up. Everyone was hungry, especially the milk run crew. They realized that all the stress had suppressed their appetites, but when the stressful event was over, their appetites quickly returned.

They ate and planned out what to do that afternoon. They would build a coop and inventory each household's supplies. People were taking guard duty without being told; it was just something they instinctively knew to do. Everyone would meet back for dinner at 6:00 p.m. and then go to the meeting at the Grange.

Cole was the only one without any chores. He was enjoying it out at the cabin. His whole family was there and his sister was taking care of him. No school. That was the best part. He was in regular classes, but school was hard for him. All those people talking to him and making him talk. He wanted the quiet and to only be around people who knew him.

Grant realized that Cole also had to work, even though he had a disability. It would be good for him and everyone else would appreciate that Grant's son wasn't getting any unfair breaks.

"Come here, little buddy," Grant said to Cole. Grant motioned for Manda to come over and join them.

"Yeah, Dad," Cole said.

"We all have jobs out at the cabin. What could be a job for you, Cole?"

"Playing?" Cole said with a smile. He wasn't dumb. He just couldn't talk too well.

"Nice try." Grant looked around. There were pinecones all around. They would burn nicely. It was May now, but would be cold in a while. They would need things to burn. "You can pick up pine cones. I'll show you where to put them. We can use them to burn for heat in the winter."

Cole nodded. He was happy to have a job.

"One thing, though," Grant said. "You can't leave the gravel road. You can't go past the guard shack," Grant said, pointing to the shack, "without your sister or one of us grownups. Got it?"

Cole nodded. It was so much easier to nod than to talk.

"Okay, pal," Grant said. "You can gather a few pinecones every day. You can still play, but just not all the time. Once the pinecones are done, we'll have you do other things." Grant thought about Cole gathering up all those apples that just fell onto the ground in the late summer. That was past the guard shack, but Manda could go with him. Armed, of course.

Cole would be the little gatherer. He could also run messages throughout the Over Road cabins. He couldn't relay messages because his verbal skills were so low, but he could tell people to come to a certain cabin and talk to someone or he could deliver a note. That kind of thing. Cole and Manda would also make beds, clean bathrooms, sweep, dust, and vacuum. They would set the table, wash dishes and cook some meals themselves. They would also cut and stack firewood. They would assist with canning and dehydrating food.

Grant realized that Cole and Manda, the upper middle class suburban kids, didn't really have any chores back at home. They sure would out there. It would be good for them. And it would be a real help to the grownups. The kids were open to doing chores. They both realized that their help was needed.

One thing the grown-ups would need to talk about was school for the kids. Abstract learning—calculus, comparative literature—would have to wait a future time. At least they wouldn't be wasting their time with what passed for history before the Collapse. Grant had called it "Anti-American Studies." It was pure indoctrination with no educational value. Out here, with no school and probably no internet or textbooks, they could maintain what the kids already knew with refreshers on the basics. Luckily, a year ago Grant had picked up an encyclopedia set for next to nothing. That had tons of great knowledge in it and it made for interesting reading even for grown-ups when there was nothing else to do.

Grant realized how lucky they were that the kids were sixteen and thirteen. They already had a good chunk of their education. A makeshift school or semi-organized home schooling would be a topic for the next neighborhood meeting.

Dinner that night was deer steaks and some leftover salmon from lunch. Mary Anne and Eileen made biscuits. Everyone seemed to be getting along well. People were sharing things and offering to help each other. Grant hoped it would last.

"Time to get to the meeting," Mark said, looking at his watch. Grant thought it was good that Mark was taking leadership role on some things, like the meeting. It was also good that Mark, who was well respected by the Pierce Point full-timers, would be representing them at the meeting. John was liked, but not as well known. He and Mary Anne kept to themselves more than Mark and Tammy.

Grant thought about what to wear. That was such a pre-Collapse thought: dressing right for a meeting. But he didn't want the Team to come across to the full-timers as too "military." That would be a threat to them. The Team was wearing 5.11s and earth-tone t-shirts in colors like green, brown, and tan. Not camouflage, thank God. Actually, they didn't have any camouflage, except for some outerwear. Their day-to-day clothes were 5.11s and similar things. They looked like military contractors. That was actually okay, Grant thought. Let the full-timers know that they have some skills—but not too many skills.

Grant would wear 5.11 pants, but with a hunting t-shirt with a Mossy Oak camouflage pattern. Mark had hunting pants and a regular t-shirt. John had jeans and a hunting shirt. That was how guys out in rural areas dressed. Hunting clothes were a "two-fer": clothes for hunting and for everyday wear. They only had to buy one set.

Grant needed to talk to the Team about the politics of the situation. This first meeting with the full-timers would be key. First impressions were everything, especially when the stakes were as high as they were right then.

Grant tagged along as the Team finished dinner and headed to the yellow cabin to get ready to go the meeting. He motioned for Chip to come with him. He didn't want to have the political discussion in front of Mark.

When the Team was in the yellow cabin, Grant said, "Hey, guys, could I talk to you for a minute?" They looked like something was wrong or they were in trouble.

"Everything's cool," Grant said, "I just need to go over a plan with you. This meeting tonight is a big deal. It's the full-timers' first impression of us. We might scare them. We're very tactical and they're a little more on the duck hunter side." Grant didn't think his description was entirely accurate; these country boys were far more effective fighters than one might think. Grant wanted to compliment the Team and, at the same time, emphasize the distinction between them and the full-timers.

"We are way better trained than these guys and way better armed," Grant said with a "no duh" tone. "I don't want them jealous of us or thinking we're a threat to them. Remember, people aren't sleeping, they're afraid and men are more aggressive during times like this. They might be looking for a reason to hate us. Now, at the same time, they need us and our gear, so they'll probably be cool. Regardless, I did lots of big meetings at my old job and know how to handle these situations."

The Team nodded. At some level, they were all thinking the same thing about easing into it with the full-timers. Watching Mark and Rich interact at the gate showed them that the Team was part of the larger Pierce Point security force, not a separate little unit.

"Here's my approach," Grant said, "Let me know if you agree. I think we should be ourselves. We are good at this tactical stuff. We don't need to hide that, but we should respect the full-timers, especially their leaders, like this Rich guy who was at the gate. He's an ex-cop. Mark said he quit about six months ago because of all the corruption. Mark is a leader, too. We need to take the lead from them, but we can be open about the fact that we know our shit. Let's face it; we will end up being the SWAT team out here. But, we don't need to throw it in their faces. Let them come to the conclusion on their own that we should be doing that shit."

The Team nodded some more. "So I'm thinking that we go there tonight with just pistols showing," Grant said. "Don't even bring ARs."

"Seriously?" Wes said. "What if we can't trust these guys? I mean, I think we can, but I don't want to take any chances." The Mexican grocery store incident earlier that day had him thinking that long guns were pretty nice to have in an argument.

Grant thought about it. What he didn't want was for the full-timers to see a group of military contractor-looking guys show up with tricked out ARs. "How about if we keep the ARs in the truck?" Grant suggested.

"That will require one guy to stay with the truck and guard the ARs," Pow said. "Hell, it would probably be a good idea to have someone doing that for all the cars there."

Good point. "Sure," Grant said. "Let's do it. You can bring ARs, but keep them in one truck. One of you can stay with the truck. When it's time to introduce ourselves, someone run out and get the truck guard." Grant knew that specific duties instead of vague "somebody be the guard" plans were best.

"Who wants to guard the truck?" Grant asked. Bobby and Scotty raised their hands. They hated meetings.

"Bobby it is," Grant said. He looked at Scotty, "His hand was up slightly faster," Grant said with a smile. He wanted to foster healthy competition among the guys on the Team. It kept people on their toes.

"I think you guys are dressed okay," Grant said, looking at them in 5.11s and earth-tone t-shirts. "Here's my idea on that. We can be a little different with 5.11s and that kind of thing, but no camo right now. That will freak them out. They might think we're militia whackos. We don't need that impression. Camo should be for outerwear when we're going out to do something or are hiding in the woods. And by 'camo,' I mean military camo. These guys wear hunter camo, which is always going to be okay for us, it's just that I don't think you guys have any." The Team nodded. They viewed hunting camo as "duck hunter" wear.

Grant went on, "Maybe after we have their confidence and respect, we can start wearing whatever we want, but that will take time. Do you guys think I'm crazy about this?"

"Nope," said Pow.

Grant pointed to his own hunting camo tee shirt. "I will wear some hunting camo to kind of blend in with these guys." They chuckled.

Grant pointed to Chip who had Carhartt jeans and a black tee shirt. "I think it's great that Chip is wearing his working-man clothes, which is all he has." Chip laughed. Chip never dressed like a "tactical" guy, even though he had all the tactical skills in the world. At his age, Chip would dress any damned way he wanted. And with all the guns he usually worked on, he needed clothes that he could get oil on and that wouldn't rip.

Grant continued, "I'd like to take the lead with these guys since I'm the one who has a connection out here. I'm a resident, even if I'm just a cabin person. You guys, though, are total strangers." And one of you is Asian, Grant thought. Probably not a big deal, but when it came to a first impression that the Team were outsiders, probably being the only minority in the room would be a factor. In time, everyone would love Pow, like everyone always did.

"You guys are doing great on the political stuff," Grant said to the Team. "Mark and John love you guys. I just wanted to script this meeting a little bit. It's what I do," Grant said.

Chip said, "I can talk more than the young guys, if that's okay with you gentlemen. I look like the full-timers. They'll relate to me." And Chip was one of the most charming guys around. He made a living selling guns. He knew how to talk to guys, especially rural, working class guys. He was one himself.

"No prob," said Scotty. "We want to fit in out here. It's our home now."

Good. Grant was relieved.

"Gentlemen, let's go do this," Grant said.

Grant went over to Mark's. "Ready when you are," he said.

"Let's go," Mark said. "Take my truck?"

Grant thought it would be good if the well-armed strangers rolled up in Mark's truck.

"Of course," Grant said. He motioned for the Team to pile in. They had their ARs and tactical vests in their hands.

"You're not bringing those, are you?" Mark asked, a little concerned.

"Not into the meeting," Grant said. "We'll keep them in the cab. My guys need to have their gear. You never know what can happen there, on the way there or on the way back," Grant said with a shrug.

"As long as they stay in the cab," Mark said. He and Grant were on the same page with concerns about introducing "militia"-looking guys to the people of Pierce Point.

"Oh, and Mark," Grant said, as they got into Mark's truck, "these people at this meeting are your guys, so please take the lead with them. I told the Team that we are guests out here and that we are volunteers to Pierce Point and that we will be a part of the group effort, not doing our own thing."

That was music to Mark's ears. "Thank God you said that," he said. "I was just about to have a heart-to-heart with you and say the same thing. You boys are a little more tactical than we're used to out here. That will be a big advantage, especially when it comes to scaring off bad guys, but tonight is not the time for it."

"Way ahead of you," Grant said. "That's pretty much what I told them. They'll just have pistols on."

"That's perfect," Mark said, lifting up his shirt and showing his concealed revolver. "Let's saddle up. It's ten 'till."

The Team was in the back of Mark's truck. John, Paul, and Chip got in the rear back cab. Grant was in the front passenger seat.

Drew stayed behind. They needed a guard. Besides, Drew was a retired accountant. This security stuff would be primarily handled by others. He could take care of himself and guard the place while they were gone, but he wasn't trying to be a cowboy. Everyone had a role, an important role. It's just not that everyone needed to be a gunfighter.

In fact, too many gunfighters would mean people weren't eating, getting medical treatment, and things weren't getting repaired. Having all the gunfighters in the world wouldn't do much good if the tactical bad-asses were puking their guts out from food poisoning because everyone was too important to wash the dishes. Every single person out there had an important role.

After a short drive on the beautiful May evening, they arrived at the Grange. The parking lot was full. Almost all the vehicles were trucks. Men, and some women, were getting out of their rigs and going inside. The men looked like rural guys; tough and self-reliant compared to the people in Olympia. The women looked like country girls who knew how to take care of themselves. A few were wearing pistols. Most of the men were. No one had long guns for this meeting.

The Team definitely stood out, but not too much. They were the only ones in 5.11s. They had tactical pistol belts with the same Raven

Concealment holsters. A trained observer could see that their pistols had small lights attached to them; the outline of the lights was visible through the holsters. No one else had those. But the guys, especially having Chip with them, didn't look odd. They just looked different.

As they went in, Mark realized that he didn't know everyone, either. Some of the faces were familiar, but that was it. Most of the full-timers were like Mark: rural residents in hunting and work clothes. Some had jeans and tee shirts. There were even a few who looked like cabin people.

Seats were going quickly. The sign inside said "Capacity: 120" and it looked like the place was just about full. A dozen or two women were there. Pow motioned for the guys to yield their seats to the ladies. That got noticed by the crowd as a positive thing.

Rich Gentry was at the front of the room with a little podium. He was comfortable there, as he had given many briefings before and this was like being back at work at the Sheriff's Department.

"All right, let's get this thing going," Rich said looking at his watch. "Thanks for coming out tonight. This is a meeting of what I guess we'll call the Pierce Point Security Committee. I hate committees, but I love security, as in I love not having thieves, rapists, and murderers in my neighborhood," Rich said, deciding to shock people into the reality they were there address.

"That's what all this is about. Keeping out bad people. This is not a militia or anything like that."

Everyone nodded.

"First of all," Rich said, "is there anyone here who disagrees that we need a guard and patrol?"

Silence.

"Good," Rich said. "By the end of this meeting, I'd like to have some volunteers to man the entrance to the Frederickson Road on a shift basis and some men," he looked at two women in the front row, "well, some people to patrol inside the development. Once we have enough guards, we can start working on training and communications."

Grant knew that this meeting was about more than just guards at the entrance and a patrol. Leaders would emerge from this meeting. It would set the tone for the governance of Pierce Point. By "governance," Grant knew that meant how food was distributed and shared, how medical care was handled, communications, and, eventually, what side—government or Patriot—Pierce Point would take.

But first things first, Grant thought. Security first, governance second, and politics last, if ever at all. It was all about surviving out there. Politics was a luxury for people who didn't have to worry about surviving.

Grant was itching to have a role in the meeting, but he didn't want to overdo it. He was a cabin person and brought a group of well-armed strangers there. He was a lawyer and most people hated lawyers. Grant had to be careful. He'd been in some tricky political situations, but this one was the most important one so far. He had the oddest feeling that the politics of this meeting would be child's play compared to what was coming in a while.

Grant knew that he had to get a big role for the Team. They were exactly what Pierce Point needed. He wasn't going to let his Team just blend into the neighborhood. What a waste.

I put you and them here for a reason.

Whoa. He hadn't heard the outside thought for a while. He understood it loud and clear.

"For those of you who don't know me, I'm Rich Gentry. I was a sheriff's deputy for eleven years until about six months ago. I left because some things were going on that I couldn't be a part of. I'll just leave it at that." It was apparent that having to leave the force still pained Rich.

"I still have lots of friends on the force," Rich continued. "They tell me that there basically is no more law enforcement out there right now." He let that sink in for a few seconds with the crowd. No more law enforcement. Grant knew it, but suspected that most in the room hadn't confronted this fact first-hand like he had. No more law enforcement was such a shock that it would take quite a while for most people to fully accept the new reality.

"We have to be law enforcement for ourselves until this all gets sorted out," Rich said. "This doesn't mean vigilantes. It means structured volunteers with some training and accountability to the community. None of you are expected to be like what law enforcement was. No six-month academy, but you need to know the basics. And you need to know when to use force and when not to. That last part is key. We are not a thug squad, beating and killing people. I've seen enough of that in the past."

Grant was so glad this Rich guy was laying the foundation for the neighborhood security force like this. Perfect.

I put him here, too.

Of course. Grant felt stupid for thinking this was pure chance.

95

"Here is my plan in a nutshell," Rich said. "I'm not a dictator, so I want to lay it out, see what you think and get started on putting a guard and patrol system together. To get boots on the ground tonight, as a matter of fact. Okay, the nutshell."

Rich looked at everyone in the room and continued, "We have at least a half dozen guys." He looked at the women and said, "and when I say 'guys', I mean men *or* women. As long as people have some rudimentary training, they can volunteer for this. Anyway, we have about a half dozen guys, armed of course, at the entrance to Pierce Point Road. We have a car across the road. We'll work on a real gate that can swing open and shut, but we can use a car for now. We need communications between the gate and a headquarters. We need enough people in reserve that we have guards to take shifts and to man the gate if someone is trying to shoot their way in."

That thought caught a few people by surprise. They probably thought a "security" meeting would be like some homeowners' association discussion of locking their doors and maybe some unarmed "neighborhood crime watch" crap that worked great when 911 answered calls in two minutes except, those days were gone.

Even out in Pierce Point, there were still plenty of people who hadn't fully grasped that things were totally different now. They weren't bad people, they just needed to process the changes. It was weird: back in Olympia, normalcy bias was the enemy. Grant fought against it. He was outnumbered by all the weenies who thought things were fine. He was in the minority there. But out at Pierce Point, he was in the majority. He didn't have to fight as hard against normalcy bias, although it still existed.

For the first time since he fled Olympia, Grant realized he wasn't furious at the people with normalcy bias like he had been in the past. As long as they didn't cling to "normal" and let it affect their decision-making on important things, they'd be fine. If they did cling to it, they'd be dead and get many others killed along with them. That's the part that he would be watching for. Grant wasn't on a crusade to have people think like him, but he was on a crusade to get through this and people with normalcy bias would put him and his people in danger. It wasn't personal. It was survival.

"There are two other things we need security-wise," Rich said. "The first is a patrol that can respond to things door-to-door. These need to be the best trained because they are dealing with our families. This is where a no-thug requirement is key. The patrolmen need to be very well trained with firearms, tactics, and respect for people." Rich was looking directly at the Team. He had singled them out the second he saw them, but he needed to know if the well-armed guys in Mark's truck were thugs or not.

"I will personally train and lead the patrol," Rich said.

Grant wondered how Pow would react to that. Probably pretty well. Pow was glad to just be in a safe place and having some training would only make him happier because he could do an even better job. It beat the shit out of selling insurance, which is what Pow had done during peacetime, just a few days ago.

"The second thing we need," Rich said, "is a way to hold prisoners and, I guess, find out which ones are guilty."

Here's your role.

Grant suddenly knew exactly why he was in that room and in that neighborhood. He had that odd feeling again that this was just the beginning of the role he was to fulfill.

"Chances are, we're gonna need a judge and a jail. At least some way to resolve disputes and lock up people who are violent or thieves. As I see it, the jail won't be fancy," Rich said. "In fact, if you're caught stealing from us or hurting us, then I'm not real concerned that you're comfy or even well fed. But we're not animals. We won't mistreat prisoners. This will mean a facility and some guards."

Rich kept going. "The judge part will be pretty easy. Nothin' fancy on trials. I just want someone or some people who can objectively look at things. I don't want innocent people punished. Don't worry. We won't have lawyers and arguments and technicalities and week-long jury trials. Unless you guys want that, in which case we'll try to make it happen." Rich knew that the level of due process out there would be a topic of debate. He was hoping that if there were a lawyer in the room that he or she wouldn't be a spaz who loved process over substance.

"Any questions?" Rich asked.

A hand went up from what looked like a cabin person. "What about the beach? That would be a way for people to come in and out."

"Good point," Rich said. "We'll need a beach patrol." He pointed to the person asking the question. "You and me will get together after the meeting. You can coordinate the volunteers for what we'll call the beach patrol. We'll get some boats and some beach walkers. Thanks for bringing that to our attention."

Another hand went up. "What kind of guns do we need for this?"

"Another excellent question," Rich said. "We're not a military force. We don't need military weapons, although those are certainly welcome," he said, looking at the Team. "If you're familiar with your shotgun, hunting rifle, or handgun, then that's what we need. I'd much rather have guys who know their weapon well than have people with the latest and greatest gizmos who are unfamiliar with those gizmos. People who haven't shot ever or in quite some time, will get trained. Some people probably have a couple extra guns. We could start a 'gun library' where people without a gun can check one out for a period of time. We would keep them in a central place, like a makeshift and secure armory. That way, the person loaning the gun to the community doesn't have to worry about it walking off. Or if people make arrangements to borrow a gun and keep it with them, that's great, too. But it's up to the person loaning the guns to loan them to the armory or directly to a person."

Rich paused. Grant couldn't tell if he was thinking of all of this as he went or if he had thought it out in advance. Either way, it was impressive. This guy was a leader.

"Guards borrowing guns from the gun library is fine and I can't fault those loaning guns to want to get them back," Rich said. "But I have to say that my preference would be for direct loans to people. This way, people would have the loaned gun with them in their homes. Armed homeowners will be our best defense against crime. Don't forget, the majority of crime will be among neighbors, not from outsiders."

It was silent. People either hadn't thought of that or didn't want to hear it.

"Yep, I know it sounds bad," Rich said, "but it's true. We need to keep bad people out and we need to have a plan for if a gang tries to breach the gate, but most crime will be internal." Rich let that sink in. These people needed to know that. They needed to be realistic. These were the times that called for realism.

Someone asked, "What about communications?"

Rich smiled, "I expected that question from you, Curt. Ladies and gentlemen, Curt Copeland here is a ham radio operator. A very, *very* valuable person to have in a situation like this." Grant wondered if this was the guy who lived at the house with the huge antenna array that he and Pow had noticed.

Curt just smiled. He loved that he was a valuable person right then. Ham radio operators often spent years at their hobby with no one understanding how important they would be in a disaster. Curt was glad he had a chance to shine. He wished things hadn't broken down, of course, but since they had, he was glad to be there with many ways to communicate.

"Curt, what are your thoughts?" Rich asked.

"Well, I can keep in contact with the outside world with my various equipment," he said, not wanting to bore everyone with the details of his various radios. He could literally talk to the space station with his gear.

"Curt has plenty of handheld radios that we can use. Isn't that right, Curt?" Rich said. It was obvious they had talked before the meeting. Good.

"Oh yes," Curt said, "I have about a half dozen handhelds that operate on the VHR and UHF ham bands. They're easy to use. Very good reception, even with the highlands up here and the beach down there. Especially when we bounce them off the Frederickson repeater."

Rich looked at the Team again. "Some of you have CBs, too. Raise your hand if you have one." About a third of the room raised their hands, including the Team. "Great. CBs are fine for short range communication and getting info from nearby people outside of Pierce Point. They aren't secure, of course, but I doubt the bad guys will be monitoring all 40 CB channels to hear us. Besides, all the stuff we need to have secure will be done on the ham bands and then we can relay it in some simple code via CBs."

That reminded Rich, "Oh, if any of you are going into town anytime soon, please try to buy all the CBs and antennas you can. It would really help us out. If the stores are out, which is likely, then don't worry about it. I just wanted everyone to know how valuable CBs are right now."

Rich waited for another question. There wasn't one. "Okay, now we come to personnel," he said. "This is the most important part. Equipment is great, but if we don't have good people, none of this will work."

Rich pointed to Curt. "We need lots of people with diverse talents, like Curt here. He isn't prior military or law enforcement, but you can see how valuable he will be. So regular civilians are very much needed."

Rich paused. "With that in mind, military and law enforcement experience is a definite plus. So who here is prior military?" About a quarter of the hands went up. Rich pointed at the first person he saw and said, "What branch, what did you do, and when did you get out?"

Men and a few women around the room described their service. All branches were covered. Lots of Army, but it was the largest branch. Some Air Force and a couple Marines, including Mark. Quite a few Navy and even two Coast Guard. None of the people in the room were active duty or in the Guard or Reserves. Two people said they had neighbors in the Army National Guard and one said her neighbor was in the Air Force Reserve, but that they weren't at the meeting.

The veterans had done many different jobs in the military. Four had combat specialties in the Army: two infantry, a scout, and armor. Another, a Marine rifleman named Ryan McDonald, was a combat veteran from Afghanistan.

John raised his hand and said, "U.S. Navy. Machinist. Got out in 1968."

Mark said he was a former Marine sniper and left in 1975. He grabbed his belly and said, "I ain't in Marine shape anymore. I couldn't lie in the forest for two days and make a shot at 800 yards anymore, either."

When it came to Chip's turn to talk, he said, "I'm Chip. Army. Supply sergeant but saw some combat in Southeast Asia. Got out in 1970." He didn't mention the part about building ARs for a living and having a few dozen "assault rifles" in Grant's basement. He knew it wasn't necessary to mention that now. There was still too much at stake; too many unknowns. Not even to mention that Grant was a wanted man. Blend in whenever possible, Chip would always say. Be the gray man; a fighter or resister who doesn't attract attention so he can get the job done.

One veteran was particularly interesting. Rich smiled when it came to this guy's turn and said to him, "Sergeant Morgan, why don't you introduce yourself?"

The man in his early forties with black hair and in great shape said, "I'm Dan Morgan, formerly of the United States Air Force. I was in Security Forces, which used to be called Security Police. We defended air bases and other sensitive installations, and conducted counterterrorism. I was MWD, or Military Working Dog. A dog handler. I retired as a Senior Master Sergeant. I am currently — or, I guess, formerly — a volunteer for the Sheriff's Department's K9 team. I say formerly since I don't think there is a Sheriff's Department anymore."

Dan paused. "Anyway, I train their dogs and kennel them here. I have several great dogs." Dan smiled, "Defending an air base or an area like Pierce Point, it's all the same. I got some tricks up my sleeve that Uncle Sam taught me." He was beaming. He was happy to use his skills and save his friends and neighbors in the process.

Rich said, "Dan and I know each other from Oath Keepers." No need to hide that anymore, Rich thought. He was off the force and besides, the cops had enough on their plates. Arresting political people wasn't high on their list of things to do. Rich smiled, "Welcome to the Security Committee, Dan." Rich and Dan had obviously talked before the meeting.

Nice, Grant thought. He was feeling like he was in good hands. Could this set up get any better?

Rich asked, "Okay, any law enforcement, past or present, here?" Grant winced at the "present" part; he was technically wanted, or whatever POI meant. He was hoping there were no cops in the room.

Four hands went up. One guy said, "I was a reserve Sheriff's Deputy in the 80s but I haven't done it in a long time. I wouldn't count myself as 'law enforcement.'"

A man said, "My neighbor is currently a county sheriff's deputy. I haven't seen him in about a week."

Another guy, who looked like Jimmy Buffet, said, "I'm Dick Abbott. I'm a retired LA County deputy. Out on disability. Lost most of my hearing in a shootout twenty years ago. Don't know that I'll be much help, but I'll do whatever is asked of me."

The third hand was a woman in her fifties. "I'm Linda Rodriguez. I am retired from Seattle Police Department. I was a dispatcher."

"Great," Rich said. "Glad to have all of you." He was, indeed, happy to have so many veterans and some law enforcement. "Now, any other people who have some unique skills?"

There were two nurses and an EMT. "Great. We'll definitely need medical skills," Rich said. Mark and John looked at Grant for him to announce that they had an ER doctor out at Pierce Point. Grant slightly shook his head. He wanted to talk to Lisa before he announced her occupation. He didn't know why she wouldn't want to be the neighborhood doctor, but he just thought he should ask her if she wanted a part-time job out there.

"There's Randy Greene, the foot doctor," someone said. "But he's not out here. Yet."

Rich said, "Okay any other skills out there that will help us out?"

Chapter 89

Meet the Team

(May 8)

When Rich asked if anyone else had unique skills, the Team looked at Grant. Grant whispered to Mark, "Introduce me and I'll take it from there." Mark nodded.

Mark stood up. "My neighbor here, Grant, has some guys to introduce. These guys are solid, I can tell you from personal experience." That was a big boost from a local.

All eyes were on Grant. He stood up and said, "I'm Grant ..." Should he give out his last name? What if someone looked him up on the POI list? Well, it would get out some time and there weren't exactly any cops around with time on their hands to take him in. He paused and thought.

Grant decided right then and there that he would die with his boots on. If they wanted to come get him, he'd fight it out, so he might as well give out his last name now. He was betting his life on the fact that there wasn't any more law enforcement left.

"Grant Matson. I have a cabin out here but, as Mark Colson will tell you, I'm not exactly a city boy." Mark gave the crowd a thumbs up. "I live next to Mark on the far north end. I brought some good friends out here with me. Actually, they rescued my family from Olympia and convoyed them out here, running into a sticky situation on the way out." That was a bit of an exaggeration, but these people needed to know that the Team weren't just Billy Bobs in a pickup truck. They weren't military or law enforcement, either. Somewhere in between.

Grant pointed to the Team. He introduced them and noted that another one, Bobby, was out in the truck guarding some valuables. John went out and got Bobby, who came in for his introduction and then left.

Grant almost forgot Chip, who was kind of on the Team. Grant pointed to Chip and said, "We shoot a lot with Chip, too. He is very good." Chip put his hand up in an "aw shucks" gesture.

The next part was hard. How could he describe the Team so that people knew they could do things without being nervous about them? Grant didn't want to seem like he was searching for the perfect words, which indicated he was holding something back or trying to spin something. So he just said what he meant.

"We are … well, we train together a lot," Grant said. "On the range. We have been lucky enough to get the law enforcement shooting range in Olympia on Sundays and we've made good use of it. The SWAT guys have taught us a lot. Bill here, or 'Pow' as everyone calls him, is a handgun instructor." True, but he didn't get paid for it. Grant was exaggerating a little to establish their credibility; it was a little risky, but he thought he had to do it.

"We've been training together for two years," Grant said. "We're not formally trained law enforcement, but we're pretty darned close. We don't claim any super-specialized skills, but … well, we're pretty good. We will do whatever we can to help the effort here."

The crowd was looking over Grant and these young men he brought with him. They all seemed clean cut and well spoken. They had given their seats to ladies. They called people "sir" and "ma'am." They had guns and holsters that indicated that they were serious about this stuff. They didn't have a "strut," but they were confident. Grant sensed that the Team was initially making a good first impression with the crowd.

Rich, always the curious cop, asked, "What do you do for a living?"

Grant answered, "I am … well, I guess I *was*, a lawyer." A few people looked like they hated him already. "Not a scumbag lawyer, like most of them are," Grant quickly added. "I don't even like lawyers." That got a couple of laughs. "Out here, with what's going on, I'm not a lawyer. My job now is protecting my family and feeding them and helping my neighbors as best I can. I plan on spending a lot of time hunting and fishing and helping with things like guard duty and anything else that is asked of me."

In that moment, Rich realized who their judge would be, but he didn't want to hand out that job until he got to know Grant. It was an important job; a bad judge would be counter-productive. Rich would keep his eye on Grant and these guys of his for a while.

Rich said, "Welcome to you and your guys. I'd like to see what kind of skills you have and then we'll see where we can put you." Fair enough, Grant thought. He nodded at Rich.

"Well, now you know the basic plan," Rich said to the audience. "We also know some of the skills people have out here. You can go now if you want; I don't want to keep you. I will be taking names for guard duty, beach patrol, and the internal patrol. When I know how many people we have for each and the skills we have, then we can start doing more detailed planning and figure out what training we need and who will do it. This was just a meeting for the basic plan and introductions. The detailed planning will go on tomorrow and then we'll meet back here at the same time, 7:00. I'll take all the planning volunteers I can get. Come up and see me. Any other questions?"

There weren't any.

"Good night and stay safe," Rich said.

People started milling out. There was a big line to talk to Rich. Rich saw Grant and said, "Can you and your guys stay for a while? I'd like to meet them."

"Sure," Grant said. This was a good sign.

"And I'd like Mark and John to stay with you guys, too," Rich said.

John said, "Which is good because we all rode together."

Mark and John were chatting with their neighbors, most of whom they didn't know very well. Mark spent some time talking with Ryan McDonald, the Afghanistan Marine. Ryan was in his late twenties. He had been a substitute teacher, but had rarely had any work for the past few years. He cut firewood and did odd jobs. He lived by himself in an immaculate mobile home in Pierce Point. Ryan looked like an ordinary guy; he didn't have a crew cut or "USMC" tattooed on his arm. Grant overheard Ryan say to Mark, "Bronze star, sir." He must have been in a fight or two and done nicely, Grant thought.

Grant was sure to say hi to as many people as he could and introduce the Team. They were saying "sir" and "ma'am" to everyone and making a great first impression. This was key. Grant didn't want his guys to be stuck doing menial things they were overqualified for. That would lead them to, maybe, want to go back to the city, as crazy as that would be. These guys wanted to use their skills. Grant needed his guys to be very happy where they were. He needed the Team to be the Pierce Point SWAT team, or at least to be on the SWAT team. They would share the roles with qualified people, like Ryan. But just about anyone could man the gate. Guys who had shot for a long time together, in semi-SWAT-like training situations, should be the ones knocking down doors.

Knocking down doors? Grant realized that the Team had never actually done things like that. They'd cleared imaginary rooms where Ted drew the boundaries of the room in the dirt, but they'd never actually done it in a real house or been shot at.

Oh well. No one else had (except Ryan McDonald and maybe Rich Gentry). The Team, while inexperienced in some areas, was more experienced than almost everyone else, overall. This was a time to make do with what they had. Pierce Point had Rich Gentry, Dan Morgan, Ryan McDonald. And the Team. Not bad.

After a while, Rich came up to Grant. "I'd like to meet your guys. Now, tell me how did you all meet?"

Grant told Rich about Capitol City Guns and how they started shooting at the law enforcement range and the things they practiced.

"What are their backgrounds?" Rich asked. Grant explained that all of them were civilians with no formal training. This was interesting to Rich. He had never run across civilians who just trained like this on their own. He had heard of militia wannabe guys who did this, but he could tell Grant's guys weren't like that. They didn't wear military clothes and seemed eager to help instead of fantasizing about killing people like they were in a video game. Rich kept wondering what the catch was.

"Can you guys come by the gate tomorrow?" Rich asked. "Maybe show us a bit of what you know. Bring your full gear."

"Sure," Grant said. He looked Rich straight in the eye. It was time to set himself exactly where he wanted to be in the Pierce Point pecking order. He said to Rich, "You have things pretty organized out here. My guys want to be part of your system. Not some rogue group. We are an asset out here. We want to have a good role because we'll do a good job. We've worked very hard and have some impressive gear that will help the effort. It would be a waste to put us on the gate, in my opinion, although we will honor your decision." Grant owed it to his guys to try to get them the best jobs possible, but he also wanted Rich to know that the Team was not some rival, renegade group.

This was politics; not the political party kind of politics that had driven the country into the crapper, but the kind that was about getting along with everyone in tough situations, while not selling out. Grant was good at it. He had to be. It was how people would survive.

Rich smiled. He appreciated Grant's acknowledgement of his authority and he appreciated that Grant was trying to get his guys the best spots possible. Grant was a leader; a leader of a small unit that wanted to fit into a larger one. He was the perfect kind of leader to have within an organization. Rich also had a sense of how valuable the Team would be to Pierce Point's security. He said, "I think I have an idea for your guys, but I'd like to see their stuff tomorrow. Fair enough?"

"Fair enough," Grant said. He could tell this was going to work.

Chapter 90

A Case of Tuna, Big Boy

(May 8)

On the way back home, Grant told the Team that they would have a tryout the next day. They were very excited. Mark and John were happy, too. Their friends would be contributing a lot to the effort. Paul was silent. He wasn't pissy, just quiet. Grant assumed it was because he knew he was too out of shape to be doing the cool stuff.

Grant asked Mark and John, "Is there any way the Team can sleep tonight instead of doing guard duty? I want us to be rested for tomorrow."

Paul's eyes lit up. "Hey, I can take guard duty tonight. No problem."

"Hey, that would be awesome, Paul," Grant said. Paul was stepping up. He had been doing everything he could since they got out there. He had a heart of gold. He fought like hell to get his daughter from his druggie ex-wife, he worked hard around the cabins, and now he was volunteering for a boring night of guard duty. Grant made a mental note to find plenty of things for him to do.

"We'll brew some coffee when we get back," John said.

"I've got something better, at least something that won't use up our coffee," Grant said. "I've got some caffeine pills for just these kinds of occasions. One tablet is 200 milligrams of caffeine; about one strong cup of coffee. Would you like a couple?"

"Yeah. Thanks," Paul said. After a while he said, "With a serious guard station at the Pierce Point gate, I think we can go down to one guard at our shack. Besides, every cabin is full of well-armed people."

Everyone nodded. This was the first time they had thought that the community-wide security was making their individual security better. They didn't need two or three guards in the shack all the time. There was a sense that the community was improvising and coming up with solutions to problems. They had all been immersed in chaos for the past week. Chaos they could not have imagined before all of this. But now things were slowly settling down. Finally, something was working out.

They pulled up to their cabins and Drew was there with his lever action carbine. He waved them in. They hadn't been overrun by biker gangs in the two hours they had a retired accountant with a cowboy gun guarding their families. Maybe things weren't so dire.

"Pancakes tomorrow morning at 8:00, gentlemen," Grant said. It was getting dark now. He was tired. He had been moving and thinking all day and was ready to take a load off.

Grant walked into the cabin and Cole said, "Hi, Dad. How was your meeting?"

"Nice talking, little buddy," Grant said. He loved to hear Cole communicate so well. "I got home in time for tucking."

"Thank you, Dad," Cole said.

Lisa was getting the kids ready for bed, although it was still a little light out. It was hard to say they needed to go to bed so they could get up for school because there was no school.

"How was your meeting?" Lisa asked. She was a little afraid her gun-loving husband would volunteer for some crazy militia thing.

"Really well," Grant said. He described the level-headed former cop Rich, how organized things were, all the military and law enforcement people involved, and how the Team had a tryout tomorrow. "I'm looking forward to it."

"So you're going to the tryout?" she asked.

"Yes," he said. "I'm part of the Team and our skills are needed." He had decided on the ride back from the Grange that he was going to tell Lisa he was with the Team and would be patrolling with them. He knew she would flip out. The couple of days of domestic bliss would be over. He was trying not to get upset.

"Okay," she said with a smile. "Just be careful." She didn't want Grant to do this, but she was trying hard to avoid getting into an argument. At the same time, though, she knew it made sense for him to do it. She was proud of him for taking such responsibility for everyone's safety. She just wished it was someone else's husband doing it.

"The community asked if there were any medical people here," he said. "I didn't want to volunteer you without talking to you."

Lisa had been expecting this conversation. A few times, when they were driving on long trips for a vacation, they would come across a car accident before the ambulances got there. Lisa would get out and "go to work" as she called it. She had come to accept that as a doctor, an ER doctor no less, she needed to help people. But she wasn't always exactly thrilled about it.

"There's no decent hospital or even clinic here and I don't have insurance," she said. "What am I supposed to do? Treat people with third world supplies and get paid in chickens?"

Yes. Exactly. But Grant didn't want to say that. "Well, you have skills. Life-saving skills. We can't just let you sit it out while people die or suffer needlessly."

Lisa got mad. She didn't want to go be a doctor out there in Hillbillyville. She wanted her old state-of-the-art ER back in Tacoma.

But she knew she had to save all the people she could. Of course she would do that. But under primitive conditions. The whole situation sucked. Damn it. Nothing was right. She would have to treat people like they were in Haiti or something. Why couldn't things be normal again?

As mad as she was, she couldn't come up with a solid reason to disagree. She wanted to help people—there was never a question about that—but treating people out there would be such a nightmare. She was insecure because she knew exactly what to do with all the equipment and supplies of a modern emergency room and with all the help of a team of ER nurses. What if she didn't know how to treat people without all that stuff? It was scary.

"I could do a walk-in clinic," she said, after thinking about it for a few minutes. "Check-ups. That kind of thing. No organ transplants," she said, laughing at that last part. The laughter broke the tension.

"Deal," Grant said. "No organ transplants. There are a couple of nurses and an EMT out here. You wouldn't be doing this alone."

"Where would we do this?" Lisa asked. "Certainly not in our cabin."

"Our" cabin? Grant was glad to hear her referring to the cabin as their place. Not Grant's cabin, like she had before. She was slowly accepting that she would be out there for a while.

"And waivers," Lisa said. "I want people to sign waivers. You can write them up." She was surprising herself that she was actually agreeing to do this. But she knew she had to. Try telling a mom that her child would have to die because Lisa didn't have insurance.

"Waivers are no problem," Grant said. "There are no courts anymore, but I'll do one. No problem. That sounds reasonable."

Grant paused. "By the way, I don't think you'll be doing this for free. You can ask for food and other things for doing this. People will be glad to pay for medical care. And, just think, no taxes," he said with a smile. Hey, there had to be some kind of upside to doing third world medical care in exchange for chickens.

"Yeah, I guess," she said. "But I won't turn anyone away who really needs it." She paused and smiled, "I won't give some middle aged guy a testicular exam without getting a case of tuna." She winked and whispered, "Do you have a case of tuna, big boy?"

Grant blushed. He had not seen that coming and he planned to take her up on that offer later.

Thank God she was okay with this doctor thing. He went into overdrive to make this work. "I'll talk to Rich in the morning. We'll figure out a clinic facility. We'll get an inventory of medical supplies. I have some rubbing alcohol here, for example."

She looked at him. "You have rubbing alcohol? What else did my psycho survivalist husband pack up out here?" She was so happy he had taken these precautions. She was just having some fun with him.

"You'll see, my dear," Grant said. He started to describe all the things in the storage shed. He emphasized the fact that he bought all these things with the money it took to buy an ounce of gold back when it was just $900. "A two-quart pack of rubbing alcohol was $4.99 at Costco up until recently," he said with a smile. That's as close to gloating as he would come.

"Well, you're still psycho but I'm glad I have some rubbing alcohol," she said and then winked. "That way I can thoroughly sterilize my hands after giving testicular exams to all your friends."

Grant looked around at where the kids were.

She read his mind. It wasn't hard. She looked at him and whispered. "Yes, when the kids go to bed. My parents are upstairs, but I'll try to forget that."

This setup out at the cabin wasn't ideal, but the basics were getting taken care of. Like sex. Oh, and food, water, shelter, and security. And sex.

Chapter 91

Show Time

(May 9)

How would they get more food? Grant woke up at 2:30 a.m. wondering that. They, the Matsons, had months of food for themselves, but that wasn't enough. The Colsons and Morrells had a month or so of food. The Team had practically nothing. Drew had plenty of cash, but would the stores have food to buy? Would the inflated prices mean the cash would be gone quickly?

Grant laughed at himself. Before the Collapse, he would wake up in the middle of the night on occasion worrying about a work problem. Back then, he thought that if work would just go away after society imploded, he'd be set. All his work problems would go away and everything would be fine.

He realized that wasn't true. Now he didn't have to worry about something at work, but he had to worry about getting food for his family. Not necessarily a good trade.

Well, look at your assets, he thought. You can offer security. That's worth something. It's worth more now than having a lawyer argue about the meaning of words. Lisa can offer lifesaving. That's sure worth something.

"I have a new job," Grant whispered to himself. That was it. He had a new job. He would hopefully get paid in meals and maybe some gasoline. His wife would similarly get paid. They had emergency "savings" in the form of the food in the storage shed. Not bad.

So how would everyone else on Over Road get food? Tammy had a normal job. People needed electricity. That would be a huge priority of the government. Imagine the political problem if a government supposedly in charge couldn't keep the lights on and the water running.

The hunting and fishing was nice, but no one really expected that to sustain the seventeen people on Over Road. Everyone in the area would have the same idea. Game would get scarce fast. That happened during the first Great Depression. Old timers told stories of squirrels getting rare. The same with fish. The days of seeing closed oyster shells with live oysters in them on the beach would soon be over. The hunting and fishing was great for a meat "anchor" one meal, like the deer steak BBQs at the Colsons. Gas was in short supply and travel was dangerous, so people in Pierce Point couldn't just drive a few miles to a place with no people and hunt and fish there.

The chicks and chickens were great, but they would only produce a meal or two per person each week, if that. A definite plus, but not a complete solution.

Gardening and permaculture, which was food that returns every year like apple trees, was great. It was only a supplement, though. It would take a few months for the crops planted now to mature in the late summer or fall. And, more importantly, there weren't too many clear patches for crops. They were in a forested area that dropped into the sea. The few clear patches had houses on them or were overrun with weeds. Grant started thinking about some clear patches a few roads away. They should start a community garden on those patches. Pay the owner of those lots (if they could find them) some rent in the form of produce. He would bring that up at the next meeting.

The stores in town. Grant kept thinking that the stores, with their virtually bare shelves, would still have to be the main food supply for most people. America wasn't the rural, self-sufficient country it was even a few generations ago. Grant remembered hearing on the Survival Podcast that America was now a net importer of food. The country imported more food than it exported. That was unbelievable. When Grant was a kid, America fed itself and most of the rest of the world. But politicians decided it was better to give American farmers subsidies not to farm than it was to actually grow food. In the insanity of the pre-Collapse political world, that actually made sense to those in power. And the farmers, most of them working for giant agricultural corporations, didn't mind cashing the checks. Everyone was a winner—except if the unthinkable happened and America actually had to feed itself. How is feeding oneself "unthinkable"? Besides, according to pre-Collapse thinking, the U.S. could count on the Mexicans to send all the produce the country needed and save a dollar on each tomato. What could ever go wrong in Mexico that would cause a disruption in the United States' cheap food supply?

Hopefully the government, as inept as it was, would figure out a way to harness the enormous potential food production America still had and get it out to the people. What an impossible task, even for a competent and honest government. It would be even harder for this government. But the political pressure to feed people would be enormous. The government knew that if people were hungry and had nothing to lose, they would rise up and kill all those government people who were keeping them hungry. Feeding the people was a military necessity. Grant remembered reading Mao's book on guerilla warfare describing food production as a military necessity.

Even if the government could pull it off, people would have much less to eat. They would have different food. No more tomatoes from Mexico for salads that people ate a bite from and then threw out. Now, a tomato a week might come from a neighbor's garden. It would taste far better and not have who knows what sprayed on it, but it wouldn't be as plentiful. All the junk food that sustained so many people would be gone. It cost too much to produce and required ingredients from all over the country, which couldn't just roll down the road on semis now that gas was $15 a gallon today, and maybe $20 tomorrow.

Grant tried to go back to sleep. He started thinking about all the food his family had. All the various meal combinations they had. All the nutrition. All the vitamins he stored out there. He had done a hell of a job getting ready for this. A hell of a job.

He woke up when the sunlight came into the bedroom. He got dressed, which now included his pistol belt, and tried to get up quietly and start cooking pancakes. He still had some time before people started coming over.

Grant went out onto the deck and just stared at the water. It was perfectly quiet in the cabin. He thought. And thought. First he thought about the looters he had killed. He hadn't thought about them since it happened. He wondered if there was something wrong with him for not worrying about them. He regretted having to do it, but he kept coming to the conclusion that he did the right thing. They were trying to kill him and Ron and eventually others in the neighborhood. He hoped that he remained at peace about killing them. He didn't want to have nightmares.

Then Grant thought about all the "coincidences" that led them all there. All the people he knew and trusted who had come together. All the skills they had out there. All the supplies and gear they had. Grant talked to God. He thanked Him. The conversation was private. Grant never talked about these things with anyone.

Drew and Eileen started to stir. The kids would be up soon. Chip came over with a cup of coffee.

"Mornin', sunshine," he said. "This old man is looking forward to an audition this morning."

"So is this slightly less old man," Grant said.

Grant started making pancakes. People were trickling in. It was a happy scene.

They talked about the news. No one had been terribly interested in it lately, so they didn't think about it, although some things were happening of interest. Tammy said that some Feds had come to the power company and told them that the utility would be staying operational, no matter what. The power company had first dibs on supplies like parts for the equipment and gasoline. In fact, Tammy was happy to report, employees of the utility would get free gas from the company's big gas tanks they had for the equipment trucks. The Feds said that "critical workers" like the power company people had to get to work so they would get all the gas they needed. The power company wouldn't be using the gas to go out and read meters or clear brush around the lines anymore. They would just concentrate on keeping things running. The Feds told them not to even bill people for power anymore. No one could pay and it would be a waste of time to try to collect. The Feds explained that the government would be taking over the utilities and giving away power, water and, in some places, sewer and internet. Tammy concluded that, in exchange for the Feds getting to own and control everything, people would get "free" necessities like utilities and, the Feds hinted, basic food once they got that production on line. She said food would be distributed by using something called "FCards."

The "free" utilities, some basic amount of food and a military (what was left of them) was all people would get out of the federal government. All the parks, NASA, historic preservation, and studies about the mating habits of blue winged pecker snapples would be gone. So would Social Security, Medicare, Medicaid, and welfare. No one really was surprised at this forced paring back of the federal government. The budget cuts leading up to the Collapse made it clear that those things would be gone soon. They were going, going, gone now.

"They say this whole thing is temporary," Tammy said softly and sadly.

"Yeah, right," Manda said as she laughed. Everyone was thinking the same thing, but didn't want to say it. Leave it to a sixteen year-old to just say it.

"Oh, one more thing," Tammy said. "They said this situation is called the 'Crisis.' They said the terrorists are calling it the 'Collapse.'"

"Then I'll call it the 'Collapse,'" Grant said. "That's what it is. A

'Crisis' is just an excuse to give more power to the government. They created this mess and now they want..." He could feel a political rant coming on, so he stopped. This kind of politics was irrelevant now.

Paul chimed in. "I've been watching the news and it really seems like things are mellowing out a bit. Most people are staying in their homes. Lots of 'neighbor helping neighbor' stories. I'm not sure I believe everything I see on TV, but it doesn't seem like a zombie apocalypse."

"True," Grant said. Paul was right: it was not a complete and total collapse. Grant realized that it seemed like more of a collapse to them, out there in Pierce Point, harboring a POI fugitive and taking matters like getting food into their own hands. But for most grasshoppers just sitting in their homes and watching TV, it was not a big deal. Yet.

Grant decided to be positive. No reason to shatter the hopes of Lisa and others. So Grant said, "Let's hope this is just a temporary 'Crisis.' But we need to be prepared for anything. In fact, we have a meeting with Rich now. Mark and John, I'd like you guys to come because Rich knows you."

Mark volunteered to drive. He loved hanging out with these guys. "I'll get my stuff and get the truck started," he said.

Pow said, "Okay, gentlemen. Full kit and ARs and meet back at the yellow cabin." "Kit" was a tactical vest with magazine pouches full of loaded magazines. For the most part, the Team had kit made by Tactical Tailor, which was located near Ft. Lewis. Except for Chip, all the guys had tactical vests. Grant went into the master bedroom and got his kit out of the suit bag. Lisa thought he looked weird in it, but it was starting to seem more and more normal.

Pow had a tactical vest with body armor plate inserts. They were the level IIIA ones that could stop an AK-47 round at point blank range. Pow was the only one with body armor. That had been on everyone's list of things to get as the Collapse was nearing and they knew they'd need advanced gear like that. Body armor was legal to buy, except for felons. But it was expensive. Scotty had spent his money on radios and first aid equipment. Wes and Bobby got lots of ammo. Grant had the cabin. So Pow got the one set of body armor. "There has to be a door kicker," he said. The door kicker should have body armor.

The pouches on the tactical vests varied, based on personal preferences. But each one held six thirty round AR magazines. The tac vests also held varying numbers of pistol magazines. Each had a

Camelbak water bladder with about three liters of water. A vital and often overlooked item was a drop pouch. It was a nylon pouch that opened up and held empty magazines. That way, they didn't drop valuable empty magazines on the ground; they had a place for them. Other items included flashlights and extra batteries, both for the flashlights and for the Aimpoint or EO Tech red-dot sights.

Rounding out the standard equipment was a Zero Tolerance folding knife and a Surefire weapon light mounted on every AR. It was a high-output flashlight mounted with a LaRue Tactical mount on the left side of the hand guard that allowed the Team to put a 110-lumen beam of light on whatever they were pointing their AR at. Each member of the team had a molded Raven Concealment holster for his pistol.

The knife, Surefire weapons light, and Raven Concealment holster were a "membership card." Each member of the Team had them. It was a way to signify who was in the "club." The Team never intended to have standardized gear to set themselves apart. It was just how things evolved: someone would get a good piece of gear, like a Zero Tolerance knife and then everyone else would get one. Pretty soon, it was a "membership card."

The Team assembled at the yellow cabin. Dang, they looked impressive. ARs and kit. No one was in jeans. All 5.11s or, in Chip's case, Carhartt pants. No one looked "mall ninja"; they looked like military contractors.

"Armed serenity" was what Grant called this feeling. He got that term from nutnfancy's YouTube videos. It described when you're out with your guys, armed to the teeth, and doing what you love. You're calm and confident and know that what you're doing is important. Armed serenity. That term was perfect for this moment—and for hundreds of other moments for the Team out there at Pierce Point.

Grant looked at his guys in their kit. They were badass, but clean cut. Exactly the two things Grant wanted to convey to Rich and the rest of the community. Effective, but controlled. That was the message Grant wanted to give to the Pierce Point people: the Team was effective, but not radical.

"Let's go show them duck hunters how we do it," Pow said when they were leaving the yellow cabin and heading to Mark's truck.

Grant had to stop that.

"Hey, man," Grant said, "I get the 'duck hunter' thing and totally agree," Grant said in a rare public rebuke of Pow. "But the locals can't hear us talking like that. This is their playground. We're the guests. I don't want the duck hunters jealous of us or thinking we're mall ninjas. We need them as much, or more, than they need us. So you guys need to do what you did last night at the Grange, which was perfect. Lots of 'sir' and 'ma'am' and 'how can we help.' Does that make sense?"

Grant knew that the local boys and girls had skills and were a huge asset. "Many of those duck hunters," Grant said, "are badass in their own way. They know this area like the back of their hands. They've been shooting since they were little kids. They have used the same rifle or shotgun for years and know it well. They can stay out in the cold and rain for hours waiting for something to move and then take it with one shot. That will make them great guards."

The guys didn't appear convinced. Grant continued, "So while we're way better at many things, I don't want you guys to write off the duck hunters. When you're hungry and there's duck for dinner, you'll appreciate the duck hunters."

The Team smiled. They got it. They could be very good at what they do, they just didn't need to be dicks about it. Appreciate the help their hosts were providing. After all, the Team was out there to help people and not insult them.

Pow realized that Grant was right. The Team was … a team, and all suggestions were welcomed. Besides, Grant was kind of in charge out there. It was his place. He and his neighbors were feeding them.

Pow said with a smile, "No problem, brother. We'll low-key it and then go do our thing. Frickin' well, I might add."

Grant smiled. Thank God the Team had been together for so long and knew and trusted each other so much. Grant couldn't imagine a pick-up team of some guys who just met trying to pull all this off. It took a seasoned team.

Grant knew how to motivate and manage an elite group. He did it with Squadron 3 back in Civil Air Patrol. Motivate the guys so they retain their swagger and want to stay part of the elite group, but at the same time, don't alienate the regular units and make them jealous. Respect the regular units because they're much better than the elite guys think.

Grant realized that the Team was Squadron 3 all over again. He had one of those funny feelings where he realized that all those seemingly random life experiences he'd had, like Squadron 3, were actually forerunners for things he'd need to do now when it really mattered. Another "coincidence."

"Oh, hell yeah we'll do it well," Grant said, returning to the present moment. Grant looked around to see if Mark or any of the other locals were around. They weren't. Grant said, "Let's go show these duck hunters how we do it." That fired everyone up. Which is exactly what Grant intended.

As they were walking to Mark's truck, Wes said, "We need to live here, too. I'd much rather get along with everyone." Wes had been looking for a place to fit in. That place hadn't been his dad's house. It hadn't been all the different high schools. It hadn't been his job with all those near strangers. It was the Team and now it was Pierce Point.

Chip said with a smile, "Hey, I'm Uncle Chip out here. They love me. I can fit in with duck hunters just fine."

Pow, who was a leader of this group, too, realized that he needed to have a role in this. He pointed to everyone and said, "We're cool with the duck hunters, right?"

Everyone nodded.

"Then let's go. Show time," Pow said with a giant grin.

They piled in Mark's truck. Manda and Cole waved. Lisa had gone inside. She didn't like to see Grant with all those guns. It reminded her that he had killed some people and he would be in danger. But she couldn't stop him. She would if she could figure out a way, but she knew the "gun things" needed to be done. At least for a little while – until everything got back to normal.

They went past the guard shack. Paul and Mary Anne were there, rifles in hand. They waved and Mary Anne snapped a picture.

As they went down the road, Grant felt so alive. There was something exhilarating about riding in the back of a truck with extremely well-armed friends. It never got old. He had done it with the Team when they would drive downrange to set up the steel targets that were too heavy to carry. He loved the truck rides with the guys. When Grant would see pictures on TV of military contractors riding together in pickups in Iraq or Afghanistan or even the Somali men in their trucks, he understood the bond they had. He understood it. And he loved it.

A little way past Over Road, they saw their first residents. They were an older man and woman out walking, holding hands. Their jaws dropped when they saw the truckload of well-armed men. Each of the Team said, "Morning, sir" or "Morning, ma'am" and tipped their hats, which were tan baseball caps with a Velcro patch of an American flag on the front. Any resident seeing this would be relieved to have these guys in their neighborhood.

Once they passed the couple, Grant said to them, "That's exactly how to do it, gentlemen. Those people will go back and tell their neighbors that there is a team of nice SWAT guys here to help. Exactly what we need. Thanks."

Grant hoped he wasn't obsessing over this political stuff, but first impressions were everything. And they were dead if the Pierce Point people turned on them. The Team and Grant's family would need support from the Pierce Point people. There was no way they'd make it through this without help from the community.

Grant decided to have some fun with this and make a point at the same time. "You know, guys, the more buzz there is about the nice men in the truck, the more the chicks here will want to meet you." Smiles all around. Chicks had been motivating young men for several thousand years. "Even for you, Chip," Grant said. Everyone laughed, especially Chip.

As they went past the houses on the road to the Grange, Mark drove slowly. He figured the residents should get a good look at them. Mark loved being a part of this, even if he was only the driver. The guys waved and smiled at everyone. They tipped their hats and said, "Good morning." They felt like heroes. All the training and expense was paying off. This was what they were supposed to be doing in such a disaster. It was what sheepdogs lived for.

When they pulled into the Grange, there were already several trucks there. The Team jumped out of the bed of the truck while keeping control of the ARs on their slings. They had done this plenty of times before. They'd never shot at anyone or been shot at, but they had the rest of this down. The locals looked at them in shock. Who were these guys? Were they here to help?

Mark was the guide. He was the connection with the locals. He looked for Rich. Rich was in the Grange with a clipboard. Ryan, the Marine, and Dan, the Air Force dog handler, were standing there talking to him.

"Hey, Rich, my guys are here," Mark said. He loved calling the Team "my guys."

Rich smiled as the Team walked in. They looked like the Sheriff's SWAT team Rich had been on briefly, except that they didn't have matching clothes. They also looked like they would follow orders. Perfect. Rich already knew that these guys would have door-busting duties, with some guidance and additional training from him.

"Great," Rich said. "Thanks for coming by this morning." He

knew these guys, especially the young ones, were itching to come by and show their stuff so "thanks for coming by" was a little joke. "I'd like each one of you to tell me about yourself."

Grant started things off as a signal to Rich that he was the overall leader.

Grant said, "Sure. But first, I want to make an important point." Grant looked Rich right in the eye and said, "None of us are prior military or law enforcement. We taught ourselves some things. We got to use the law enforcement range in Olympia. We had some military and other people train us informally. I think we're really good, but we've been practicing on steel targets that don't shoot back. I know it's unusual for civilians like us to train themselves, but we did. We're at the service of the community."

Rich nodded slowly. So did Ryan and Dan. They were encouraged by the apparent luck of this, but they wanted to see if these guys were for real or just mall ninjas.

Grant pointed to Wes, who was next to Rich, and said, "Introduce yourselves."

Each guy gave his name, where he used to live, what he used to do, and how long they had trained with the Team. The last guy to introduce himself was Pow.

"Pow," he said. "That's what everyone calls me." He paused, not sure if he wanted to say the next thing. "I used to sell insurance." Rich, Ryan, and Dan laughed. Pow laughed, too. It was totally at odds with the gun fighter standing before them.

"Hey," Pow said, "there's lots of crazy shit going on now. An insurance salesman turned gunfighter is just one of them."

Grant pointed to his AR. "We have standardized equipment, pretty much. All of us run ARs and most of us have AKs and tactical shotguns if we need them. Pow has a sweet bolt gun." Grant was referring to Pow's sniper rifle in .308. Pow could hit six-inch targets at 600 yards with that thing.

"We all run Glocks," Grant continued. "I am the freak of the group in .40; everyone else is in 9mm. We have at least 10 magazines for every weapon. We have enough ammunition out here for … a while." Grant didn't want to describe all the valuables they had for someone to steal. But if he couldn't trust Rich and the others, who could he trust? Chip looked at Grant. Of course, the basement full of ARs, parts, and ammo would not be mentioned.

Rich smiled. "You guys know that, as of yesterday, all these guns are illegal." The guys shrugged. "Yep," Rich said. "Governor signed an executive order. For real."

Rich smiled, "But I'm happy as hell that you have them and I'm no longer a police officer, so I don't give a shit about any of that. Especially unconstitutional executive orders. Let what's left of the police come and try to get them."

Ryan whispered something to Rich. "Can we do a little marksmanship test with you guys?" Rich asked.

"Sure," Pow said. Rich motioned for them to follow him. They went out the back door of the Grange. There were no houses around the Grange and there was a hay bale with a paper plate set up about twenty-five yards away.

"The residents know we'll be shooting?" Grant asked. "I don't want them to think there's trouble and come streaming out to shoot us."

Dang. This guy thinks of everything, Dan thought. "No problem," Dan said. "We told them to expect some training fire. But that's a good thought."

"Okay, how about five from each of you," Rich said.

Bobby was closest to Rich, so he would go first. He yelled, out of habit, "The range is hot!" meaning they would be shooting live rounds. He effortlessly swung his AR up, clicked off the safety, and put five rapid-fire rounds right into the center of the paper plate. After firing he did a "search and assess," where he kept looking through his sight and scanning the area around the target for additional threats, just like they had trained. After a few scans, he lowered his rifle and clicked the safety back on. Smooth as silk.

Each of the guys did the same until that paper plate was shot out in the middle. There were three holes a couple inches from the edge of the plate. Almost all holes were in the very middle.

Rich, Ryan, and Dan were impressed. Not in awe; they could shoot the same, but they were impressed that insurance salesmen, hospital techs, and equipment rental guys could do this kind of shooting. Not to mention a lawyer. Dan got another paper plate and, after making sure no one was still about to shoot, called out "range is cold" and went to the hay bale to change plates. As he was doing that, Ryan said, "It's pistol time."

They moved up to about ten yards in front of the hay bale and did the same thing. Every shot hit the paper plate. They shot their pistols with their ARs on their slings. They looked effortless when shooting and moving. It was obvious they had done this hundreds of times.

Dan said, "Show me dry how you transition from primary to secondary." "Dry" meant no round in the chamber. This would be a test to see how they transitioned from the primary weapon, the AR, to the second, the pistol, in the event the AR ran out of ammo or jammed. Each of the guys made sure their weapons were pointed in a safe direction, removed the magazines, ejected the live round, and reinserted the magazines. They did a press check to ensure that there was no round in the chamber and put the safeties on the ARs (the Glocks didn't have a manual safety). This test was as much about safe weapons handling as it was about marksmanship.

Each guy did a perfect or near perfect transition, letting the AR fall to his side while suspended on the sling and then drawing his pistol. It was obvious that they knew what they were doing.

Ryan dragged his heel in the gravel to make a line. "This is a door. Show me an entry." Marines did a lot of urban training and clearing a room was a basic component of that.

Wes and Bobby were standing closest to Ryan, so they teamed up. They demonstrated a two-man stack and how to clear a room. When they wanted to come out of the room, they yelled, "Exiting!" Grant yelled back "Exit!" This was the command to prevent guys exiting the room from walking out of a room only to be shot by another team member. Their technique wasn't perfect, but it was impressive.

"Where did you guys learn this?" Rich asked. He couldn't believe they didn't have any training on this.

Grant said, "We hung out at Chip's gun store with a Special Forces guy named Ted. He came out to the range and taught us all kinds of shit." Grant couldn't help grinning. He was proud.

Rich, Ryan, and Dan were silent. They felt very lucky that these guys just happened to be living in the neighborhood. Rich wanted to see if he could get even luckier.

"So where is Ted?" Rich asked.

Just as Grant was about to answer, Chip shot him a weird look. Grant paused.

Chip said, "He's in Texas. That's where he said he'd be going." This was news to Grant and the Team. Chip had never mentioned this. Grant could tell this was something Chip didn't want to discuss.

Dan asked, "Have you guys ever been shot at?"

They shook their heads. Grant raised his hand. Oh crap. That was stupid — telling people about the shooting — but he'd already raised his hand. Might was well follow through.

"I had to defend myself and a neighbor a few days ago back in

Olympia," Grant said. "A group of about a dozen armed young punks were charging my friend, Ron, who was guarding the entrance to the neighborhood. I drove my car at them, got out, used the car for cover, and ... I used my pistol. Three confirmed dead, not sure how many wounded. I didn't enjoy it. Ron was pretty happy about it, though," Grant tried to smile but he couldn't. This wasn't a joking matter.

Grant collected his thoughts. "I credit my training with these guys for getting me out of the situation. I knew exactly what I needed to do. I wasn't afraid of gunshots because I'm around them every other Sunday afternoon with these guys. I was shooting at steel targets that night. They just happened to be people."

Rich and Ryan had shot people. They knew what it was like. Even the most justified shooting wasn't pleasant.

"Sorry, man, I've been there," Rich said.

"Me, too," said Ryan.

"Well, it's over," Grant said. "I don't want to do that again, but I sure as hell will if more bad guys charge me and my guys. They had guns and clubs." Grant shrugged as if to say, "What else can you do?"

Dan came over to whisper to Rich and Ryan. They nodded.

Rich said, "We think we have a role for you guys. I'll want to see more of you and, quite honestly, get to know you. So you're officially probationary. But I'm thinking of using you guys for SWAT duties, if necessary. Entries, that kind of thing. Would that be okay with you guys?"

"Okay? Hell, yeah!" Pow said, a little too excited. The other guys were elated. Mark was beaming at "his guys."

Chip wasn't smiling. "Thanks, Rich, that's very kind of you, but I'm too damned old for this. I'm ... well, I'm in my sixties. I'm in decent shape for an old man," he said with a smile, "but my door-bustin' days are over. I can patrol and train others, but I don't want to slow these guys down." No one disagreed. They all thought Chip was great, but if a guy thinks he'll slow the team down, that needs to be taken seriously.

Grant, who was in his forties, wasn't so sure about busting down doors, either. He'd have to think about it. But, man, he really wanted to do it. If there were bad guys threatening his people and he had a chance to stop it, he would. It was fighting bullies, something he'd been doing all his life. Plus, there was a little pride, perhaps even a little midlife crisis. He wanted to show everyone that a forty-something lawyer could take down bad guys like a twenty-something could. That kind of thinking would probably get him killed, but he was thinking it.

Pow said to Chip, "Well, you can do security onsite during an entry, at least. Make sure those bastards don't run away from us. We need a guy we can trust out there for that."

Chip couldn't resist. "Okay, maybe that kind of thing, but I'm not the first in the stack."

Dan said, "We'll have tons of uses for you, Chip. You worked in a gun store, huh? You know gunsmithing?"

Chip smiled, "A little. Do you need an armorer?" That was the military and law enforcement term for the person who maintained and repaired a unit's firearms.

Dan nodded.

"Then I'm your armorer," Chip said.

Rich said, "I gotta be honest. There's another role for you guys," he motioned to Chip, "all of you guys."

Rich pointed out toward the surrounding houses. "I want the residents to feel safe. You guys look like you know what you're doing. Those ARs look pretty badass out here. I'd like to have you on patrol to let the residents know that they have some guys like you on their side. I want the shitbags or potential shitbags in Pierce Point on notice that we've got some contractor-lookin' men out here."

The guys on the Team were loving this. Rich continued, "See, there are two threats here we need to deal with. The first is from outsiders trying to get in. Dan has the gate organized tight and those dogs will keep the gate sealed. The beach patrol will be good for keeping the beaches secure. But the second threat and maybe the bigger one, is from our own people. The petty criminals out here and maybe the masses once food gets tight."

Rich looked at the guys and asked, "How would you feel about patrolling, interacting with the residents, and then being on call for SWAT duties?"

"Yes, yes, and yes," Scotty said with a huge grin.

Dan said, "We'll be working with you, accompanying you, and watching you. We have a lot of experience to share with you. Let me be honest. If you guys suck, or are cowboys or treat the residents with any disrespect, you're on guard duty at the gate. Or worse."

They all nodded. They were being entrusted with a lot of responsibility. They felt honored and determined to do the best job possible to keep their jobs.

Rich was standing next to Grant. Grant pulled Rich over to him and whispered, "Are you giving us this role because we're good or because we're all you got?"

Rich smiled and whispered back, "Both."

Chapter 92

What Do You Call Yourselves?

(May 9)

The Team and Mark stayed at the Grange the rest of the day. They went over a map of the whole Pierce Point development that someone had found. They talked about the locations of the few known druggies. They talked about how Dan was running the guard station and went down to get a tour.

The Team would be the "inside guys," meaning security inside the gate. Of course, the largely well-armed residents would have a big role in their own defense inside Pierce Point.

Dan led the "outside guys," who were the guards at the gate and the beach patrol.

Around lunch time, something a little strange happened. A couple of ladies came to the Grange and started cooking in the kitchen. The Grange had a large kitchen for feeding many people.

The ladies had sandwiches for the guys and fresh baked bread, which smelled amazing. It was whole wheat, which most of the guys didn't like before the Collapse, but, now, it was great. Some of the nearby families had small farms and though they didn't grow wheat, they had been buying and storing it for a few years, expecting something like this. They were happy to feed the guys who were protecting them.

Grant recognized that as long as the residents had food, the Team would be fed. The same was true of having an ER doctor. This was a big relief to Grant. He didn't have enough food for his family and the Team. He had a good bit and it could stretch through shortages from other sources, and the hunting, fishing, and gardening would help, too. But if he and his guys were spending all day patrolling, they couldn't be gathering food. They needed to be fed. It was a fair trade. Those farms the ladies in the kitchen came from wouldn't last long without security.

Grant liked this "new economy." Feed me and I'll protect you. It beat the shit out of working in an office and paying almost 50% of what he made in taxes to a corrupt government.

Throughout the day, various curious residents came by the

Grange. Rich would introduce them to the Team. The guys were doing a great job of "sir" and "ma'am." They were being humble, yet confident.

When one of the first groups of residents came by and asked Rich what the guys were called, Rich looked at Grant and said, "That's a good question. What do you call yourselves?"

"The Team," Grant and Pow said in unison.

"Not real imaginative. But it works," Grant said.

Rich simply said, "This is the Team."

In just a few hours, Pierce Point was buzzing about "the Team." Some speculated they were a SEAL team, which would have made the guys laugh if they'd heard that. The day flew by. The guys were in heaven. This was what sheepdogs like them were made to do. Things didn't seem so bad when nice ladies were fixing them lunch and everyone thought they were cool gunfighters.

In the late afternoon, they had gone over about everything they had to go over. "Come back here for a 7:00 meeting," Rich said. "I want to introduce you to the community and to do some other things."

The Team and Mark got into the truck and slowly went back. Once again, Grant thought about how fantastic it felt to ride in a truck with his guys and an AR. He felt so alive. People were waving on the way back. The Team was loving it.

Let's see if Lisa is loving it, Grant thought. Now the hard part of the day began. Training to run into houses full of well-armed drug dealers? No, that wasn't the hard part. Grant telling Lisa he volunteered to be on an amateur SWAT team—that was the hard part.

Oh well. He had a job to do and his wife's approval couldn't be the determining factor. Her approval might have been required when things were going fine. But not now. You're the man, he remembered the outside thought saying back when he decided to prep. You have to protect them. Don't worry about being popular. The outside thought was right.

They pulled up to the guard shack. Paul and Mary Anne were there and waved.

Grant took the magazine out of his AR, made sure there wasn't a round in the chamber, and locked the bolt open. He unshouldered it and carried it carefully with the barrel down as if to show Lisa and the kids that he was being especially careful. Waving an AR in the house would piss off Lisa and it wasn't safe, anyway.

Lisa was sorting the kids' clothes. "Hi," she said. "How was your stuff?"

"Great," Grant said. "How was your day?" Just like he used to say back when they had real jobs.

"Got lots done," Lisa said. "The kids have enough clothes, but not as many as they did back home. They have enough for normal human beings, but not for their old selves," she said with a smile. This was good. An acknowledgment that they had unnecessary stuff in their old suburban life.

Lisa looked at the clock. "It's 4:00. Aren't you hungry? You didn't come home for lunch."

"Some ladies made us lunch at the Grange," Grant said.

"Oh, nice," Lisa said. "Why did they do that?"

Because we're protecting them, Grant thought. Here goes the pitch about the SWAT thing.

"My new job," Grant said.

That surprised Lisa. Previously, a "job" meant a new law firm or something like that and there weren't any law firms out here.

"Job?" she asked.

"Yeah, it's cool," Grant said with a shrug, downplaying how awesome he thought this all was. "I'm getting fed and the guys are, too, so we don't need to draw on the food we have out here." So far, so good.

"What's your job?" Lisa asked, skeptically.

"I'm helping that cop, Rich Gentry, with law enforcement," Grant said. "The guys and me are patrolling. We're basically for show. Our scary guns scare off bad guys." She might believe that. It was what she wanted to believe. She was extremely intelligent, but people could be counted on to believe things, even unlikely things, if it's what they wanted to believe.

"Really?" Lisa asked. She'd have to think about this for a while. Her husband as "law enforcement?" He is a lawyer. Or was.

After a few seconds, she asked, "Are you guys deputized or whatever?"

"Nope," Grant said. "There is no functioning police force to deputize us. We'll be making citizen's arrests, if it ever comes to that and it probably won't. Again," he pointed to his AR, "it's the scary guns that scare people." He hated to lie, but it was for the greater good.

Grant continued, "We've heard that some of the petty druggies have already left Pierce Point. See, in the past, when it took the sheriff's department a half hour or more to respond to a call out here, the druggies weren't too afraid of the 'law.' Now that there are no criminal defense lawyers or the ACLU to protect them, they've decided to go to the city where all their druggie friends are, anyway." Sounded plausible.

"Oh, okay," she said. "But you're not going to be shooting at people. Right?"

"Oh, no," Grant said. "Hey, most cops never shoot their guns in a twenty or thirty-year career. Except, you know, practicing at the range."

Lisa had heard that statistic somewhere. It was what she wanted to believe here. "Okay," she said. "But don't volunteer for anything dangerous? The kids need you and … I need you."

She was starting to tear up. This had been a very stressful time for her. Her perfect life had been uprooted and was probably over forever. Her beautiful home had been destroyed, a neighbor had attacked her and her son, people with assault rifles were all over the place, her autistic son was out in Hickville during what felt like a war, they couldn't go to the grocery store and … she had to go to the next house to do laundry. Everything was upside down. Now her prestigious lawyer husband was an unpaid cop or something. The possibility of him getting shot was too much.

"I won't, honey," Grant said. "I'm just doing this for the few weeks or whatever until things are better and we can go home. We'll fix the house up. I'll sue the shit out of Nancy Ringman," he said with a big smile.

Lisa burst out laughing. That was her old husband. Suing people. Things were normal again. Kind of.

Chapter 93

Steve's Vacation

(May 9)

Steve Briggs was on his way home. His cell phone rang. Interesting. Cell service had been very intermittent.

It was Todd at corporate. He was a good guy, with an MBA on his way up the ladder at Ready One Auto Parts. Steve realized he better take the call.

"Hey, Todd, what's up?" Steve said.

"Steve, how are things in Forks with all that's going on?" he asked.

"Okay, I guess," Steve said. "The credit card system isn't working and we haven't had a shipment in about a week. People have less and less cash to spend. But everyone is calm. No angry customers or thefts. How are the other stores doing?"

"Terrible," Todd said. "Shipments aren't coming from our suppliers, most of which are in southern California. It's beyond bad down there. I-5 is a mess, but it's getting better. The cops are preventing people from driving needlessly. All that's getting through is food and medicine and some military vehicles. Auto parts are a low priority compared to that, so we have basically realized that we can't supply our stores. The internet isn't reliable enough now, so we can't reorder inventory even if we could pay for it and have it shipped. Oh, and the whole credit and debit situation makes it worthless to stay open. So we're shutting down the stores. Sorry, man, but we have to."

Steve knew this was coming. He was surprised it had taken over a week. He had a plan, though.

"Of course, Todd," Steve said. "Understandable. I'll shut 'er down. Lock it up tight. That kind of thing." He paused, "Let me guess, all my employees and I are laid off as of now."

Todd was silent for a while. "Yes," he finally said. "Sorry."

Steve was not too concerned, actually. He had plenty to get by on so he was actually fine with a little vacation. The collapse of the United States was a "vacation"? Well, it kind of felt that way when you had enough to get by, although it was hell on earth for most people. Steve tried not to think about them.

"Understandable, Todd," Steve repeated. "No hard feelings. We'll be back in business in a few days or weeks, or whatever. Hey, look at the positive side: cars break down. In a while, when we're back in business, people will be lined up at the store to buy parts." Steve knew this wouldn't happen anytime soon, if ever at all, but he wanted to make Todd feel better. Poor guy. Todd was making these calls all day long.

"Yeah, I hadn't thought of that," Todd said. "Steve, we love you up there in Forks. You've done a hell of a job for Ready One and we appreciate it. Hey, is your family okay?"

"Oh, yeah, we're fine," Steve said. "Lots of deer meat in the freezer. I'm eating more smoked salmon than ever. Not a bad way to go. What about you guys there in Bellevue?" Steve asked. Bellevue was the wealthy suburb of Seattle where Todd and lots of other executives lived. Steve had been to Todd's house once for a company event. It was an amazingly beautiful home. Todd's wife, Chloe, wasn't bad either.

Todd was silent again. "Things could be better, but they're not terrible. The stores are running out of things, but people are pretty calm. There's lots of money in this town. Most people can pay ridiculous prices for things. The lack of ATM cash and the on-and-off credit card system is making buying things hard, but it's not impossible. Chloe is freaking out about all the things that are closed like school and, get this, soccer practices for the girls." Chloe was a little on the yuppie side for Steve's tastes. Freaking out over soccer practice being cancelled. That sounded about right for Chloe.

Steve decided to raise a controversial subject with Todd. He figured he'd probably never work with Todd again, so what the heck. "Hey, Todd, you got a gun? Just sayin'."

Todd got defensive. "No. I never thought … well, Chloe doesn't like guns."

Steve normally wouldn't get on a guy about things like this, but he knew that Todd really needed a gun.

"Can you get one?" Steve asked. "I hope I'm not sounding like I'm on you about this, but, Todd, you need a gun. Things will get nasty pretty soon." He didn't say what he really wanted, though, which was "think about Chloe and the girls."

Todd just sighed. He knew he was screwed. His chances to get a gun were about zero. There weren't any gun stores around Bellevue. One had tried to open, but the city council wouldn't let them because it wasn't "the kind of thing we like to have here." There were plenty of porno stores, but a gun store didn't meet "community standards."

Even if there were a gun store, Todd was still screwed. With the Governor's executive order, guns were illegal. Todd didn't know anyone who had a gun, either. He'd never fired one, so he was afraid they would blow up in his hand or something.

"We'll be fine without one," Todd said. "We have the best cops in the state. They make over $100,000 a year here. We've paid good money for them to protect us. They will. Besides, not to be a dick, but you've seen my neighborhood. Not exactly a high-crime area." Todd was doing a good job of convincing himself that they'd be fine. Just like they always had been. Crime happened elsewhere.

Steve knew he couldn't help Todd. Steve finally said, "Yeah, you're right. Didn't mean to scare you. You guys will be fine." He wondered if he sounded convincing. At this point, all Steve could do for Todd was try to convince him that nothing bad could happen.

Todd had to go. He had a bunch of other calls like this to make. He didn't look forward to them. "You take care now, Steve."

"You bet, Todd," Steve said. "A country boy can survive."

Todd had no idea what Steve was talking about.

Chapter 94

Hoarders

(May 9)

Nancy Ringman was a piece of work. Two days ago, immediately after Ron Spencer had seen the Matson's trashed house and heard what Sherri had told him about Nancy's odd behavior, he had gone to Nancy's house to confront her. She denied doing any of it. Flat out lied. And she acted like Ron was the crazy one for suggesting that she'd do something like that. Her voice was dripping with condescension. He wanted to punch her in the face. He'd never actually done that to a woman before. He'd never wanted to. He'd never had a reason to.

The final straw came when Ron was leaving Nancy's house. She actually said, "Ron, I'll bring up your concerns about whoever vandalized the Matson house at the neighborhood meeting. We are getting a Freedom Corps group together. Maybe you'd like to serve on it. The Freedom Corps would find the vandal or vandals. And perhaps you can help us catch Grant Matson. He's on the POI list, you know." She was actually smiling when she said that. She was a crazy, crazy bitch. Ron had never used that word before. It wasn't worth his energy to use it now.

Ron walked out. He wouldn't take the POI bait from her and get mad, which was just what she wanted. She would use his being mad to convince everyone that she was the calm one to whom they should listen.

On his walk from Nancy's house to his, Ron started to realize how outnumbered he was. Nancy might just succeed in turning the neighborhood into her fire-wardens-with-funny-hats Freedom Corps group. Most people in the Cedars were government workers. They were used to some government structure for anything to get done. They didn't have many independent thoughts. They had never relied on themselves for their own safety. This Freedom Corps thing was perfect for them. Taking direction from an aggressive and manipulative political hack. They did that all day at work. It would be "normal."

For the first time, Ron realized that the greatest threat to his family might not be from the looters outside the Cedars, but from his neighbors inside the Cedars. He could see how this would play out. He needed to suspend the fight against the looters and start it against Nancy. He hated politics and neighborhood meetings, but he had to do this.

He told Sherri what had happened. She said, "I'm coming to this meeting, too. I won't let her treat us that way." Sherri knew that Nancy would claim Ron and his "testosterone" were trying to intimidate poor little Nancy. Sherri could say things that Ron couldn't because she wasn't a man.

Ron talked to Len before the meeting who, along with some others, were feeling the same about Nancy. This meeting would be a showdown.

They assembled for the meeting at Nancy's house. There was some guy there with a funny hat. It was a hard hat with a "FC" sticker on it for "Freedom Corps." Oh, God. Were they serious? Funny hats and everything. Ron actually laughed out loud when he saw it.

Nancy started. She absolutely loved having a crowd and power. "Thanks for coming," she said. "I have a special guest with me. He's Clint Peterson of the Freedom Corps. He is our official Freedom Corps, or "FC" as we call it, representative. I know Clint from our work on the Governor's campaign. He's at Revenue," meaning the Department of Revenue. "He's here to tell us about the FC and how we can all help get this situation back under control so we can return to normal. It's all been so hard on everyone."

Clint Sillyhat, or whatever his name was, droned on for a while. Ron kept thinking about his great grandfather's description of the American Protective League during World War I. Most people had no idea how bad the government and lots of willing citizens, infringed on civil liberties during World War I. The APL was a group of hundreds of thousands of citizens who worked closely with the government to "keep an eye" on undesirables, such as those opposing President Woodrow Wilson. The APL had semi-official status. Federal authorities bragged about having a cadre of Loyalist APL people helping the government. Some APL members carried badges. The FC was the APL all over again.

When Clint was done with something about "neighbor helping neighbor" and asked if there were any questions, Ron's hand shot up.

"How," Ron asked in his nicest voice, "will your little Freedom Corps protect us from the looters that came here a few days ago and tried to kill me? Specifics, not platitudes, please."

133

That surprised Clint. In his world of polite bureaucratic meetings, people didn't talk that way.

Nancy answered Ron's question. "Oh," she said sarcastically, "your way worked so well, Ron. How many died? Three, at least. And there were bullets flying all over the place." Nancy's voice changed to her concerned mother tone. "Ron, you are brave and all, but you're not a trained professional. You need resources. The FC has resources."

"Like what? Tell me the resources," Ron said. "Tell me, Nancy. Tell me."

Silence. Ron was on a roll. He went on. "Does the FC have the resources to catch the Matson vandal, Nancy? Gee, who could have done that? Maybe the person who attacked Lisa Matson and her special needs son right before the place was trashed? I hope the mighty FC catches him — or her."

People were stunned. They'd never seen mild mannered Mormon accountant Ron so angry. Sherri just glared at Nancy. No one had ever seen Sherri angry.

Clint started to talk, but Nancy put her hand up to him. She'd handle this.

"Well, Ron," Nancy said coldly, "I can understand why you're so concerned about security here. You have a lot to lose, don't you?" She pointed in the direction of Ron and Sherri's house and then she pointed to Ron and Sherri.

"You know what they have there, don't you?" she said to the audience. Nancy looked like she was about to punch Ron and Sherri.

"Tell us what you have in your house, Ron," Nancy yelled. "Tell us."

Ron and Sherri had no idea what she was talking about. They shook their heads. Ron finally said, "Huh?"

"Tell everyone about the food you little Mormons have," Nancy yelled. "Oh, is 'LDS' the term you prefer?" she said sarcastically. "Tell us about the one year worth of food that your Grand Pooh-Bah tells you to have in your home." Nancy was screaming at this point.

Ron and Sherri didn't have a year's worth of food. They didn't follow all of their church's teachings to the letter. They had no more food than anyone else.

Ron was stunned. He could feel the eyes on him. "I don't have any food. A year's worth? Where would we put it?"

"I don't know," Nancy said. "It's your religion, your fundamentalist religion. Your macho, shoot-em-up religion. You want to shoot people rather than share your food." She went back to the condescending tone, "Not very 'Christian,' is it, Ron? What would Jesus do? Shoot the hungry?"

Ron could not speak. He could not believe what was happening.

"Shut up, bitch!" Sherri jumped up and yelled. That stunned the room. Nice Mormon homemaker Sherri just dropped the "b" bomb.

She started walking toward Nancy, pointing her finger and saying, "You will not threaten my family. You will not turn everyone against us. I will not let you…"

When she got close enough to hit Nancy, Cliff stepped between the two women. "Calm down. No one is threatening anyone," Cliff said.

"The hell she isn't," Sherri said. No one had ever heard her swear, even if it was a minor swear word like that. Sherri pushed the rather weak Clint aside and pointed her finger right at Nancy. The two women were about a foot apart.

"Stay away from my family and don't attack my religion," Sherri screamed. "Understand? Understand?" Sherri was shaking with rage.

Nancy stood there. Calmly. This was exactly the reaction she was hoping for from the fundamentalists. Poor Sherri, Nancy thought. She has been subjugated by the fundamentalist male power structure. She has been so subjugated that she was violent against someone like Nancy who was trying to help her be free from it.

Nancy went with the concerned mom voice again. It seemed to be working well. "This is the kind of hostility we don't need here."

Sherri turned around and walked out. Ron came with her. As they left, Nancy yelled at them, "People need to share now. We all need to sacrifice. You need to help the community with all your food. Don't hoard it."

Len stood up. This was crap. "Nancy, you're way out of line. The Spencers are good people. I've been to their house numerous times. They don't have a year's worth of food lying around."

"That you can see," Nancy interrupted him. "That you can see. Their religion teaches them…"

"Stop with the religious shit," Len said. No one had ever heard him swear either.

Three others stood up. Ken Kallerman, the Fish and Wildlife Department biologist, said, "We're LDS, too and we won't tolerate this." He pointed at Nancy and said, "Stop it right now." No one there had ever seen Mr. Scientist raise his voice.

Nancy was silent for a while, evaluating the field of battle to decide her next attack. Clint started saying something but, once again, Nancy put her hand up to him and he stopped talking.

"You fundamentalists are free to leave," she said to Ken. "We don't need your intolerance here. Don't try to leave with your food. It belongs to the community."

People were stunned. People had been worrying about food because there was the $200 limit at the store, but they still had several days' worth. It wasn't like they were starving.

Finally, "Judge" Judy Kilmer, the administrative law judge who was tight with Nancy, said, "Nancy, what's wrong with you? Are you okay?"

With that comment, Nancy knew that her control of the Cedars was over. At least for now. Judy Kilmer, who was on Nancy's side, said what everyone was wondering. It was obvious that Nancy had snapped under the pressure and stress of recent events. Everyone was on edge with all that was going on, but targeting people for their religion, trying to turn people against them and telling them to leave was too much.

Nancy knew she couldn't turn the Cedars into what she wanted at least, not at this meeting. She had overdone it. Her intentions were good, she told herself. All she wanted to do was to prevent the fundamentalists from hoarding food and imposing their will on everyone else. But these stupid people weren't ready for the cold hard truth, which was that the Mormons wanted to take over with their guns and testosterone. She needed to regroup for later, when the stupid people would finally see it.

"I've been up for a few days," Nancy said, quickly deciding to make a small political retreat. "I've been working so hard for all of you." She started sobbing, which was genuine.

She hadn't had her anti-depressants for several days either, but she didn't think that was the problem. "I'm just trying so hard to make everything perfect for all of us."

Judy came over and hugged her. "You'll be fine, Nancy. Let's just get some rest." Nancy was sobbing, but smiling inside. They were falling for it. Judy was one of the stupid people, too, Nancy thought. Nancy made a mental note not to trust Judy.

Nancy had big plans and they didn't include being slowed down by idiots. This was just round one.

Chapter 95

Jason's Briefing

(May 9)

Jeanie had two good nights of sleep in a row. Whoa. That was a record. She hadn't felt this good in two weeks.

She had her organic oatmeal and fruit for breakfast. The night before, they had veal kabobs with rice pilaf, which was very nice. They even had ice cream for dessert. Life was not bad at Camp Murray.

Jeanie hadn't seen her boss, Rick Menlow, since they got there. She had no idea where he was. All she knew was that she was working hard to get the State of Washington's message out to the people through the media. She was very good at her job. She was proud to help with the effort. Lots of people were doing great things—some of them dangerous—to make life better for everyone, but those great things had much more impact if the public knew about them. Keeping the public calm and upbeat was as important, if not more important, than a load of spare parts getting up I-5 to some water treatment plant or whatever the crisis du jour was there at the Command Center of the Washington Department of Emergency Management.

As an insider, Jeanie was one of the people who got the 7:00 a.m. morning briefing. She was starting to actually look forward to the morning briefings. This was a fascinating time to be alive and she was right in the middle of it.

Jason was giving the briefings every morning. He was an interesting guy, who graduated from Yale and worked in Washington D.C. for several years for the State Department. He had only recently come out to Washington State. Jeanie thought it was odd that he had some important federal job, but now had come all the way out to Washington State.

Jason was in his early thirties. He dressed very well, kind of East Coast. He was a handsome man, which reminded Jeanie that she hadn't talked to her boyfriend in several days. They traded texts that said they were fine, but that was about it. She missed him. But she knew he was doing some important work with his National Guard unit.

Jason started off pretty chipper that morning. "Well, more good news. We have pretty much got I-5 flowing with essential cargo. Same thing with I-90." That was the interstate going from Seattle east to Spokane and connecting Western and Eastern Washington State. "Local police and, in some cases, National Guard are at the onramps making sure only approved loads move. Like fuel, food, water, medicine, essential parts, communications equipment, military vehicles ... those kinds of things."

Jason put his hand up for emphasis. "The bad news is that civilians can't travel on the interstates and they're not real happy about that, which is why law enforcement and the Guard are there. There have been some incidents, but that's not public information."

Damned civilians, Jeanie thought. Getting in the way like that. Didn't they understand how important the government loads were? It was weird. "Conservative" Jeanie, who used to be ostracized for wanting smaller government, was rooting for the government. But she had decided that *this* government was okay. They were helping people.

Then Jason dropped a bomb on them. "Here's something that's definitely not public information. One Guard squad at an onramp in Lewis County was ambushed. Seven killed, three disappeared. Probably taken prisoner."

"Prisoner?" National Guard troops were being taken prisoner? What? Was this a war or something?

Jeanie let that sink in. She couldn't process it, but she was starting to see that there was at least a war-like feel to all of this.

Wait. A squad was ten troops, Jeanie knew from past conversations with Jim. Ten well-armed National Guard troops were ambushed, killed or captured, and there weren't any bad guys found dead? Either the Guard squad didn't know how to fight or the attackers were very good.

Oh, crap. Then again, nothing would surprise her anymore. Some once-in-a-lifetime amazing thing seemed to be happening hourly.

"Utilities are remaining on, which, I gotta say, is a little surprising," Jason continued. "We are keeping parts and crews flowing to electrical and water plants. Hell, I mean heck, even sewage treatment is working."

"Gasoline and diesel are a really big deal," Jason said. "The price on the open market ... well, there isn't really an open market. I've heard up to $100 a gallon, but there isn't really any place to get gas. We are getting fuel to federal, state and local fueling stations. Like a city's gas pump for police cars. Places like that are getting gas. We have diesel under guard at truck stops, so our vital trucks can refuel at all the usual places. The civilian truckers are not too happy. There have been some problems." A dozen pissed off truckers were a formidable force, as some truck stop owners, local law enforcement, and Freedom Corps were finding out.

Jason looked at his notes. "Speaking of trucks, we're commandeering them. Oh, I mean 'requisitioning' them. Thanks for the word of the day from yesterday, by the way. We don't have to requisition them too often. Most of the truckers will run a load for us just to get the fuel to get closer to their homes, but they're not the most trustworthy drivers now that most things they're hauling have become worth 100 times what they were just a few days ago. We prefer to have people we can trust driving the rigs." It sounded so stupid for uptight white-collar Jason, with his DC metrosexual clothes and hair, to call a truck a "rig."

"Food," Jason said. "That's a big one, too. The good news is that America has a bunch of food in warehouses. The bad news is that the warehouses are pretty far from where most people live, but with the interstates basically being turned over to the trucks, things are actually getting out. Perishable food is a little sketchy. There have been electricity outages periodically, especially in southern California where a lot of the goods are. But most perishables are okay and many trucks are refrigerated. We are focusing on staples and non-perishables. We're getting food to government installations, of course," that went without saying, "and we're getting grocery stores in larger population centers supplied."

Jason checked his notes again and said, "More good news. On two fronts: fuel and food. Fuel is scarce but we're, well, actually the Feds, are arranging for our domestic oil production to get to the refineries. We imported about two thirds of our oil before the Crisis. A good hunk of that came from Canada, who is still selling to us. Another hunk, unfortunately, came from Mexico and, um, obviously, Mexico is having trouble producing anything right now. So we have almost half of our oil from ourselves and Canada. But here's the good part: oil consumption is a fraction of what it was pre-Crisis. No one is driving. No more fifty-mile commutes from the suburbs to the office. So, we actually have enough oil and refining capacity to run things. Well, essential things. We requisitioned the oil, refineries, and trucks to get the fuel out."

"There's a catch, though," Jason said, looking troubled. "Most of the oil and many of the refineries are in Southern states that aren't exactly cooperating with the federal government right now. But the oil and refineries are run by companies who are loyal to the United States. More importantly, the Feds have extremely potent military strength in, and around, the oil and fuel facilities. So, bottom line, we have enough fuel now and in the future for vital uses, such as government."

Vital uses such as government, Jeanie thought. That sounds right. It used to sound wrong. But, now with the Crisis...

Jason took a breath. He smiled as he began discussing the next topic. "Regarding food, this is a political gold mine. The Feds have basically nationalized the farms. Most are owned by big companies who have worked with us before." That was an understatement. Federal farm policy and subsidies, had made the giant agribusinesses very wealthy and powerful. They were now returning the favor to their friends in government. "The Feds are buying food on an emergency basis. We're getting unemployed people to the farms and putting them to work. Kind of a jobs program. The regular farm workers realize they have nowhere else to go and, believe it or not, we actually think we can get some potatoes and wheat out of Eastern Washington and to some places for some processing. Not processing into french fries or chocolate cakes, but some food that people can eat in a few weeks. Mashed potato and biscuit mix and that kind of thing." Jason smiled even bigger, "Courtesy of your government." The political message was unmistakable.

His demeanor changed. "Here's the problem. The smaller areas, rural areas, the hick areas. Well, they're a second priority for food deliveries, to be honest. We can't do it all. If you're on the I-5 corridor, you probably have enough food. If you're in Hickville, where the teabaggers are pretty much revolting, then you'll have to wait until the civilized people get a first chance."

Civilized people? That statement jarred Jeanie. But, then again, the government was doing the best it could to get the most supplies to the most people and to the ones who supported the effort. Besides, Jeanie thought, the rural people were better equipped to take care of themselves. Seattle, with all the rioting welfare recipients who had been cut off, was a powder keg. Keep that place calm and let the teabaggers take care of themselves, she thought.

Jason went on. "One big problem is medical care. The hospitals are overrun and have been for quite some time. Most medical supplies have run out. Re-supply is a priority and some have been getting through. So many Americans are on a medication of some kind. Most of them have run out by now. People are dying. They just are. We have no solution for this. There's not much we can do."

He continued. "Crime is a problem, to put it mildly. Lots of people on mental illness medications are off their meds, as I mentioned."

Jason took a drink of water. "One item that is a state thing is the rioting and looting. Downtown Seattle has a lot of it; mostly petty criminals. There are well organized gangs running pretty much wild in the larger cities. Kind of like the L.A. Riots, I'm told." Jason was young enough to somewhat remember the L.A. Riots, but not really. "That's a National Guard thing. We have that under decent control. We have control during the day. The freaks come out at night."

Jeanie raised her hand. "Is there media coverage of the night riots? I mean, I haven't seen any video of it."

Jason said, "And you won't. We have an arrangement with the broadcast media and the papers. They understand they shouldn't show that stuff. It will just scare people and encourage the looters and terrorists."

"What about cell phone footage getting onto YouTube?" she asked.

"YouTube and other websites are not a problem for us. We have arrangements with them, too." Jason left it at that. The wasn't any need to scare every one about how the Feds had a virtual switch — the "internet kill switch" as it was talked about before the Collapse — that could shut down any website they chose.

Jason went on. "Oh, and the terrorists. Yes, there's been some of that. The Red Brigades and now some 'Patriot' groups. Militia teabagger whackos. The 'Don't Tread on Me' people. Assholes." What Jason didn't say was that the "teabagger" terrorism was great for the government, politically speaking. It was almost like some of it was staged, Jason thought to himself with a mental wink.

"There's some interesting graffiti popping up," Jason said. "The Right is spray painting things like, 'There is no gov't,' and 'Gov't can't protect you.' It's in gold or yellow spray paint, like the color of their 'Don't Tread on Me' flag, the Gadsden, I think they call it."

"Red paint is the Leftist graffiti," Jason explained. "Those are the predictable ones like 'Rise Up,' and 'Revolution.' That kind of thing."

Jason paused. "Here's a highly classified topic that's being discussed. The Governor has issued a variety of executive orders to provide emergency powers, but she hasn't declared full-on martial law. Should she declare martial law?"

Silence. Jeanie's first thought was "yes." People couldn't have normal liberties without order. And there was no order out there.

Someone from the Governor's Office asked, "What are the political ramifications?" That debate on went on for a while. The general consensus was that most people would want the Governor to take bold action. They would understand that martial law was temporary.

"It will take their minds off the budget," one of them said.

That's right, Jeanie thought. The State of Washington doesn't have any money. So she asked, "How is all this going to be paid for? I mean, we don't exactly have any way to pay for this."

"We'll worry about that later," said the chief of staff for the State Treasurer. He had been used to saying that. It really meant, "We have no idea how to pay for anything."

"There's an answer for that, too," Jason said, with yet another smile. "FCards. We are using the trillions of dollars of money people have in their bank and retirement accounts that they can't use right now due to the Crisis." The government could demand that people sell things to it for whatever price it set—and it had all the country's money to use. That would solve a lot of problems, at least for a while.

Jason got serious again, "So, to answer your question of how do we pay for this, the answer is with FCard credits. The military, police, Freedom Corps members and key civilians, like us, will get FCard credits. There will be enough in the stores we can go to."

"There should be enough food in the regular stores for the regular people," Jason said. "It will take an FCard for them to get food." Jason smiled, "That's their incentive to get with the program. You know, play ball."

Jeanie realized that FCards were the ultimate entitlement. The authorities controlled the FCards. Therefore, they controlled the people. It was better than anything they did in the past, like having only a portion of the population dependent on them with welfare. The FCards were the ultimate entitlement and the ultimate control.

A military person asked, "How do we enforce martial law? I mean, we have a squad taken out by some hillbillies or a gang or whatever. We can barely keep I-5 and I-90 flowing. I'm a logistics guy. How do we pull off martial law?"

A discussion ensued. It centered on the fact that they had no choice. It wouldn't be a well-enforced martial law. It would be a "better-than-nothing" martial law.

The question kept coming back to who would enforce it. Jason said, "Well, we have the Freedom Corps. We could use them."

The military guy rolled his eyes. "A citizen auxiliary?" he said. "Are you serious? This is a very bad idea. Sorry, but it is."

It was quiet for a few moments.

Jason said, "I'm hearing that martial law is not a preferred solution because it will be hard to pull off, but it might be necessary, anyway. Do I have that right?" Most people nodded. Jeanie found herself nodding, too.

Jason walked over and closed the conference room door. Whatever he was going to say must be juicy. If the door stayed open for "the Governor is thinking about declaring martial law," Jeanie wondered what the next topic could possibly be.

"Oath Keepers," Jason said softly. "They are becoming a real problem. Everyone familiar with them?" Everyone in the room had heard of them and nodded silently.

"The question is how many regular, Guard and Reserve units, and police departments are loyal and how many are Oath Keeper units."

More silence. Was this really happening? "Loyal" military units? In America?

"The Feds are having real problems with this," Jason said. "Oath Keepers have most of the units in the South. Texas and surrounding states have privately told the President that they are 'opting out.' That means secession."

Silence.

One of the staffers, a thirty-something, very well-dressed woman, said, "So the rednecks want to leave the U.S. Let 'em. Why should we worry about what southerners are doing way up here in Washington?"

"The military up here, many of them at Joint Base Lewis and McChord across I-5 from us are from the south," Jason said. "Have you ever been driving around here, near the bases and noticed all the Texas, North Carolina, and Georgia license plates?" Jason asked. "A lot of the military guys up here are Southerners."

The staffer who asked the question said, with an attitude, "I don't exactly hang out at military bases."

"Well, those license plates show that the military, even at bases up here, is chock full of Southerners," Jason said. "So, if they are loyal to the Southern states, we have a real problem. They're thoroughly mixed into the military everywhere."

Jason tried to smile. "This 'opt-out' thing of the Southern states is probably bluffing. Some political game." He didn't believe that, but he was trying not to be an alarmist. Then he got serious again.

"We don't know, with precision, which units would go with the Oath Keepers," he said quietly. "It's not like some units have declared allegiances or anything. The intelligence people say the situation is fluid. We have been told not to count on the loyalty of any given military unit. Not that most are defecting, but we shouldn't count on them."

More silence. The military guy who spoke up earlier looked dismayed. He could not believe what he was hearing.

He spoke up. "My loyalty to my commander in chief, the Governor, since I'm a Guardsperson, should not be questioned..."

"Of course not..." Jason interjected.

The Guard guy continued, "But, since you asked my opinion, I will give it to you now that I have factored in this latest revelation. Do not declare martial law. Do *not*. Oath Keepers will view it as war. The people will view it that way, too. It will be the thing Oath Keepers use to peel off units. You will have a civil war on your hands."

Civil war? What? Shit.

Jason started to laugh. "Civil war? Really? You can't be serious."

"Yes, sir, I am," he said. "Do not declare martial law. That's my advice to the Governor since I was asked for it." He stared at Jason until Jason looked away.

More silence.

The meeting broke up. No one was talking. They were too stunned.

Jeanie tried to sum up what she had learned. She would be talking to the media all day, so she needed to get her story straight. The truth was that in the short term, things were going reasonably well. Better than they had been. Food and fuel was getting where it needed to go. Well, it was getting to the Seattle metro area and to government installations. In the medium term, they had a plan for getting more food and fuel out. They even had a way to pay for it with the FCards. Well, not "pay" for it, but to distribute it. The majority of the people would be taken care of. This wasn't the end of the world, just the end of the world as everyone knew it. The pre-Crisis world was gone, but people would still eat.

The long term was a little scarier, with the Southern states talking about "opt-out." And there were even loyal versus Oath Keepers military units. But, if things worked out, like food and fuel distribution, then there would be a lot less reason for people to fight a

… she couldn't even use the term.

Chapter 96

Marty and His Boys

(May 9)

Joe Tantori was living through history. He knew something was up about two weeks ago when the Marines and sailors he trained for their guard duties at the nuclear facilities started cancelling their classes without saying why. Even his longtime friends on the bases wouldn't chat with him. Something was up.

At first, the law enforcement guys didn't seem to be getting the same memo that the military guys were; they kept coming to their classes like nothing was happening. There had been budget cuts, but they still kept coming. They needed to learn the military-style gun fighting that Joe and his staff taught. They had been told to expect "civil unrest" in the future and they had the money to spend on training for it.

Then, right around May Day, the law enforcement guys started cancelling classes. His friend, the sheriff in a neighboring county, said, "LEOs," meaning law enforcement officers, "will be a little busy for the next couple weeks. We'll be putting your fine training to use, I'm afraid." That seemed weird.

Then, when the news hit on May Day and beyond, Joe knew what they were talking about. He knew that, without law enforcement at its normal levels, his compound way out in the country, full of guns, ammo, and fuel, would be a tempting target for thieves. Many cops and military people had seen his armory, along with all the weapons he used for training. He and his dozen employees, all military and LEO veterans, made sure the compound was secure.

Joe's facility was a natural fortress. There was only one long and winding road in with a guard shack and strong gate. The curves in the road slowed everyone down, which gave those in the woods along the road plenty of time to hit them.

Joe had tons of supplies. He and his family lived there, along with his employees. They had an absurd amount of food and two EMTs who had complete medical supplies. None of his employees had families; Joe's crew was their family.

Years earlier, with a changing political climate, Joe sensed this day was coming. He knew that people like him were getting screwed and wouldn't take it much longer.

One of Joe's most coveted possessions at the compound was a 1,000 gallon underground diesel tank. He used it for the small patrol boats they used to train the Marines and sailors on maritime operations at their facility. Joe topped off the tank about a week before May Day. When the fuel prices skyrocketed, he was very glad he had done that.

Joe, his family, and his crew had just about everything they needed. He actually felt good about what was going on. People would finally see that the emperor had no clothes. The government couldn't do shit right now, and people would have to rely on themselves. Finally! Joe knew he was better off than probably anyone else in that corrupt county. He would walk around his compound smoking a cigar and talking to his guys. He loved it. He felt like these were going to be the most important days of his life.

Ever since Grant Matson had come to the compound and they had discussed a seemingly inevitable collapse, he had struggled with whether to openly be a Patriot or try to keep below the radar. One day, a few months before May Day, Joe realized that he had no choice. He had been blessed with a fabulous compound, a team of employees who were well-trained fighters, and tons of supplies. More importantly, he had been put into a position where he knew hundreds of military and law enforcement personnel. He couldn't shake the feeling that he was supposed to be working with these military and law enforcement people to do something good.

He realized Oath Keepers was the link between the people he knew and the things he was supposed to do, so he decided to be very open that he was a member of Oath Keepers. He would try to get as many people as possible to join.

Right after May Day, he started receiving weird calls from former students. A group who were LEOs two counties away said they were leaving the force because of the budget cuts and they needed a place to go work. They were Oath Keepers, and wanted to be his "security consultants." Joe knew what was going on. He said they could come.

Word then got out that Joe was accepting "recruits." More came. They brought supplies with them. The bunkhouses for students filled up quickly.

Then Joe got a call from Marty; Gunnery Sergeant Martin Booth, who ran the Marine security forces out at the Bangor submarine base where his unit guarded the nukes. Marty, in his deep South

Carolina drawl, said, "Joe, can I come out to see you? Like, right now?"

"Sure, Marty," Joe said. "What's going on?" As if he didn't know.

"See you soon," Marty said and hung up the phone.

He wasn't in uniform when he arrived. Joe had never seen him out of uniform. He looked nervous.

"Thanks for seeing me, Joe," Marty said. "I have some business to discuss." He looked around to see if anyone was around. No one was.

"I know I can trust you," Marty said. "I'm an Oath Keeper, too, in spirit. I can't openly join, given my security clearance. I don't talk about Oath Keeper things. Given the items we have at work, it didn't make sense for me to be talking about my possibly divided loyalties."

Marty looked down at the ground and then up at Joe, straight into his eyes. "Joe, I want to bring some of my guys out here. Permanently. You understand what I'm saying?"

"AWOL?" Joe asked in a near whisper even though no one was around at the compound.

"Defecting is more like it," Marty said quietly. It was hard for him to say that. He loved the Marine Corps. He loved the United States. Well, the former United States. Marty never wanted to leave the Marine Corps. He had thought of retirement as an awful thing because he would no longer be able to wear the uniform of his beloved Corps. But now he was running from the Corps.

"I have been issued unconstitutional orders," Marty said. "We've spent the last week or so moving our precious cargo off base and back to...somewhere." Even though Marty was defecting, he still wouldn't reveal where the nukes had gone. He didn't want to harm the United States, he just didn't want to be part of what the United States was about to do to its people.

Marty continued, "All of us realized that we needed to get those weapons out of harm's way. We don't want some terrorist assholes to get them. So we did our duty and we were proud to do it. Well, the precious cargo is all out and now they want to send us to the 'Southern front.'"

"What the hell is the 'Southern front'?" Joe asked.

"Down to Texas," Marty said. "The feds are spoiling' for a fight with Texas and any states that want to join them, like my home state of South Carolina. I won't do it. I won't."

Joe was speechless. He had focused on all the crap and drama in his little area out there, but he had never thought about the national situation.

"I quietly inquired among my men," Marty said. "'Who's going to kill Americans?' I asked them. 'Who wants to fight for socialism in D.C.?' I'll be honest, I only asked the Southerners. There are some good Northerners, but I didn't want one of them to turn me in."

Marty paused. This conversation was very hard for him. "So I told them—three squads plus—that I'd come ask you if you have a place for us. We'll work for our chow. I bet you could use some motivated Marines." He smiled, "Who couldn't? Especially in these uncertain times."

Joe blurted out, "Glad to have you." He had no idea how he'd feed these guys or pay them. He had supplies for his family and the current employees, but the recent LEO defectors and now thirty plus Marines? Oh well, he'd figure it out. These were shaping up to be historic times. Roll with it. He was supposed to be doing this. Don't try to make it fit into a business plan.

Then it hit him.

Joe got out a new cigar and handed it to Marty. "I have an idea."

Chapter 97

Mrs. Roth

(May 9)

Mary Anne Morrell was a tough chick. She was a retired teacher in a rural school district where teachers didn't put up with any crap from their students. She was a sweet lady, but she didn't wait around for people to do things for her. She hunted and fished and knew how to fix things. She loved living out at Pierce Point.

She was on guard duty with the 30-30 carbine she used for deer. She was sharing the guard shift with Paul while the guys were gone for their tryout at the Grange.

Mary Anne liked Paul. He was a great father to his little daughter, Missy. She thought she noticed that Paul was losing weight, but she couldn't tell for sure.

"Not sure why we're even doing this," Paul said of guard duty. "No one has come down that road in a week, well, no one who doesn't live here." Paul wasn't complaining, he was just observing.

"Yeah," Mary Anne said, "but, until things get stabilized out there, we'll need it here. For all we know, bad guys are checking us out, but are moving on to another group of houses because they see us. Besides, I'm retired. so this is fine."

"I guess you're right," he said with a shrug. Paul was finishing up metal fabrication at a local trade school, but the school had closed like everything else had. "This is like a bunch of snow days, except it's May and beautiful out. Not bad, not bad."

John came walking down the road from their house. He had two cups of coffee and a pistol belt. He had a cowboy revolver and nice leather gun belt with cartridges on it.

"Brought you a cup of coffee, dear," he said. He offered the second cup to Paul, who put his hand up as if to say, "No thanks."

"Thanks, hon," Mary Anne said. "Everything's quiet here."

"Hey, I'll take guard duty," John said. "You should go see Mrs. Roth about those canning supplies."

"Good idea. Will do," Mary Anne said as she moved to hand John the 30-30.

John wouldn't take the 30-30. "Nah, you take that with you." It was only a quarter mile to Mrs. Roth's. Most husbands wouldn't suggest that their wife walk alone in times like this, but Mary Anne was deadly with that 30-30.

"Okay," Mary Anne said. "See you in an hour or so. If I'm not back, send in the cavalry," she said with a smile.

Mary Anne spent lots of time during her retirement visiting with people, especially those within walking distance of her house. Mrs. Roth was one of them, although she had not seen her in a few months. Mary Anne felt guilty about not visiting the old woman more, and now she was going to her and asking for something. Oh well. What use did Mrs. Roth have for the canning lids?

It was beautiful out that May morning. A perfect time for a walk. She got to Mrs. Roth's house quickly. It was a modest little house on the land side of the road, across from a very nice waterfront cabin owned by … what was his name? He was that podiatrist from Seattle. Oh, Randy Greene.

She tried to hide her rifle as she walked up to the door. There was no need to alarm the poor old lady. She knocked on the door, and could hear someone inside slowly get up and shuffle to the door. The house smelled like a "grandma house." Not a bad smell, just that distinctive grandma house smell.

Mrs. Roth smiled widely when she saw Mary Anne. A visitor. How nice. "Hello, Mary Anne. It's wonderful to see you. Come in, please." Seeing that Mary Anne had a rifle, Mrs. Roth said, "Oh, bring that in, too. No need to keep it outside. I used one of those myself back in the cowboy days when we tamed the prairies," she said with a laugh.

Mrs. Roth wasn't looking so well. She was very thin and moving even more slowly than usual.

They chatted for a while and Mary Anne asked about Mrs. Roth's health. She wouldn't say much, brushing aside the questions. They talked about the news, keeping it very general. Mrs. Roth was well informed; she had been watching the TV news non-stop, but she didn't seem too worried about anything.

Mary Anne asked her if she had food. Mrs. Roth answered, "My son comes once a week and brings me things. I don't eat very much at all anymore. In fact, eating is a chore. I'm fine, but thanks for asking."

She stared out the window. "I was a little girl during the Depression and World War II. This reminds me of those times, I hate to say. Except that then, we were all so united. We had a common cause. I don't think people are united now. The country is too big. We're bickering and greedy. I think this great country is over." Mrs. Roth said that in a flat, matter-of-fact tone.

She had lived through so much that something like the Collapse, while certainly noteworthy, wasn't the end of the world. The end of her world was coming soon due to her illness and she knew it. It put everything into context. Mrs. Roth started to remember all the people in her life who were no longer alive. She thought about them and what she would do to help them if they were still alive. She started thinking about how she could still help the people at Pierce Point. She knew she was going to Heaven soon and wanted to do all the good things she could before then. "Well done, my good and faithful servant," she whispered to herself, which was what she wanted to hear after she died.

Mary Anne told Mrs. Roth about the Matson family coming out with the Team. She had a hard time describing exactly what the Team was. Realizing now that Mrs. Roth had lived through World War II, she said the men were kind of like soldiers. Mary Anne also told Mrs. Roth that Lisa Matson was a doctor. "I'll ask her to come by and see you," she said. Mrs. Roth nodded.

There was a pause. Sensing that she had come over for a reason, Mrs. Roth asked Mary Anne, "What can I do for you?"

Mary Anne was a little uncomfortable asking for something and hesitated for a moment. "Well, we have all those people living in the cabins on Over Road, like the team of young soldiers in the yellow cabin. We need to feed them. I am gardening and there are those apples everywhere that just rot each year. I am going to put up all the food I can, just like when I was a girl."

Mrs. Roth smiled. People were going to be canning again. It was about time. All this fast food and relying on the grocery store for everything never made any sense to her.

"Oh, I have so many canning supplies I can't keep track of them," Mrs. Roth said. "They're in the shed. You can have them if you'd like. I can't stand long enough to can anymore."

"Oh, that would be great, Mrs. Roth," Mary Anne said. "Just great. That's what I came to ask you about." Mrs. Roth was making her feel less and less guilty about asking for the canning supplies.

"Oh, certainly honey," Mrs. Roth said. "I probably have ten cases of wide mouths and about the same number of pint jars. I have cases of lids. I got them fifteen years ago, but they never go bad. I thought I would can for everyone but no one wanted home canned food." She chuckled. "They do now, though!"

Mrs. Roth's eyes lit up. "I also have cases of those Tattler reusable canning lids. I got them in the 80s, a little while after they first came out. I never threw them out. I just knew that someone could use them. After living through the Depression, it's hard for me to throw things out."

Tattler lids? Mary Anne was euphoric. Unlike regular canning lids, which usually could not be reused a second time, Tattler lids could be used dozens of times. So could canning jars, making Tattler lids an absolute gold mine.

"That would be so generous, Mrs. Roth," Mary Anne said. "We could really use them. We could also use some canning recipes. Could you share some with us?" Mary Anne knew the answer.

Mrs. Roth's eyes lit up again. "Oh, yes, dear. I would be thrilled to share my recipes." She realized that this would be one of the ways she could live on down on earth even after she was gone. People would talk for decades about "Mrs. Roth's canned stew" and "Mrs. Roth's apple butter." She could tell Mary Anne the stories about her family and how the recipes came about. This was the best thing that had happened to her in years. She was so happy. She felt renewed. It was making the prospect of her approaching death that much easier.

"Let's start by having you go out into the shed and inventory what I have," Mrs. Roth said. "Then we can start on the recipes. I have a book of canning recipes and some up here," she said, pointing to her head. "You can write them down. My mind is still sharp. I can give them to you by memory. And I might share a story or two about them."

"That would be great," Mary Anne said. She wanted to hear Mrs. Roth's stories. She could tell that this was one of the best days Mrs. Roth had had in many years. And everyone would benefit from the canning recipes and, especially, from the supplies.

Mary Anne was stunned at how many canning supplies Mrs. Roth had. She had eleven cases of quart jars. With twelve in a case, that was a lot of jars; enough for many families each year. She also had nine cases of pint jars, also twelve to a case.

Mrs. Roth also had almost ten pounds of paraffin wax. Mary Anne knew that for some things, especially jams and jellies, she could melt about a quarter inch of wax on top of the jar and seal it that way, without having to use a canning lid. Wax could be reused to stretch it even further. Mrs. Roth had enough paraffin for lots and lots of jams and jellies; more than the families on Over Road probably would eat in a year.

Another prize was Mrs. Roth's stores of pectin, which would allow Mary Anne to make jams and jellies that would gel instead of being runny. Mrs. Roth had Pomona pectin, which had a longer shelf life than regular pectin. This was important because Mrs. Roth's pectin was about fifteen years old; regular pectin would not be guaranteed to be effective over this period, but Pomona would. Also, Pomona pectin worked with lower sugar content jams and jellies and, with sugar being as scarce as it probably would be soon, that would be a good thing. Another amazing find in Mrs. Roth's storage shed!

Mrs. Roth also had two twenty-one-quart All American canners; the ones that sealed without a rubber gasket, like the kind Mary Anne got at the farm supply store that week. Now, with Mrs. Roth's canners, Mary Anne actually had more canners than she needed, but she could give the extras to others who needed them.

Mrs. Roth also had a well-worn copy of the Ball Blue Book of canning recipes, which would be great for people like Mary Anne and Eileen who hadn't canned in a while.

The final prize was the boxes of Tattler canning lids. They were absolutely spectacular. Mary Anne counted the number of Tattlers. There were 365 of them. One for each day of the year, she thought.

"Mrs. Roth, you are literally saving our lives," Mary Anne said, trying to choke back tears.

"I know," Mrs. Roth said with a smile. Then she got choked up, too. "But you're saving mine. Making it meaningful here at the end. I'm more grateful to you than you are to me. Thank you so much for asking for my help. Thank you." They both cried; joyous crying.

In that moment, Mary Anne realized that modern American culture did not value older people. That was over, though, now that modern America had collapsed. All across America that very morning, hundreds of thousands of people like Mary Anne and Mrs. Roth were probably having that same conversation. Younger people were getting skills from the older people. Older people were receiving a well-deserved purpose and pride by sharing those skills. Perhaps it was one of the few positives coming out of the whole mess.

Chapter 98

No Kings

(May 9)

After talking to Lisa about his new job and assuring her how safe he would be, Grant only had a little while before he had to go back for the 7:00 meeting at the Grange.

Grant and the Team would go early to get ready for the meeting; it would be an important one. There would be more people at this meeting than the one the night before; they met people all that day who said that they hadn't been to the first meeting, but would be coming that night. The Team would be introduced by Rich and—Grant felt like he'd said this to himself a hundred times in the past few days—first impressions were everything. The residents of Pierce Point had to trust the Team and want their help.

Grant was still elated that Lisa had agreed to be a doctor out there. Part-time, of course. He knew that "part-time" would become full-time very quickly. He was happy for three reasons. First, it anchored Lisa to Pierce Point. She had a purpose to be out there. It would be harder for her to wish things were fine and that she could go back to Olympia when she had patients to see. Second, she would save lives out there. There was no question about it. She regularly saved lives when she was in a fully stocked ER, but out there, with primitive conditions, her knowledge would save even more lives.

Finally—and Grant was embarrassed that the politician in him actually thought this—having a doctor out at Pierce Point would be a huge political asset. It would be another reason for the residents to buy into the plan to have as self-sufficient community as possible. A Patriot community. Not in a giant ideological sense of "Patriot." People didn't need to walk around Pierce Point reciting the Federalist Papers or quoting Ludwig von Mises, but they needed to pick sides: Patriot or Loyalist. Grant knew that the more security, food, and medical services that Patriots could provide—contrasted with the security, food, and medical services the Loyalists were failing to provide—the more people would gravitate toward the Patriot side.

Grant had studied Mao and had a copy of his book "On Guerilla Warfare" out at the cabin. In it, Mao was crystal clear: a guerilla movement succeeds or fails depending on whether it can give the population what they need and treat them fairly. (Once Mao took power, he didn't care so much about the fair treatment part.)

The military side of a guerilla movement is just that: a side. A part of it. Warfare is political. It's about giving people a reason to fight and die for your side. Feeding them and protecting them are a huge part of that. And, as Mao made clear, successful guerillas focus on practical things, like food and security. They don't talk about politics.

Grant heeded this advice. He would not even mention politics. He wouldn't lie to people about his Patriot beliefs, but he wouldn't dwell on them. "Politics" — officials spending money they didn't have and grabbing power — had caused this Collapse. The people knew it. The last thing people cared about when they were hungry and terrified was "politics." Not again, they would think, we have just been through that crap. But, over time, they would see one side was helping them and the other was bullying them. Having a doctor was a big part of showing people that the Patriots were helping them.

There wasn't time for the usual group dinner at the Colsons'. Manda and Cole made spaghetti for the whole family that night. Manda was so good about getting Cole involved in everything. Grant had stored forty pounds of spaghetti noodles in vacuum-sealed pouches and had those cans of sauce. That was a lot of inexpensive food and it stored forever. Grant was proud of himself for having all that food out there. Not in a "pat yourself on the back" way but in a "so glad I can be taking care of my family" way.

Dinner was quick, but great. The Matson family all talked over their meal. Like they had ... well, never. Back in Olympia, they always had work or ballet or whatever going on.

Drew and Eileen were there, too. They were doing fine. Both were finding plenty to do out there and were really working well with the Morrells and Colsons. Grant couldn't remember a time other than Thanksgiving when the whole family was together eating and talking. It felt great; like how things were supposed to be. It took a Collapse to get us to eat dinner together, Grant thought.

After the quick dinner, Grant went over to the yellow cabin. The Team was there, except Chip. He had been hanging out more and more with the older residents like the Morrells and Colsons. He could keep up with the Team, but everyone could tell he wasn't trying to be a full-on member.

Grant told the guys, "We're being introduced tonight as a SWAT team, so let's look the part. Full kit. Strap on your ARs. Empty mags in, actions open. You can bring loaded mags in your kit, but we're around a lot of people and no discernible threat. So empty mags in. Wear your pistols, of course." Grant realized that he and everyone else on the Team—and many other males in Pierce Point—were wearing pistol belts all the time. It was starting to look weird to see people without them.

The guys looked very professional with their full kit and ARs. Grant had seen them like this on Sundays at the range, but he realized how someone seeing them for the first time would react: these guys know what they're doing. Not in a "playing Army" way, just in a "we've done this hundreds of times" calm and understated, but comfortable, way.

Pow even had a hunter camo shirt in the Mossy Oak Real Tree pattern. He must have gotten it from Mark. Grant was embarrassed to note in his mind that it looked odd to see a Korean guy in hunting clothes. Grant, too, had a hunter camo shirt. It was amazing how hunter camo made these strangers with sophisticated weaponry fit in with everyone else.

The guys were eating some sandwiches that the ladies at the Grange must have made and given them for the road. Somehow Grant had missed out on them. Oh well. He got to have his kids make spaghetti and eat dinner with the whole family. That was what it was all about.

It was time to go. Lisa got on the nicest outfit she had out there, which wasn't nearly as nice as the ones she wore to her old job. But still, she looked very professional and pretty.

Mark was driving and Lisa got to ride in the front cab of the truck. John and Mary Anne were in the back cab. The Team piled into the back of the truck at about 6:15 p.m. Paul was on guard duty back at the shack.

The ride to the Grange was spectacular, as usual. It was a little different this time, though. Instead of just being a bunch of well-armed comrades, this was a ride with Lisa, too. It felt like the "gun" part of Grant's life was merging with the "Lisa" part. Finally. It felt like things were complete. It felt perfect.

Lisa had not been out of Over Road for the few days she'd been out there. She hadn't seen all the people out in their front yards waving at the Team and giving thumbs up. She was proud of Grant and the Team. She didn't want to tell him that, though; he'd just get a big head.

They pulled into the Grange. A few people came up to them and greeted them. They seemed so glad to have them there. That would only grow when they found out that the pretty lady was a doctor.

Rich, Dan, and Ryan were in the Grange going over a map. Ryan motioned for them to come over. Mark stayed with Lisa and was introducing her to residents. He wasn't telling them about the doctor part. Grant told him that he wanted to surprise everyone at once with that.

Rich and the others had several large plat maps of all the lots in Pierce Point. The maps had lot numbers, which started at one end of the development and increased as they went farther out. It was a logical system, like street numbers. This would help them easily learn their way around the area.

The plat map and lot numbers would serve another valuable role: organization. The lot numbers could be used to conduct an inventory of skills, equipment, and medical needs. "Block watch" captains could use lot numbers to keep track of things in their little area.

Grant realized another use for the lot numbers. Eventually, if things went well and the whole community was pulling together, the lot numbers could be used to keep track of who donated to the group effort. Not "taxes" — that was a word so hated that it should never be uttered by anyone attempting to persuade people to join them, but contributions could be tracked with the lot numbers.

With the lot numbers, all it took was a series of index cards. There could be an index card called "Mechanical Skills" with a list of lot numbers, names, and specifics like "diesel mechanic." Another set of cards could be "Medical Needs" with, for example, a list of diabetics, broken down by Type I and Type II. The index cards were cheap, low tech, and took up no space. They didn't require electricity, which had been flickering on and off occasionally, but was still on most of the time, surprisingly.

Directly related to the organizational uses for the lot numbers was something just as important, at least in the long-term. Politics. Grant could foresee that Pierce Point was going to be a Patriot community. Probably not a full-on community with 100% participation; there would be many undecideds and even some Loyalists. But with an Oath Keeper like Rich in charge and Grant having a lead role, the leadership out there would be solidly Patriot. The Team were Patriots and they were taking a lead role, too. Dan and Ryan seemed solid, too. While Grant couldn't count on it — in fact, it would take a lot of work — there was a good chance Pierce Point would end up being a Patriot stronghold.

Index cards and lot numbers could be used to keep track of the helpful Patriot households, helpful undecideds, freeloaders, criminals, and hostile Loyalists. Grant had no idea if the others in Pierce Point would be thinking in terms of Patriots and Loyalists, and it was way too early to start acting on those divisions, but he was staring at a map and lot numbers that could be used to keep track of the various factions.

The index cards with lot numbers would not become a "hit list" to get Loyalists. That was the revenge-filled French Revolution approach. Instead of directly targeting Loyalists, Grant wanted to use a more nuanced approach: favoring or disfavoring people based on their contribution to the effort. And by "contribution to the effort," Grant meant whether they were a Patriot, undecided, or Loyalist. Grant wasn't making an assumption that Patriots would contribute and Loyalists wouldn't. Even Loyalist contributions would be rewarded. Fair was fair.

He wouldn't try to shoehorn his politics into the all-important topic of getting Pierce Point running as a self-sufficient and peaceful community. His goal wouldn't be recruiting ideologues. The decent people would rise to the top and be obvious to the rest of the community. Show the decent people why they are Patriots; maybe without them thinking of themselves as Patriots. Good equals Patriot. Show people the other side of the coin: freeloading shitbags are Loyalists.

There would be no waving of the Don't Tread on Me flag. It would be more like, "This guy really contributed and needs a little gasoline. What do you guys think?" Then when he came to pick up the gasoline, a Don't Tread on Me flag would be pinned up at the Grange for him to see. Nuanced. Practical. Fair. Effective.

This was the approach Grant wanted to employ out there. He didn't have dictatorial powers in Pierce Point, so he would need to use persuasion to get people to follow his lead. He had no desire to be a dictator. He'd seen enough of that and had been on the receiving end of it. He didn't like it one bit and was damned sure not going to impose it on anyone else.

Dictatorships were a real problem when a society breaks down. People in Olympia and Seattle were probably experiencing this. Grant needed a plan to handle any dictator who might spring up in Pierce Point. Back in the Cedars, he was hamstrung because he couldn't just strap on an AR, gather up the Team, and go deal with a dictator. Out here, though, he had plenty of firepower to deal with one, but his firepower would make him a threat to a potential dictator, so he had to watch his back. That was yet another reason to approach the Patriot versus Loyalist thing slowly and subtly. The best defense against a dictator was a strong and well-organized broad base of Patriots. That's what Grant wanted out at Pierce Point. He didn't want to be the king; he wanted to have a mini constitutional republic that didn't need a king.

Yes. That's why you're here.

Grant physically shuddered when he heard the outside thought. He knew he was supposed to be doing this. It was an amazing feeling. Powerful, yet humbling; exhilarating, yet frightening.

Grant snapped back into the reality of the meeting that was about to start. He could feel that it was going to be a crucial evening. He felt like the bad guys out there were not going to give up easily and let the good guys start running things. He just felt it.

Chapter 99

Call 911

(May 9)

Grant overheard Mark slip and introduce Lisa to a resident as "Doctor Matson." That reminded him that he hadn't broken the good news of Lisa's volunteering as the Pierce Point doctor to Rich, who was in charge. Grant couldn't blindside him like that. Rich needed to be the one to manage this news.

Grant quickly went over quickly to Rich and interrupted him while he was talking with Dan, Ryan, and Pow.

"Sorry to butt in, Rich," Grant said, "but I have some news you need to know. I brought my wife tonight. You might let people know she's an ER doctor." Grant smiled.

"Whoa," Dan said. "An ER doc?"

"Awesome," said Ryan. He looked over at Lisa and pointed. "Her? Doctor Foxy?"

Everyone laughed. A nickname was born in an instant. Lisa probably wouldn't mind. She was in her mid-forties and it was a compliment, and a tasteful compliment at that, which was not always the case with a Marine.

Grant filled them in on Lisa's reluctant agreement to treat anyone she could. She would accept food and other items, but only as much as people could provide. There would be no price list and no one would be turned away. Grant didn't describe his plan to use the doctor services to help turn Pierce Point into a Patriot stronghold. He would let that play out before talking about it.

"This is great," Rich said. "We have at least two nurses and an EMT. We'll have to get them together with … your wife."

"Go ahead and say it, Rich," Grant said with another smile. "Get them together with Doctor Foxy."

"Okay," Rich said with a smile. "With Doctor Foxy. I'll let you introduce her," he said to Grant.

"And, until I let her know about her new nickname," Grant said, "let's keep it to ourselves. I want to see how she reacts to it first." Rich called the meeting to order and everyone introduced themselves. There were almost double the number of people at this meeting than were at the previous night's. Word was getting out that the neighborhood was organizing and people needed to find out what was going on. There seemed to be more "cabin people" there than the night before.

Rich said many of the things he'd said the previous night. He introduced Dan and let him describe what an Air Force Security Forces guy does: defend installations. He introduced Ryan. "Combat Marine, Afghanistan" was all the introduction people needed to be able to understand what he could do. Then came the Team. Rich pointed to them, who were up front with Rich, Dan, and Ryan.

"These gentlemen are the 'Team,'" Rich said, pointing to them. "They are out on Over Road. They are a group of young men and," Rich pointed at Chip, "not so young men who have been training for about two years for a situation just like this. I'd like their leader, Grant Matson, to introduce them."

The room was silent. Everyone appeared curious about who these guys with "machine guns" were and how they would help them. Grant started off.

"Thank you for coming out tonight," he said. "I am Grant Matson. I have a cabin out here by the Colsons and Morrells." Grant pointed to them and they waved. He knew it was important to establish himself as part of the locals who were already out there. He also had another trick up his sleeve to make a good impression.

"But where are my manners?" Grant said humbly. "Before I introduce the Team, I'd like to introduce my wife, Lisa. She's an emergency room doctor."

Gasp! An audible gasp from the crowd. Then they started clapping.

"Lisa has graciously agreed to help all of us," Grant said. "Rich will be talking later about the nurses and EMT we have out here. " Grant loved to be the one to introduce the security force and doctor to all these people. That would make quite a first impression.

After the hoopla died down, Grant pointed to the Team, who were standing up by the podium with him. "These guys are civilians who have been training for about two years on the weekends with me," Grant said. "To be absolutely clear, we're not some militia or anything weird like that. If we were, Rich wouldn't let us near here." Rich nodded. That was a critical point to make, and it was 100% true.

Grant continued, "We started out shooting for fun, but then we got better and better. We have been training at the Olympia law enforcement range and are actually pretty good. We are just natural sheepdogs." Grant explained that term and told the audience that each of the Team used to have white-collar jobs. He had to get the audience to understand something that might be unbelievable to some of them: there was actually a bunch of guys who wanted to help people and trained with guns to do it.

"We decided," Grant continued, "to become an informal … well, I guess you'd call it a SWAT team. We spent the day auditioning for Rich, Dan, and Ryan and we passed their test. We are at your service." The crowd liked that and a few clapped.

"Rich and others will be overseeing us," Grant said. "We will treat everyone well—except people trying to steal and hurt you. Some of you have met the guys and I encourage those of you who haven't to say hi to them after the meeting. We'll be staying to answer any questions you have."

Grant realized he hadn't actually told people the guys' names, so he introduced them, starting with Pow. Last was Chip. "Chip will be assisting us, but he thinks he's a little old to be knocking down doors and shooting druggies."

Some people laughed. Some didn't. Grant realized that the "shooting druggies" thing was probably a little too much reality for some of them.

Rich said, "I want to emphasize that these guys are under my command. In the unlikely event there is a problem with them or anyone else, you can talk to me or Ryan or Dan. We encourage it, but don't think it will be necessary. Any questions?"

A yuppie looking guy raised his hand. He was obviously a "cabin person."

"Why do we need armed men out here? I mean, they're not police officers or anything. They have no real training. Why should we let them run around and," he used his fingers to mockingly make air quotes, "'enforce the law'?"

It was silent. Many others must have been thinking that same thing.

Rich motioned to Grant that he would answer it.

"A fair question," Rich said. "The short answer is that there is no law right now. Stores are running out of food and everything else. What do you think is likely to happen?"

The yuppie looked annoyed that he had to even answer that question. "What I don't think should happen is a little dictatorship out here with weekend commandos running around with guns telling us what to do. That's what I think."

This man is a threat. Fight him.

Grant heard that loud and clear. Polite and political Grant disappeared and fighting Grant appeared. He felt a surge of adrenaline as he went into verbal battle.

"Dial 911, sir," Grant said with an edge to his voice. "Go ahead." Grant looked for a cell phone. Dan handed him one.

Grant—in full kit and with an AR slung across his chest—walked right up to the yuppie and handed him the phone. He was purposefully getting very close to the guy to show he was not at all afraid of him. The yuppie flinched when Grant got close.

"Go ahead," Grant said. "Dial. See what happens. I'm serious. Put it on speaker phone so we can all hear." Grant paused as the yuppie stared at him, afraid to take the phone from his hand. Grant decided to soften the aggression. He had made his point and asserted his role here.

"Sir, you raise a valid point that I'm sure others are wondering," Grant said. "I sincerely ask you to dial 911 and tell us what happens." Grant waited a few seconds. The yuppie wouldn't dial, so Grant dialed 911 and put it on speaker phone.

A busy signal filled the air. Then a recording said, "All circuits are busy. Please try your call later."

After letting the recording play a few times, Grant hung up. "This, sir, is why we're doing this. Do you think criminals are going to take some time off right now?" He let that sink in.

"No, sir," Grant said, "they are having a field day. In Seattle, Olympia, and probably Frederickson. Soon, if it hasn't happened already, some criminals right here in Pierce Point will be seeing if they can get free stuff or," Grant pointed to the yuppie's wife, "worse."

"I don't think fear mongering is appropriate," the yuppie said. He was pissed, but in a passive-aggressive way.

"What do you, or did you do, for a living, sir?" Grant asked.

The yuppie paused. "I am an architect. Henderson and Snelling in Seattle."

"That's what I thought," Grant said. Some people in the audience clapped at Grant's zinger. "I'm happy for you, what was your name?"

"Thomas Snelling."

"Mr. Snelling, I am happy for you," Grant said. "Know why? You've never had to deal with criminals. Let me guess, the last time you were in a fight was … kindergarten?" Grant was enjoying this. Maybe too much.

Snelling was silent. He did not expect to have this happen. He thought he would just throw out some questions and win the argument. It had always worked in the past.

"Sir," Grant said, "Unfortunately, I have been in fights before. I've had to fight bullies my whole life. I understand how bad people think and act because, again unfortunately, I've had to be around them. Not by choice. In my professional life I fight bullies, too." Grant felt like his whole life story was gushing out.

"Professional life?" Snelling sneered. "What profession?" he expected an answer like "law enforcement" or some "lesser" profession than architecture.

"I was an attorney, Mr. Snelling," Grant said. "A damned good one. You see, sir, I fought bullies for a living in the courtroom. I would much rather keep the 'fighting' to a courtroom where we fought with words. But guess what? There are no more courtrooms, but there damned sure are bullies. And guess what else? They have guns. And knives. And broken bottles. And they want to take what you have. They're hungry. They want what you have."

Snelling was silent. This wasn't going like he expected.

"Let me ask you, Mr. Snelling," Grant said, "what kind of architecture do you do?" Grant bet he knew the answer.

"Public works. I design government office buildings, mostly," Snelling said with pride.

Grant knew it. Yet another person living off the taxpayer. Yet another person who had a vested interest in government taking from the people and giving that money to important people like him. Another Loyalist.

"What a surprise," Grant said and then realized he was getting far too political for this meeting, which was supposed to be about security. He decided to reel in the politics and get back to the topic at hand.

"Mr. Snelling," he said, "I hear your concerns. We have taken measures to make sure our security personnel are top notch and accountable. You may not know this, sir, but most people out here are very well armed. If my guys decided to run amok, as you seem to fear, then some ole' deer hunters would take care of business. We know that and welcome it." Grant let that sink in.

"Mr. Snelling," Grant continued, "my men and all the others here will risk their lives to protect you, your wife, and your property here. We're not asking you to like us. We're not asking for anything from you. We will give and give. How you respond is your choice. I trust I have answered your question?" Grant smiled.

He was in full control of the room and loved it. Dickheads like Snelling were everywhere, even in rural Pierce Point. They needed to be put in their place. No one was suggesting they be rounded up and shot; they just needed to stay the hell out of the way of the decent people trying to survive.

Good. That was necessary. Grant felt the same way.

Rich decided to take back command of the room. "Thanks, Grant." Rich looked at Snelling, "You are welcome here and we will do all we can to help you or anyone else. Are there any other questions?" A couple of the obvious cabin people sitting next to Snelling looked down at the ground. They knew they wouldn't win another exchange like that.

The meeting turned to the details of neighborhood defense and the medical clinic. More volunteers signed up for guard duty. Rich said that a medical committee would be formed to work out the details of the clinic and would report back at tomorrow night's meeting.

When the meeting broke up, dozens of residents were crowding around the Team and Lisa. They were offering to do whatever they could. Grant made sure to send offers of help to Rich. Rich, not Grant, was in charge out there. Grant was very conscious of that. He didn't want to displace Rich.

When they were leaving, someone asked if he was afraid Snelling might be in the parking lot.

Grant laughed. "Attacked by an architect?" Grant said as he gripped his AR. That got a good laugh. Snelling was exactly the kind of person who had screwed up the country. Assholes like him had no place now that the people were trying to put the country back together.

Grant saw Lisa and Ryan talking. He thought it might be a good time to try out the new nickname.

"Honey, Ryan came up with a nickname for you and I want to see if it bugs you." Grant already knew the nickname would stick whether Lisa liked it or not. So did Lisa.

"Doctor Foxy," Grant said.

Lisa smiled and then frowned. Then smiled. A forty-something woman usually didn't mind being told she is still attractive.

Grant looked at Ryan and said, "Doctor Foxy it is."

After about an hour of talking to people, Grant and Lisa finally headed out to the parking lot. There was no one around. As they were getting into the truck, Lisa stopped and hugged him. "I'm proud of you," she said. "Now I understand you. Bullies. It's all about bullies, isn't it?"

Grant didn't answer. He just hugged her. He started to cry. God. It was all about bullies. His whole life. Now he was able to protect people from bullies. It was what he was born to do.

Yes.

Chapter 100

Jobs

(May 10)

Grant woke up with the sunlight coming into the bedroom of the cabin. He always slept so well out there. It reminded him of the time he had to have a general anesthesia. He woke up so refreshed from the deep sleep of the anesthesia that it was hard to describe. That's how it was out at Pierce Point.

His thoughts quickly turned to all the things he had to do and all the things he was responsible for. It was like a job. Hell, it was a job. His new job. He was starting to see this.

That was a good way to look at it, he thought. It would help make things seem "normal" because it was normal for Grant to have a job. Treating survival out at the cabin as a job would also make him focus his energies on it, like he did with a job. Treating his new duties as a job would also be a good example for the others, especially Lisa who needed the normalcy of a job. She might even put "Pierce Point Clinic" on her resume when this was all done, he thought. That's how to think about it: things were pretty decent out there, this will be over, and we need to work now and to make it through this so we have some stories to tell the grandkids. That's how survivors think.

There were signs of a routine developing out at the cabin. There was the morning "breakfast meeting" with the Over Road crew as he was calling his family, the Team, the Morrells, and the Colsons. There was supervising others, such as making sure Manda was getting chores done with Cole. There was making sure that others had what they needed to do their jobs, like figuring out how to get medical supplies to Lisa. There was motivating people and making them want to work. It was what he'd done his whole life in his other jobs. Now he was doing it for the most important job of his life and his family's lives.

And thousands of people's lives. People you will never meet.

Really? Grant thought. How is what I'm doing out here going to affect thousands of people? That had him puzzled. But, oh well, the outside thought had been right every time. Still Grant couldn't wrap his mind around that. He could only focus on doing his new job the best he possibly could.

People started stirring at Grant's cabin. Eileen came down the stairs.

"Good morning, Grant," she said. "How did the meeting go last night?"

"Pretty well," he said. "I think. This community is really forming up nicely. Lisa was very popular. Doctors tend to be, especially when there are no doctors or hospitals around." Grant wanted to see how Eileen had been spending her time.

"So," he asked her, "what have you been up to?"

Eileen described how she was working with Mary Anne on food and gardening. They were working on planning out, to the extent possible, how the various families would eat. For example, if the Colsons got a deer, who would butcher it, how it would be stored, how to preserve it, how to distribute it, and even recipes and ingredients for things like deer jerky.

Eileen was also working with Mary Anne on gardening. They were planning what and when to plant, finding seed, and scouting out garden patches.

"Growing food is different than the kind of gardening I'm used to," Eileen said, referring to ornamental gardens, "but the basics are the same."

Eileen looked a little concerned and asked, "Can I go into town and get some things? We have the money."

Grant was worried that people would start, just a few days into this, to miss all the things of town. Eileen's question reminded him of this.

"I'll ask the security people what the situation is like in town," Grant said. "We also have to be careful with the gas. It's a precious commodity now. It takes a couple gallons to go into Frederickson and back, but I hear what you're saying. We need a way to periodically go into town. I'll get an answer for you by tonight." Grant realized that Eileen had not seen what the others who went into town had seen. Like pulling out an AK-47 or having punks follow you until you flashed a gun. Besides, not seeing the actual conditions in town, Eileen had the most normalcy bias of anyone on Over Road. She was rational, just clinging more to "normal" than the others.

"Thanks," Eileen said. "I know it's hard to do things now but I needed to ask." Maybe that was it, Grant thought. Eileen was curious and just needed someone to tell her that it wasn't possible to go into town.

Manda and Cole came down, sleepy-eyed and yawning. They

were getting plenty of good sleep out there, which suggested that they were doing okay. If they were terrified, they wouldn't be sleeping.

"Can we have some pancakes with syrup, Dad?" Cole asked. Grant hadn't seen him at all the day before. He missed the little guy, who wasn't so little anymore at thirteen. His voice was changing.

"You bet, pal," Grant said. "Let's cook them up right now." When Grant was cooking pancakes with Cole, he wasn't a killer of looters, a POI, a SWAT team member, or a guerilla political organizer. He was a dad. It felt great.

Lisa came out of their bedroom. She looked well rested and a little disoriented. She was going to work this morning at a new job. "Morning," she said. She seemed deep in thought.

Grant would try to find out later that day what was on her mind. She wasn't a morning person so, after over twenty years of marriage, he'd learned that deep conversations first thing off the bat were not wise.

Chip came over with his trademark, "Morning, sunshine" greeting to Grant. Everyone loved him.

Mary Anne followed. She explained that John was on guard duty last night and was sleeping. Grant thought that they needed a better guard arrangement. With the Team, Chip, and Grant about to do full time patrolling, it fell on Mary Anne, John, Paul, and Mark to guard, and that was on top of the gardening, repairs, driving the Team around, hunting and fishing each was doing. Drew was volunteering for guard duty, but he wasn't a gunfighter. He could fire a first shot to alert all the armed people in the houses, but that was about it. Grant needed to get someone out there whose job would be night time guard duty.

You will have that person soon.

Who? Grant wondered who could possibly fill the role of a dedicated night guard. But he trusted the outside thought.

The screen door made its distinctive sound of being opened. It was Paul and Missy. Grant hadn't seen much of Missy in the past few days. She mainly kept to the Colson house. She was only five and Paul kept a close eye on her.

"Hey, Paul," Grant said, "Manda and Cole can hang out with Missy. Manda's main job out here is watching Cole and she could easily watch Missy, too. I think Missy and Cole would get along great."

Paul thought about it. "Missy, would you like to play with Manda and Cole?" he asked.

Missy was glad to get to play with the big kids. She was shy and said, "Okay. What will we play?"

Manda lit up. "How about we play cooking? Then we can go to the beach and try to go find the duck family that lives down there. And there's a secret waterfall down on the beach. Wanna go see it?"

Missy smiled. So did Cole. At age five, Missy had roughly the language skills Cole did at age thirteen. Cole always loved the younger kids. He felt at ease around them because they didn't talk as much as big kids and grownups. He could communicate with them easily, which was such a relief for him.

"Okay" Manda said, "you can help me clean up after breakfast and then we'll go down to the beach. Sound good, Missy? Cole?"

Both of them nodded.

Paul was happy. "Thanks. Great. I appreciate it. I don't know what I'm doing today so it's good to know that Missy is taken care of."

Grant realized that he had been largely neglecting Paul. He wasn't on the Team and was, well, way too heavy to do much. Paul had been taking lots of guard duty, but there was only so much night time guard duty a person could do and then try to do things during the day. Besides, Paul had metal fabrication skills that the community could probably use. Grant was determined to put every person to his or her best use.

"Hey, Paul," Grant said, "come with us to the Grange today. I bet there is something that a metal fabricator could do for us."

Paul smiled. He had been waiting to hear that for days. "You bet," he said. "Drew and I worked yesterday on an inventory of the tools and equipment I have. We can bring that list to the Grange."

Grant felt good. He always did when he could find a way to make a "loser" fit in. Paul was a great guy, a great father. He wasn't a "loser" in reality, just in his mind. Paul was feeling left out because he was different (overweight) and that made him think of himself as a "loser." Grant had been there. He knew exactly what it felt like. Like when "loser" Grant was asked onto Squadron 3. Grant's experience as a "loser" allowed him to see hidden skills in "losers" like Paul so they could be fully integrated into the group. That was how he got the most out of everyone. Being a Forks loser was great training for his future role. As breakfast got rolling, the main topic became Lisa's new job as the Pierce Point doctor. Drew was very proud of his daughter, so he started off the conversation by asking, "So, Lisa, are you going to be the doctor out here?"

"Yep, looks like it," she said. She seemed to be neutral on the idea, not enthused but not regretting doing it. "I'm it," she said. "I just wish I had a real ER out here. I'm not sure how effective we can be without all the stuff I had back at my ER."

Grant wanted to change the subject a little, toward the positive. "We?" he asked. "Who else will be working with you?"

"Oh, two nurses and an EMT," Lisa said. "I met them last night at the meeting. The nurses are Cindy and Rory, and the EMT is Tim. Cindy is—well, was, I guess—a renal nurse at the Frederickson hospital. Rory was a general nurse there, too. Tim was a fire department EMT in California, but moved up here two months ago when his department folded down there. They ran out of money and laid him off. His sister-in-law lived here so Tim and his wife moved here. He was looking for a job when all this started."

Well, for a community of a few hundred homes they had a decent medical team. Supplies would be the hard part.

Chip was thinking the same things and asked Lisa, "Do you have any medical supplies out here?"

"Nope. That's the bad thing," she said with a frown. This was a very big concern to her. "We have some first aid supplies, but they won't last long."

Grant would later privately tell her about the fish antibiotics he secretly gotten a few years earlier and stored out at the cabin. He wanted to save those for his family, the Team, and the Over Road people. Besides, all of his antibiotics would only last a week or two if all the people in Pierce Point were using them. Might as well give the people close to him the benefits of his planning, although that seemed a little selfish. Grant thought that if he were a perfect Christian, he would give all the antibiotics away. But, he was not a perfect Christian. Far from it.

Lisa, still frowning, continued. "But, we don't have any extra prescription medications. Most people are running out of theirs and, I suspect, a few already have. We have no anesthesia. We have a little rubbing alcohol to sterilize instruments and wounds, but not much. I don't have instruments, anyway. We don't even have a place to do all this, although Rich the sheriff guy said we would probably use the Grange building for the clinic." Lisa made a "yuck" face. "It's not exactly the germ-free facility I'm used to."

Lisa realized she needed everyone to have confidence in their medical care out there. She needed to encourage them. So she added, "But, hey, people have gotten by with much less for several thousand years. We'll do fine. People just shouldn't expect all the modern medical wizardry that we have—or had."

Grant kicked into his role of encourager-in-chief. "Hey, we're way better off than those people in Frederickson," he said. "They have a hospital, but it has probably run out of supplies and the doctors and nurses have been working for a week non-stop. If they're even able to come to work. I bet people have looted their medical supplies, especially the painkillers. So, while we may not have the usual supplies out here, I bet no place has the usual supplies, either."

Grant thought about all the medical supplies they'd need. They would probably have to buy them on the black market. He was all for taking them by force from the government, but that really meant stealing them from people who needed them. Then again, any black market supplies would have been stolen by someone—probably the government—and wouldn't be going to regular people, anyway. Is stealing stolen merchandise of the real owners who can't be located really "stealing"? What if you needed it to save lives? What if others needed it to save lives? Grant would need to think about this more.

Ethics aside, Grant had a political purpose for getting the medical supplies. Having them to offer to a community was much like having a doctor: we, the Patriots, can take care of you. The government can't. Drew, the former accountant and business executive, asked, "How will a clinic work? There's no health insurance anymore. How will you and the nurses and EMT get paid?"

"A case of tuna," Lisa said with a smile and a glance at Grant. "Barter. We won't turn away anyone, of course, but we'll ask people to give us what they can. We'll take money, too, if we can buy anything with that."

Grant realized medical care would be a thing to give to those in the community who contribute, like the meals for the guards. Contribute labor or supplies to the community and you will get free medical care. Those who don't contribute must pay for the medical care. No one will be turned away, but the non-contributors will need to pay for it. Another incentive to being a full contributing community member.

This idea of free medical care for those who contributed to the Pierce Point community wasn't universal health care like the fiasco the former government forced on America. That system covered everyone—well, kind of – if you count dropping dead waiting months for life saving treatments that were needed immediately as "coverage." But it taxed everyone for it. And taxes were taken with the force of law, which was really the force of violence. Don't pay your taxes and see what happens. It involved search warrants, arrests, and jail.

The Pierce Point system was different. If you donated labor or supplies, you were making a contract of sorts with the community to get free care. It was a fringe benefit for what you were doing for the community. If you chose not to make that agreement with the community, you were on your own. You would be treated, but it would cost you.

Grant loved the political significance of the clinic. The community, led by him and Rich and various committees of people helping, were getting people medical care when none else existed. The community, working the Patriot way of voluntary exchanges instead of government coercion, was getting something done and making people's lives better. Participate in the Patriot way and things are better for you. The former government couldn't come close to providing medical care for Pierce Point residents. But the Patriots could.

Grant thought they needed to get some black market medical supplies. He was thinking of things of value they had to use to buy medical supplies. He thought of Chip and his basement goodies or they could "liberate" some medical supplies. Grant was warming up to the idea of taking medical supplies by force from the government. The government had stolen from Grant and other taxpayers for decades. Payback time. But he would try to buy them first and take them as a last resort.

Grant wanted to emphasize the point about Lisa and the medical team getting paid. He needed to encourage a semi-reluctant Lisa. "Seriously, this case-of-tuna thing will really help," Grant said. "Between the Team getting fed at the Grange and Lisa getting food and other supplies for being a doctor, I think we can really stretch our stored food out here. And, when you add in Mark's and John's hunting and fishing," Grant said that to remind those two that they needed to start bringing some food to the table instead of just hanging out with the Team at the Grange all day, "we should do fine. I am encouraged, for the first time in quite a while."

Everyone was nodding. Maybe this wasn't the end of the world. Maybe it was just a dark chapter, a low point. Maybe they'd make it.

Grant waited for the outside thought to tell him he was right. Then he realized that the outside thought was only there to encourage him when he needed it. He didn't need encouragement right now. He could see with his own eyes that things were working out. For now.

Chapter 101

I'm Going to Die

(May 10)

The Over Road crew finished their pancakes and then it was time to go to work. Mary Anne asked Lisa to come with her to see Mrs. Roth. The night before, Rich asked the Team to come down to the gate in the morning and meet the gate guards. Drew was still working on inventory and Eileen was working on food planning. She had also taken on the laundry duties. She hadn't done much laundry in the past few years with just her and Drew in the house and, in a weird way, she missed it. She used the Morrell's washer and dryer, and this gave her plenty of time to work with Mary Anne on gardening issues. They would sit in Mary Anne's house in between loads of laundry and talk about food and gardening. Although not as glitzy as gunfighting, their work was invaluable.

Manda was watching Cole and now Missy. Paul did guard duty and was going to start on metal fabrication. John and Mark would hunt and fish. Tammy had her day job at the power company and was getting lots of gas for that, which was a big plus. Out at Pierce Point, there was an order and even a rhythm; a new "normal." It didn't take long for hardworking people to figure out new things they needed to do.

On the short walk over to her house, Mary Anne told Lisa about all the canning supplies Mrs. Roth had donated.

They knocked, but there was no answer. They were worried something had happened, so they opened the unlocked door. They found Mrs. Roth in her "comfortable chair" in the living room.

"Sorry," Mrs. Roth said. "I was too weak to answer. Forgive me."

"Of course," Mary Anne said. "I have good news. This is Dr. Matson. She can look at you."

Lisa asked, "Mrs. Roth, are you okay?"

Mrs. Roth knew that it was time to tell her secret. It didn't matter at this point, anyway. "Well, I have something called myasthenia gravis. It's rare. Have you heard of it?"

Lisa had. It was very, very rare. It was when the body's

175

immune system interfered with the nerves controlling the voluntary muscles. It made it difficult to move and caused extreme fatigue. It even made it difficult to breathe because the chest muscles are weakened. Lisa thought she remembered that there was no known cure, but she hadn't read about it since medical school over twenty years ago.

"Are you on any medications for it, Mrs. Roth?" Lisa asked.

"I take Mestinon which has the brand name of Pyridostigmine," Mrs. Roth said. "I take a small pill every three hours and one big time-release one in the morning and at bedtime. I also take Cyclosporine and Cellcept. They're immune system drugs. Do you know about myasthenia gravis?"

"Yes, a little," Lisa said. She knew that Mrs. Roth needed to take her medications to live. "How much of them do you have?" Lisa asked.

"Oh," Mrs. Roth said. "I've been out of them for a few days. I'm going to die," she said with a slight smile.

"What?" Mary Anne said, shocked. "You're out? You need to get a refill."

"No, I don't," Mrs. Roth said calmly. "My son comes once a week and brings me refills. He is stuck in Seattle. Can't get onto I-5. He said the pharmacy is out of most of my medicines, anyway. He called a few days ago all worried about me. He's a good boy. I told him not to worry. I told him I had lots of extra medicine because someone out here is a pharmacist and got me several months of supply, which wasn't true. I hate to tell a white lie to my own son, but he has a family and needs to be worrying about them instead of me."

Mrs. Roth took a breath. It was hard. She continued, "No, I'll be fine. I don't want to be a bother. And, besides, I knew on May Day when everything started to fall apart that this would happen. I've been living with the knowledge that if there was a disaster and the stores closed … it would be time for me to go."

Mrs. Roth took another difficult breath and smiled. "It's all right. Really, it is. I know where I'm going and…" She looked up, "It's so, so much better there than down here." She was beaming.

"Really, don't worry about me," she said. Please, don't," she said as if the thought of anyone worrying about her caused her pain.

"Now," Mrs. Roth said, perking up, "tell me about the canning you're getting done and tell me about the soldiers. I remember when we had soldiers living in houses near us in Tacoma, right by Ft. Lewis, during the war," she said referring to World War II. "They seemed so old to me because I was just a girl, but I saw pictures of them later and they looked so young."

Lisa and Mary Anne didn't know what to say. It wasn't worth coming up with a plan to get the medicine. There probably wasn't a dose of any of her medicines in the entire state, and it would be impossible to get to where the medicine was without a military helicopter. Mrs. Roth knew she was going to die and she was okay with it. There was nothing to do. It happens to everyone, eventually.

"There is one thing you can do for me, Mary Anne," Mrs. Roth said.

"Of course, what?" Mary Anne asked.

"When my muscles won't move anymore, I won't be able to breathe. It's already hard now. I don't mind dying, but it will be scary to not be able to breathe. I'd like someone here with me when it happens. I don't want any pain drugs or anything—you probably don't have any out here—but I do want someone around. And I want to tell my stories to someone. I have a lot of time to think all day and to remember. I want someone around. Could you be here?"

Mary Anne started to cry. Lisa didn't; she'd seen enough tragedy in the ER that things like this didn't affect her like the first time she saw someone about to die.

"Don't cry, hon. Don't cry," Mrs. Roth said. She was having trouble breathing again. She struggled to put up her hand for Mary Anne to hold. They stayed there for about twenty minutes. Mrs. Roth started to breathe well again. "Thank you, hon," she said, her voice very weak. "Doctor, you're welcome to stay, but I bet you have lots of patients to see. I appreciate what you're doing for everyone out here. But all I need is for Mary Anne to stay."

Lisa had never been kicked out by a patient. "Of course, Mrs. Roth," Lisa said. "If you change your mind and need any medical help, tell Mary Anne and I'll come and do all I can. Thank you again for all you've done for us out here. Mary Anne tells me the canning supplies and knowledge are invaluable. We will never forget you."

Mrs. Roth smiled. It was the deepest, warmest, most satisfied smile they'd ever seen.

Lisa left. She'd watched so many people die, but this felt different. It would be the first death out there. But, she knew it wouldn't be the last. That was the part that scared her the most.

Chapter 102

This Never Gets Old

(May 10)

It was time for Grant and the Team to go to work. Yeah, that's right. Go to work. Grant thought about that. Go to work. It felt good to think that. It felt reassuring. They'd get through this. It's a job. A damned cool one and one he was lucky to have. But, it was a job. He needed to treat it like one.

Grant wanted his guys to think of it this way, too. They were gathering by Mark's truck getting their gear on. "Gentlemen, let's go to work," Grant said. They smiled.

Armed serenity, Grant thought. That's what it was: armed serenity. That was how he described the feeling of being with his guys like this. Grant flashed back to his childhood when he went to sleep with the .22 rifle because he expected his dad to stab him in his sleep. That's why, Grant thought, he felt so comforted by guns. He knew what it was like to need the protection. That's why armed serenity made so much sense.

They would have a new guest in the truck today — Paul. He was very glad to be riding along. He had on a pistol belt; a regular belt with an inexpensive "Uncle Mike's holster" containing a large revolver. Grant pointed to Paul's revolver and said, "That works fine." He wanted Paul to know that it didn't take a Glock with a $300 Surefire light on it in a Raven Concealment holster to be equipped to defend himself. Revolvers had been defending people just fine for over 150 years.

Paul grabbed a shotgun and asked Grant, "Should I bring this, too?"

"Nah," Grant said. "I think it will get in your way." Paul would need his hands free for what Grant had in mind for him that day. Besides, the Team had plenty of firepower without it.

Paul and Grant walked out to Mark's truck. Mark saw Paul going to the Grange and was proud. He was thankful that Grant was getting Paul involved. Mark was thankful for a lot of things lately.

Grant offered to let Paul ride in the cab since he'd probably have trouble getting up into the back of the truck. Paul shook his head and headed to the back. It was a few feet from the ground to the tailgate. He looked at the height he had to get up over, put his hand on the tailgate and threw himself onto the tailgate. The truck bounced up and down when he hit the tailgate. But he did it. He set a goal and did it. He smiled slightly. He had made his point: he would work his ass off to do what was necessary. Grant would rather have a guy with the right attitude than a perfect set of abs.

In fact, Grant noted to himself, it looked like Paul was losing some weight. His tee shirt seemed a little looser around the collar. Grant would pay attention to this and see if this apparent trend was continuing. It made sense, given the can-do attitude he'd just shown by getting into the back of the truck.

The ride to the Grange was spectacular, as always. Grant looked at the guys and said what was becoming another morning tradition, "This never gets old." They smiled and nodded. They knew how lucky they were to be there instead of the city. They knew they had an important role out there, and that they looked cool doing it.

People were waving to them along the way, though it was less of a thrill for them to see the Team than the previous two days. Most had already seen them, so the novelty had worn off. But still, people were smiling and glad to see the volunteer police force protecting them. It was that gratitude that motivated Grant. That, and the fear of the bad people outside the Pierce Point gates. And probably a few within the gates.

They pulled into the Grange. There were quite a few people there, but only two vehicles. Grant assumed people must be walking to the Grange or sharing rides. Gas was short, very short. The idea of driving alone to go somewhere now seemed like a preposterous luxury.

Paul was the closest to the tailgate. He looked at the ground, put his hand on the tailgate and jumped down, landing perfectly. It was hard for him to do, but he was going to do it. The rest of the guys jumped out of the truck effortlessly.

They went in and found Rich at a card table, looking at the plat maps. He was glad to see the Team and wondered who the fat guy was. Rich had seen him at the first Grange meeting, but didn't know his name.

Grant made the introduction. "Rich, this is Paul Colson, Mark's son."

Rich shook Paul's hand, "Pleased to meet you again." Rich wondered why Grant decided to bring him along.

Grant said to Rich, "Paul is a metal fabricator. He has some equipment back at his house. I thought you could find a use for someone with his skill."

Rich nodded. He and Grant thought the same way.

"Like," Grant said, "how about a real gate for the entrance? Moving a car back and forth takes a ton of time and too much gas."

Rich smiled. "Yeah, Dan wanted to get a swinging metal pole across there that we could open and close with just one person." He looked at Paul, "Is that something you could build?"

"Sure," Paul said with a smile. "Piece of cake. It'll depend on what kind of materials we have." Paul was thrilled about making the gate. He had a purpose now. He'd show everyone how useful he was.

"Well," Rich said, "Dan is down at the gate and I need to get you guys coordinated with the gate guards. Let's go down there."

They piled back into Mark's truck. Paul jumped up into the back. This isn't so hard, he thought. It felt good to be outside doing things and being with these guys. It sure beat sitting around the house thinking about how much he hated his ex-wife. And eating.

Rich grabbed his handheld CB radio. He told the gate they were coming. Scotty had his CB, too. They talked about what channels they'd use.

Scotty told Rich, "I have a handheld ham, too." Ham radios were far more potent than CBs but, before the Collapse, required an FCC license to operate. The licenses were pretty easy to get; it only involved a simple test. "Hams are way better for longer range and more secure communications," Scotty said. "Let me know how I can help with that."

"I keep meaning to hook you up with Curt Copeland," Rich said. "I think we can use ham units for those kinds of communications, but use CBs for routine stuff." Rich thought, in a perfect world, everyone would have a ham license and a ham handheld radio in their preps before the Collapse. But this wasn't a perfect world. CBs were a decent alternative.

"I'll get with him," Scotty said. He wanted to show off a little. He asked Rich, "What's his call sign and what frequency is he on?"

Rich told him. Scotty got on his ham handheld and, in a few seconds, was talking to Curt, who was two miles away and behind a slight hill from the Grange. Everyone had thought they'd have to wait until the end of the day and then drive over to Curt's house in order for the two to talk. Nope. It took ten seconds and not a drop of gas to talk using the ham units. Grant realized that, with the distances involved,

Scotty and Curt could have probably talked on the CB, but the ham was pretty cool. And secure. Well, not truly secure, but not as easy to listen in on as a CB. Sensitive communications couldn't be blabbed on a CB when bad guys could be listening. Odds were that criminals didn't know how to run a ham radio or, if they did, that they didn't have the exact frequency the good guys were talking on.

Mark's truck with the Team, Paul, and Rich came down the hill to the entrance to Pierce Point. There were several cars and trucks parked at the volunteer fire station about a hundred yards from the bridge that had the car across the road. There were about fifteen armed guys and few women there. Mostly shotguns and hunting rifles, although one guy had an AR and another had a Mini-14. They were talking, but were clearly paying attention to the gate and bridge. While people were chatting and social, it wasn't a BS session. It was a serious job.

Grant thought about how much things had changed. Ten days ago, a group of armed people guarding a community would have seemed hugely out of place. In fact, Grant had never seen it before, except when watching footage of Hurricane Katrina. He saw it more recently on TV down in Texas and California with the Mexican refugee situation. Then one amazing day he saw it with his own eyes in his own neighborhood. He saw it again a few days ago when he came to Pierce Point. Now it was starting to seem normal.

The gate guards were happy to see the Team, who, with their ARs and gear, looked much more professional than the rag-tag gate guards. But, the gate guards looked like a badass group of good ol' boys (and girls). What they lacked in gear, they made up for in attitude. Perfect, Grant thought. All these guys need is a basement full of ARs and they'd have a pretty decent fighting force.

Exactly. Now you see what's going on.

Grant started getting this strange sensation that he could predict what was going to happen in the future. Seeing the guards, a prediction formed in his mind, but he didn't want to say it out loud because it seemed outlandish.

Rich found Dan and Ryan and motioned for Paul to come over to them.

"Paul here is a metal fabricator," Rich said to Dan. "Would you like a nice metal swing-out gate instead of that piece of shit car?"

Dan grinned. "Hell, yes."

Rich asked Dan, "What kind of gate materials do we have?"

Dan and Paul talked about the materials they had and how to

make the gate. Paul was in heaven. He was needed. This was one of the best days of his life.

While Dan and Paul were coming up with a plan for the gate, Rich was introducing the Team to the guards. Many had already met them at the Grange meetings, but some had been on guard duty and hadn't had the chance. The guards were less wowed by the Team than the civilians were, but they were glad to have the well-armed and seemingly, well-trained, Team around. Everyone was getting along well. The Team realized that these gate guys, with their duck hunter guns, would be the first line of defense if Pierce Point were attacked. These guys were putting their lives on the line to protect everyone, just like the Team was. They had different jobs and gear, but every one of them was equal. They were all risking their lives for others, which is all that mattered.

Scotty was talking to the woman who appeared to be in charge of communications. They were working on which CB channels to use. Grant took the rest of the Team to the gate and talked to the guys behind the car about the defenses there. They had a great field of fire into the road that fed onto the bridge. They had guards and patrols along the "river," which was actually a large creek.

One of the gate guards pointed up the hill to the treeline and said that they had snipers up there.

"How many?" Grant asked.

"Enough," the guard said with an evasive smile. "Some of my hunting buddies who like to sit in the forest for hours at a time and watch things. Their old ladies aren't around to nag at them out here so this is like a vacation for them. A couple of them are older guys who can't walk around and stand all day. They can find a comfy shady patch up there and watch for anyone who somehow makes it past us, or who tries to get across the river. They've got a CB so we can talk."

Grant asked the guard, "How far of a shot is that?"

The guard pointed to his hunting laser rangefinder. "217 yards, more or less." He smiled.

Hunters concealed on a forested hill with a CB; low tech, but extremely effective.

Some dogs started barking. It sounded like they were in the volunteer fire department building. Bobby motioned for Grant to come into the building.

When he walked in, Grant saw Dan with his AK slung over his shoulder and something far more ferocious: three German Shepherds. Grant surmised that these must be the K9s Dan was training. They were impressive animals. Dan calmed them down quickly. He knew these dogs well and they knew him.

"Dan, tell the Team about your dogs," Rich said. Rich was very proud of Dan and the dogs.

"Well, I run three dogs at the gate here," Dan said. "These are attack dogs. I have detection dogs at home that are trained to sniff for drugs and explosives, but we don't need them here. We need attack dogs."

Dan pointed to his three dogs. "They're named Cairo, Boris, and Adis." Each dog looked with approval at Dan when he said its name. "We patrol the river. These guys can pick up the scent of anyone coming, or attempting to come, across the river. If I release one and tell it to 'fetch!' it'll go after whoever is unlucky enough to be hiding or running away. There is nothing more terrifying than an eighty pound snarling German Shepherd coming at you doing about twenty miles an hour. I've seen Taliban shit their pants, literally crap their drawers, and throw up their hands when they hear and see a dog coming. The bad guys weren't afraid of men with guns. It was the dogs that got them to surrender." Dan was smiling.

These dogs were a huge asset; better than a machine gun or surveillance cameras. Or both.

Grant asked Dan, "So this is what you did in the Air Force?"

"Yep. Base defense," Dan said. "I worked with dogs the last eight years of my twenty-five years in. Now I train the Sheriff Department's K9s on a volunteer basis. When I was in the Air Force, I did the usual stuff, which included law enforcement on base. But a lot of what we did was more like infantry, except that we were more defense-oriented than typical infantry, which is offense-oriented. We had a big ol' air base to defend with fences and mines sometimes. That's where the dogs come in. They can find intruders and attack them. Arabs are terrified of dogs, which came in handy … where I was a couple of times." The U.S. used air bases in various countries that did not want it known that they were helping the Americans, so the locations of the bases were secret. Dan, out of habit, wasn't saying where the bases were.

Dan petted a dog and said, "Dogs are perfect for defending an area. Perfect. Detect and attack. You can't ask for anything more than that when you're repelling bad guys."

Dan looked out at the gate and the surrounding area and drew in a deep breath. "This is exactly what I've trained to do and I'm glad to be doing it again. Not that I want any of this to be happening, but at least I can add something here for my neighbors." Grant remembered from their earlier conversation that Rich knew Dan from Oath Keepers. That meant that Dan wasn't just a guy with some experience and some dogs—Dan was a Patriot who was in this for all the right reasons.

Grant and the guys were afraid to pet the dogs. Dan said, "Go ahead, pet them. Let them know your scent and that you're okay." The dogs seemed to sense Dan's acceptance of the guys and instinctively knew that they weren't a threat.

They heard some activity at the gate, so Grant went outside to see what was happening. A pickup with some guys was waiting to re-enter Pierce Point. The guards waved and someone moved the car blocking the entrance. The pickup slowly drove in and the guys got out and started to visit with the guards. They looked like good ol' boys in work clothes with hunting rifles and various pistols.

Grant came up to the group just in time to hear one of the guys say, "It's getting bad in town." A crowd was gathering around him. People were starved for information about conditions out there.

"Here's the good news," the guy said. "As you come into town just after the city limits, right at that little park, there is a roadblock kind of like this one. Lots of men with guns," the guy motioned with his hand toward the guards, "like this, but more guys." He paused and then said, "They have blue strips of cloth tied around their arm." People were organizing themselves to solve a problem; no government was needed for this. "I saw one cop in uniform there with them so I guess it's a posse or something."

The guy continued. "They were checking IDs. They saw that we were from here so they let us in. They told us to be armed because they couldn't keep control of everything going on in town. We went down Strauss toward Martin's." Martin's was the name of the local grocery store. "There was a pickup load of some pretty mean looking Mexicans. They didn't bother us, but I wouldn't want to piss them off. Lots of people are carrying guns, which looked weird. But what looked weirder was the people who didn't have guns. Who walks around town now without a gun?" The idiots who didn't own a gun, Grant thought. Even out there in the rural part of the state, plenty of households didn't own one.

One of the guards asked, "How are the shelves at Martin's?"

"Pretty bare," the guy said. "We waited in a long line in the parking lot to go in. There were a few of these blue ribbon guys walking around the parking lot to control the crowd. People were pretty calm, but some were bitching about the line and the lack of this and that. It was pissing me off. Shut up. It's hard enough to go through this shit, but to have some welfare queen complaining…the fatter they were, the more they bitched." Like any other rural part of America, there were plenty of welfare recipients in Frederickson. Most were white.

"When we came up to the door at Martin's," the guy continued, "we had to check our weapons. We left them with Jimmy," he said pointing to one of the guys from his truck. "I ain't trusting those things to anyone. Hey, tell them what someone said to you while we were inside."

Jimmy said, "Some guy, some yuppie lookin' guy, asked how much we wanted for Derrick's .357. He said he had $1,000 in cash. Can you believe that?"

Everyone looked over at Derrick, who had his .357 in a holster. He pointed at his .357 and said, "A week ago, I would have said, 'sold!' But now there's nothing worth buyin' for $1,000. There's almost nothing left in Martin's."

The guy who had been telling this story said, "Yep. Shelves are pretty much bare. Just stuff that no one wants to eat. Health food shit. Oh, and the racks of greeting cards are untouched. No one wants to send a birthday card now," he chuckled. "Besides health food, about the only stuff left is weird shit like Chinese food." The guy saw Pow and said, "No offense."

Pow shot back, "No problem, bro. I like steak and fried chicken." That lightened up the mood.

Grant asked the guy, "What are prices like?"

"Dunno," the guy said. "We didn't find anything we wanted to buy. They had a sign up about the $200 limit. We left. What a big waste of time. We went around town some more just to see what was going on. I mean, I wanted to come back with something. But we got nothin'." He thought for a second and then said, "I even heard a couple of shots. Sounded like a pistol. 'Pop!' 'Pop!'"

"Well," he continued, "the gas stations were closed. That's when I got pissed. I had wasted all that gas to come to town and there's nothin' to buy." For the first time the guy started to look concerned.

"We're screwed if this doesn't straighten out soon," the guy said. It got quiet. Real quiet. People had been busy with the camaraderie of guard duty and all the excitement about defending their community. Now it was sinking in. There was nothing in town. They were on their own.

Chapter 103

Facebook Friends

(May 10)

The good news kept coming in to Camp Murray where Jeanie Thompson had been working almost non-stop for several days. People were upbeat as they got ready for the 7:00 a.m. briefing.

Jason came in wearing the same suit he had worn a few days before. Jeanie was reminded that her quickly packed suitcase only had a couple of changes of clothes. Oh well, they were saving lives so fashion would have to take a back seat. Besides, everyone else — except the Governor — only seemed to have a few changes of clothes.

Jason had a smile for the first time in days. "Well, we have some good news," he announced in the conference room where the morning briefings took place. "Actually, quite a bit of it. The first polling since the beginning of the Crisis is in." He was smiling.

"People are looking to their government for help," Jason said with a huge grin. "They want us — by a 78% majority — to exercise emergency powers. That's right: They want us to do what we're doing and probably do more of it."

Everyone in the room was smiling and a few were high fiving. Not Jeanie. All the others were career Democrat staffers. They were ecstatic about the polling, but Jeanie didn't believe the numbers. She wanted to believe them. She was part of the government and could see how central planning, like they were doing, was getting food onto the store shelves and gasoline to the gas stations. But 78%?

Jeanie asked, "What is the sample size?"

Jason got a piece of paper from his stack on the conference room table and said, "Six hundred and fifty-two. Registered voters. Contacted by phone. Seattle metro area."

That's why the 78% number was so high. They had contacted the Seattle metro area, where all the liberals lived. And by phone? Jeanine thought, who answers their phone and spends time with a pollster when all this is going on? Old people sitting in their houses? Scared soccer moms sitting in their houses because the authorities told them to? Certainly not people who have evacuated or are waiting in lines at grocery stores. Also, "registered" voters were just about everyone, given the "Motor Voter" laws that encouraged everyone getting or renewing a drivers' license — felons and illegal aliens included — to register to vote. Everyone was a registered voter, but fewer and fewer people were voting in each election. Most people had come to the conclusion that voting did no good. Looking at what was happening around them, they were right. Jeanie dared not say this aloud. It was hard enough being the "token Republican" at the headquarters of Washington State government. There was no need to draw any more attention to herself, though she did know that this poll was absurdly optimistic. For the first time, Jeanie thought that not even insiders like her were getting the truth. What else was being hidden from them?

The poll results provided a sense of vindication to everyone else in the room. Government was not only working during the Crisis, but people wanted more of it. Government took care of people and the more desperate they were, the more government the people wanted. This was great. For the government.

Jeanie was thinking about how she might be getting lied to on a daily basis and how she then turned around and told those lies to the media all day long. Was she being used? She kept thinking about that.

While she was halfway paying attention, Jason went over the other positive things that were going on, or were supposedly going on.

Semi-trucks were working pretty much exclusively for the government now. Food, fuel, and medical supplies were being transported from warehouses to distribution centers in large and medium-sized cities with the help of the military.

"Well, most of the military," Jason said with a frown. "There have been some pretty high incidents of absenteeism." What Jason didn't say was, "especially in the South." Whole units were missing down there. The National Guard in the Southern and mountain Western states were pretty much not showing up for federal duty. They were forming "State Guards" and not following federal orders.

But, things varied. Some units were following orders, others weren't. There were no clear dividing lines. It varied by state, branch of the military, unit, and down to the individual. Most military people were busy, feverishly doing their jobs to help. When they were working sixteen hours a day loading food onto trucks to get to hungry people, they weren't thinking about politics. But, little by little, they were thinking about their families and starting to think they needed to be with them. They started to think they needed to leave, even just for a few days to check in on their families. They promised themselves they'd come back to their unit, but few ever did.

Many in the military could see up close all the insanity around them, like the political decisions that were sending aid to favored states and parts of states, especially the cities, while ignoring the rural areas. Lots of them started to wonder why they were helping, especially when their families needed them. More than one thought, "What am I fighting for? Socialism?"

Jeanie had to snap out of it. She couldn't be doubting what she was doing. She had to just do her job. People depended on her for information that was saving lives and keeping people positive, so this didn't turn into a ... it was hard for her to finish that thought. She didn't want to think about it. She wanted to focus on doing good things.

Her cell phone rang. It was Jim. She had better take it; she hadn't talked to him in days. She got up out of her chair and went out of the conference room.

She whispered, "Hi."

Jim, hearing her whispering, whispered, too. "Are you in a place where you can talk?"

Jeanie said, in a regular voice, "Oh, yeah. I was in a meeting. But it's not a big deal. Where are you?"

"I'm not supposed to say," Jim said. "In the state, though." He was tired and Jeanie could tell from his voice that he wasn't happy.

"Is it safe where you are?" she asked.

"Yeah, I guess. But..." Jim started to whisper himself, "they won't let us have our weapons. They're locked up. Even the guards are carrying unloaded weapons. It's like they don't trust us." Jim, who was still the conservative Jeanie used to be, knew why. The brass didn't trust the troops. This was for show. Or, more precisely, slave labor. The troops were being used as laborers who could be trusted to show up. Pretty much trusted, except not trusted enough to have weapons. Jim felt used.

"I'm doing computer work," Jim said. He was working on the POI list and trying to find where POIs were, but he couldn't tell Jeanie that. There hadn't been much computer activity since the Crisis began. But, occasionally some wanted person would place a cell call from their phone or get on Facebook and publish a manifesto and then they'd know where he or she was. They'd try to send someone out to get them, but the roads were clogged and local law enforcement was too busy to do anything. There weren't nearly enough federal agents to chase all these leads. And the FCorps was useless, so POIs weren't getting arrested.

Jim thought the computer work he was doing was a total waste of time. It was pretty much a big game to let his commanding officer send in daily statistics to headquarters saying they located X number of POIs. Everyone felt great about it up the chain of command. Of course, nothing was actually getting done about it.

Jeanie started to whisper herself. "Did you see Grant Matson and the other WAB guys on the POI list?"

Jim was silent. Crap. He had not seen them on the list, but he had been concentrating on tiny little pieces of the list, the ones who were stupid enough to use their cell phones or get onto the internet under their real names.

People Jim knew were on the POI list? That meant, at some point, the brass might know that he knew them. This wasn't good.

"Really? No way," said Jim. "We were over to Grant's house, like, last year. That's got to be some kind of mistake. We're finding mistakes on the list. That must be one of them. There's no way Grant is a 'terrorist.'"

Jim wasn't supposed to say that part about them finding mistakes. Not on an unsecure phone line; a cellphone, no less.

Jim and Jeanie were silent for a while, trying to think of what to say. What do you say? Their friends were wanted and they were deep inside the government and supposed to be finding them. That wasn't a typical conversation topic for a long distance love affair.

After a while, Jim said, "It's a mistake. It has to be. Um, Jeanie, you're not a Facebook friend with them are you?" Jim didn't want to give away anything about how they were using Facebook.

"No, I unfriended them when Grant left the Auditor's Office," she said. "Menlow didn't want us to have any links to WAB. And, yes, I know about Facebook and how we are using it."

"We" are using it. Jim noted that Jeanie had said, "we." Oh God. Jeanie and him were spying on their friends, all to secure a steady paycheck.

Oh, shit. Shit. He remembered that he was a Facebook friend of Grant's and, he thought, maybe Brian Jenkins, Tom Foster, and Ben Trenton. Jim couldn't remember because he didn't use Facebook much and hadn't logged on in quite a while. If Jim were a Facebook friend of some POIs, he'd lose his security clearance, or maybe worse. Or they'd try to use him to lure the POIs into custody. He felt sick. He felt like someone had kicked him in the stomach. He felt the adrenaline running through him like a poison. He couldn't talk. He tried to tell

Jeanie he had to go, but his words were mush. He had to check Facebook.

"Are you okay?" Jeanie asked when Jim was mumbling.

"I gotta go," Jim finally said. He hung up.

Jeanie could tell that Jim was terrified about something, but she didn't know what.

She went back into the conference room. Jason was still talking about the polling and how great things were going, but Jeanie didn't believe him anymore. There was no way all these wonderful things were really happening. She was trapped in Camp Murray — there were literally machine guns and barbed wire surrounding her — so she couldn't get out and see what was going on out there. She started to wonder: what was *really* happening? She suddenly had the worst feeling that she was on the wrong side.

Chapter 104

Meanwhile, Back at the Farm

(May 10)

What was that sound? It was like a chicken or something. Tom Foster hated waking up, but this was even worse. He was being forced awake by a "cock-a-doodle-doo" sound, like from a movie. He opened his eyes. He was in a strange bedroom. It was a rooster. Shit, they really do crow at the break of dawn.

Tom was not a morning person and was not a country person. He liked late nights and the city. But, he didn't like people burning down his office and trying to kill him and his family, even more than he disliked waking up at the crack of dawn in the country. So a chicken waking him up at dawn on a farm where he was safe was just fine with him.

His wife, Joyce, was stirring. She had been going non-stop out there. The house was brimming with kids and adults. Lots and lots of activity. There were all kinds of farm things to learn out there. Plus, she needed to stay busy to take her mind off of all that was happening. Their house had probably been burned down and people were likely looking for her family. She constantly worried that someone at WAB would tell the authorities they were hiding out at the Prosser farm. These were the worst days of her life. She was constantly afraid. She tried to busy herself with work at the farm to take her mind off of all of her terrifying thoughts.

Others started stirring with the rooster crowing. Joyce wanted to be the first one up to help Molly with breakfast. She was getting ready, but it was weird getting dressed in someone else's house. It wasn't like a hotel. It was her house now. Well, her room, at least. She didn't have most of her things. She didn't have any makeup. Oh well. No one else was wearing makeup out here. No one cared. And there was no one to see her out of her makeup.

Tom was still in bed, trying in vain to go back to sleep. Joyce kissed his forehead and said, "I'm so glad we're all out here together." Tom smiled. Maybe it wasn't so bad out there.

People started shuffling into the kitchen for breakfast. Some of the kids were running around. Where did they get all that energy?

Jeff Prosser was thinking about all the work they had to do. All this work would be even harder given the fact that all his "farm hands" were city people who didn't know how to do anything. That was okay. They were friends who were in desperate need. This is what friends do. Even when they're only the mailroom guy. Yep, Jeff felt with pride, he was the mailroom guy who had saved the day.

The families talked about the chores they needed to do. It was May, so they had a garden to tend. Joyce and Karen made the point that all of this would be over soon, so maybe they didn't need to have a garden to get them through the winter; Jeff politely said that they should plant one "just in case."

The garden was a big one; half an acre. They grew just about everything that would grow in western Washington State. Lots of hoeing and weeding. After Joyce and Karen accepted that they should plant the garden "just in case," they really enjoyed turning it into a huge source of healthy food for their families. They had enjoyed gardening in their beautiful yards back in Olympia and decided to make the food garden at the farm into a masterpiece.

Molly really appreciated the help in the garden. When the crops came in, she would have plenty of help canning and drying all the produce. They'd eat the best food of their lives, Molly thought. No preservatives, no chemicals, no ripening in trucks on the drive up from Mexico. Just fresh, non-genetically modified fruits and vegetables.

The Prossers had a few dairy cows. Jeff's kids would show the city kids how to milk a cow. It was a completely foreign experience for the city kids, but they caught on. Molly was glad for the help with the dairy cows. They had to milk them by hand since they didn't have a milking machine for just the three cows they had.

The Prossers getting those three dairy cows had been a big decision a year ago. Back then, Molly thought that some milk cows would be good to have "just in case." Right about that time, WAB was cutting back the hours of employees, including Jeff, so saving money on milk and dairy products made sense. Besides, the price of "store bought" dairy products had been creeping up faster and faster. With the value of the dollar tanking as the government created trillions of dollars to buy its own debt, investors looked for something "real" to put their money into instead of the U.S. dollar. They found commodities like gold, oil and agricultural products. Pretty soon, speculators were buying dairy products and other food commodities. The price kept increasing. Right before the price of dairy cows went way up, Jeff and Molly got some and were very glad they did.

Now, the Prossers and their guests had fresh milk and lots of it. They even churned the cream to make butter with an electric churn Molly's mom left them years ago.

The kids were invaluable little laborers out on the farm. In addition to milking the cows, they were in charge of gathering the eggs from the hens. They had planned on selling the extra eggs, but now, with all the guests, they used the extra eggs for breakfasts. They had beef cows, too; about thirty. Beef cows were one investment that outperformed the stock market enormously. They had more beef than they knew what to do with. Even with the guests eating lots of it, they still had enough to sell.

The Prossers sold the extra beef to neighbors. Now, with cash not having any real value, Jeff figured they could trade the beef for gasoline, chainsaw oil, fence posts; whatever they might need out there, which wasn't much. That was the beauty of the farm: it didn't produce a lot in economic terms, but didn't take a lot to keep it running. They were largely self-sufficient. Not completely; they still needed electricity and running water and would need to go to town for things like tractor parts.

They had electric heat in the house, but Jeff was too cheap to run it, due to the fact that electricity prices had quadrupled in the past few years. A ton of "greenhouse" gas regulations had kicked in and utilities were not allowed to use the great and nearly free electricity source in the Pacific Northwest: hydroelectric dams. The utilities shut down the nearly free electricity of the dams and had to buy power on the open market, competing with California utilities for a limited amount of electricity and bidding up the price. With the cut in hours at WAB, that electric bill became a big deal.

Jeff had a woodstove in the farmhouse. His dad got it in the 1970s and it was very efficient. They had tons of firewood on the property. Down by the creek, alder grew like weeds. Alder wasn't the best firewood, but it would do. They had lots of cedar and spruce farther out toward the hill, but it was a long haul back to the house.

Jeff was glad he had the tractor. It made hauling logs or cut wood across a sometimes soggy field much easier than trying to use a truck or, worse yet, carrying it all on foot. He had a winter's worth of wood already cut, but with the free labor out there he might as well get even more cut. His guests needed to work for the room and board, he thought with a chuckle.

Another chore was guard duty. They were nearly at the end of a long road of farmhouses. There was a gate at the entrance to the road to keep cattle from escaping. It worked well to keep people out, too. Up on the high ground where they were, the Prossers could see a car coming down the road for quite some distance. But still, they needed a guard out there. Jeff had made a deal with the neighbors: they have an armed person watching the gate during the day and his house would take care of the night. He did this because he didn't want his POI guests to be seen during the day even by the neighbors, though he had grown up with and trusted them. Who knew what guests the neighbors would have during the Collapse and where their guests' allegiances might lie.

Jeff had a little Motorola radio set so a guard could communicate with the house. After a few times out on nighttime guard duty showing people the lay of the land, he let the WAB guys take it over. Jeff needed to sleep. He figured he was doing plenty for the WAB families by harboring fugitives and letting them live out there for free. They could pull nighttime guard duty in exchange. They didn't seem to mind the trade. In fact, they were extremely grateful.

The WAB guys hadn't spent much, if any, time with guns. That was okay. Jeff went over the operation of a shotgun, which would be good at the gate-to-car distances involved for a guard at the gate. A rifled slug from a 12 gauge could punch through most car doors. Jeff had a standard Remington 870 Wingmaster. It was a great duck gun or a looter gun.

Jeff showed them how to shoot his lever-action 30-30 carbine. They did fairly well, but weren't exactly marksmen. Jeff had a limited amount of 30-30 ammo, about 250 rounds, so he got the WAB guys familiar with the lever-action 30-30 by shooting his lever-action .22, a Marlin 94. He had been shooting that gun since he was a kid. He knew exactly where each round would go. Jeff had thousands of rounds of .22 ammo, which he bought one box at a time over the past few years. They used the .22 frequently out there on rabbits, squirrels, and crows. Besides, Jeff loved shooting that lever-action .22.

The guys took their pistols with them when they were on guard duty. Karen didn't like seeing the guns and asked that they not be visible to the children. The kids didn't seem to care about the guns, though. They had been afraid of them at first, but quickly realized that guns were part of what happened on the farm. They were tools. After a while, Tom and Ben quit trying to accommodate Karen and she didn't say anything. Brian, however, kept his pistol hidden as his wife wished. That was okay. At least he was carrying it, which was what mattered.

Jeff had two pistols. The first was a snub-nosed .38 revolver that he used when he needed to carry a concealed gun. He didn't have a holster; he just put it in his pocket. He couldn't remember if his concealed weapons permit had expired or not. Oh well. They weren't exactly required anymore. Besides, he only needed a permit if he was in town and he didn't plan on being in town.

Jeff's second pistol was his pride and joy: a Ruger Blackhawk in .357. It was a "cowboy" gun. He had a Western holster for it and loved it. He loved all things cowboy and wasn't afraid to wear his cowboy pistol and carry his cowboy lever action rifle. It was his damned farm and that's how it was. No one cared. Jeff had lots of .38 ammo. It also worked in the .357. He wished he had a lever-action carbine in .357/.38, too, but he never got around to getting one before the Collapse. That was okay; his 30-30 worked just fine. He had almost 200 rounds for his 30-30. It was enough for hunting or an attack or two on the farm.

Rounding out the "arsenal" was his 30-06. It was scoped and could take down elk, which came by quite a bit, at 200 or more yards. That had been the longest shot he'd taken with it. Jeff didn't shoot it much; he didn't need to. But it was sighted in perfectly. He only had about 100 rounds. This would be the gun he used from the house out to the road, if necessary. He hoped it wouldn't be.

Just then, someone knocked on the door. He grabbed his shotgun and went to the door. It was Dennis, Jeff's cousin who lived down the road. Jeff's family owned all the land on the road and subdivided it a few years ago when that was still possible before environmental regulations prevented it. Dennis' mom, who was Jeff's aunt, got one of the lots. When she died, Dennis got it.

Dennis was a nice guy, kind of quiet and shy. He was a nondescript bachelor in his thirties. A hard-working guy who was perfectly comfortable on the farm, but not so much in town. Dennis had come over to Jeff's house to see if he could help show the new people some of the things they'd need to know. He was also coming over because he was lonely and wanted to be around some new people.

Jeff told Dennis that the people staying with them had left the city because of the violence. He told Dennis not to mention to a single person that they were out there. There had been a misunderstanding with the authorities that would get straightened out when all this cleared up.

Dennis was a hick, but he wasn't stupid. He knew that Jeff worked for WAB and that WAB was hated by the state government. He was glad to help the effort. He, too, hated all the superior-minded city people who kept taking and taking from the people out in the rural areas. Dennis just wanted to be left alone, but the environmentalists kept telling him how to live. They wouldn't let him raise cattle out there. At 500 yards, it was too close to a stream. That stream had been fine for the 140 years the Prossers had been on this land. Dennis wasn't political, but he was glad to be helping in some small way to get even with the people who were destroying his country. If that meant harboring some fugitives when the cops were stretched too thin to do anything about it, that was fine. It was more excitement than he'd had in his whole life.

Tom, Ben, and Brian were huddled together and talking before breakfast. Jeff introduced Dennis to Tom, who was scoping out Dennis' truck.

Tom asked, "Hey, Dennis, does your truck run on diesel or regular gas?"

"Diesel," Dennis said. "Why?"

"Good," Tom said, "Jeff has plenty of diesel in that underground tank. So you can make trips to town, right?" Obviously, the POIs couldn't show their face in town, but Dennis could. He had no ties to WAB. Even Jeff, the mailroom guy, had WAB ties. Only Dennis could go into town.

"Yeah," Dennis said. He didn't like to go to town and knew that it was dangerous right now, but he could go. For a good enough reason.

Ben said, "Dennis, we need you to get something pretty important."

"Yeah? What?" he asked, trying to hide his excitement.

"Can you go to an office supply store and get some blank CDs?" Ben asked. "You know, the kind you can record music on. As many as you can."

That was weird. Making music CDs? "Why do you want to do that?" Dennis asked.

Ben told Dennis what they were doing with the CDs. Wow. This was exciting, Dennis thought. He couldn't wait to go to town.

Brian gave Dennis a bunch of cash. Brian didn't want his wife to see how much he was handing Dennis; she'd get mad. Karen was not loving this farm living. She was used to suburban living. She was grateful to be away from the protestors, but she felt so odd out at the farm. Giving Dennis the last of their cash to buy blank CDs would have been too hard for Brian to explain. So he didn't. He just did it.

"I'll go right now," Dennis said. He needed to go to his house and get his pistol. He wanted to be ready for what was sure to be the biggest adventure of his life.

Chapter 105

Fine in Forks

(May 10)

By now, it was obvious to everyone in Forks that things were going to be bad for quite a while. This wasn't a temporary little thing. It was the biggest thing that had happened to the country since World War II; maybe bigger.

Politics was not much of a topic in Forks. Right, left, Patriot, Loyalist—none of that really mattered. People were pissed at how the government had let all this happen, but they'd been pissed for years leading up to the Collapse. They started getting angry a few decades before when the environmentalists started to shut down logging—the lifeblood of Forks, Washington—because of the "endangered" spotted owl. There were plenty of spotted owls; the locals saw them flying around all the time. The endangered species listing was just an excuse to turn most of the Olympic Peninsula of Washington into a park for city people to play in when they drove their Subarus out from Seattle to go bird watching. For spotted owls, of course.

People in Forks had been watching the size of government grow, too. There were more and more controls on the land and taxes kept going up. More and more people worked for government; directly or as contractors. Longtime hometown businesses went out of business. More and more people went on welfare and weren't even trying to find work. Many people were making questionable disability claims and going on the state-funded workers' compensation system. Rural and isolated Forks was not immune from the slide into government dependence that was going on in the rest of America. But, it wasn't as bad there. People still knew how to live poor and take care of themselves. Most of them, at least.

Steve, the manager of the now-closed auto parts store in town, was amazed that all economic activity had stopped; just stopped. No one was buying and selling anything. Well, they were, but not like before the May Day Collapse. People still traded deer meat for gasoline and that kind of thing, but, they'd increasingly been doing that in the hard economic times leading up to the Collapse. Now it was the only way to do it. No supplies from the outside world, and no cash. Barter was it.

The news wasn't worth watching, anymore. Steve wasn't sure he could trust it. During the first few days of the Collapse, the news had story after story about terrorist attacks, power outages, riots, looting and states threatening to "opt out" of the union. At first, most of the terrorist attacks were blamed on the left-wing Red Brigade and some splinter groups of public employee unions. The union thugs—a handful of radicals out of the millions of unionized public employees—were furious that their jobs and pensions had been cut off. No one was very sympathetic to them given that Americans' 401(k)s were now basically worthless after the stock market crashed. After a few days of stories about the Red Brigade and union thugs, the news quit mentioning them. Either the left-wing attacks stopped, the news wanted to quit scaring people or the news decided to start blaming attacks on "right-wing" and "militia" groups. Which they did. That became the theme on the news. The "Right" was going on a rampage. Some believed it, though many didn't.

Don Watson, the ham radio operator in Forks, kept them abreast of the latest rumors from the outside world. People were saying that some military units were mutinying. They were killing their officers. It didn't sound like many were doing this. Most were either working hard at the relief efforts or sitting out the political stuff, waiting to see which side would be stronger. Some military units were defecting and joining gangs, which was what had happened a few years earlier in Mexico. Whole military units in Mexico would just start working for a drug cartel. Steve didn't know if American units doing this was true or just a bunch of crazy rumors. There were so many rumors and most didn't turn out to be true. After a while, most people quit trying to stay up on the rumors and tried to keep their heads down and just survive what was happening. Rumors were an unnecessary distraction, and usually only served to scare people with an endless list of "what-ifs."

The power was on most of the time, but would go off for a few hours at a time. One of Steve's friends at the electric company said that when the hackers periodically attacked, the government would shut down the power in the rural areas first, where there were fewer people to inconvenience and scare. Seattle had power almost all of the time.

Steve saw on the news that the government had started something called "Freedom Corps." Whatever, he thought. Wear your silly hats. No one in Forks would be caught dead in one of those. They didn't need the Freedom Corps in Forks. The people there were taking care of things on their own. Pretty damned well, as a matter of fact. The last thing they needed was a new government agency. That's what got them into this mess in the first place.

There was one bright spot in Forks: the police. The city police and the sheriff's deputies were local guys. Everyone knew them. There were a couple of yahoos on the force, but most were solid. They weren't abandoning their jobs because they couldn't. They lived in Forks. There was nowhere else to go. Defending home and family meant defending Forks.

The police quickly set up a volunteer "posse" force. They had lots of men willing to join up. In fact, they had to turn some away. There weren't any neighborhood guards because the posse served that function. Besides, Forks was one giant neighborhood. Might as well have a city-wide guard force instead of a measly neighborhood one. Everyone knew each other, so it was possible to trust people. People in Olympia would have a hard time trusting someone who came from another part of the city to guard their neighborhood. That wasn't the situation in Forks.

Steve was a posse captain. He had about fifteen guys working for him. They patrolled on foot because gas was too precious to waste driving around. They carried pistols and sometimes shotguns or rifles. They didn't have a colored cloth tied around their arms like many of the communities were starting to. They didn't need any identification; everyone knew who the posse was.

Steve used the auto parts store as a headquarters. He had the swing shift of guards. Just like the swing shifts from the days back when they logged in Forks: 3:00 pm to 11:00 pm. This was a pretty active time for guarding since lots of crime started after dark, which was about 9:00 pm in mid-May.

There wasn't a lot of crime, though. Some stealing. Mostly kids; the welfare kids, to be honest. There were other people stealing, but the "shitbags" as they called the welfare kids and their families, were usually the culprits. They usually stole firewood stacked at someone's house or siphoned gas from parked cars. The town used the school for a makeshift jail. Stealing got someone about thirty days in jail, along with shame from the community. Everyone knew who was in jail and would make sure to stay clear of them once they got out.

The criminals usually weren't violent. One burglar—an adult shitbag and notorious alcoholic—broke into a single mom's house. She shot him with a shotgun. That same night, a kid stealing firewood pointed a gun at a posse member. It didn't end well for the kid. The shootings jolted Forks. The welfare people were getting more and more pissed at the posse and the good people of Forks didn't care. They backed the posse. But, things weren't heading for a deep split in town because most people were related. It wasn't uncommon for a welfare recipient to be the cousin or nephew of a posse member. That kept a lid on the divisiveness. It didn't eliminate it, but it limited it.

People in Forks were helping each other in ways they never had. Steve made sure to go check on Patty Matson, Grant's mom. She was doing fine. He hadn't been over to see her since Grant's dad died and Grant had come to visit. It was things like this that made life a little bit more meaningful in Forks. People were helping each other. It had been too long since people acted so decently toward each other.

The three churches in Forks seemed to be working as usual. They were mainstream churches without any real theological differences; they got along fine. Attendance before the Collapse had been light. Mostly old people went to church in Forks. The Pacific Northwest was known for having some of the lowest church attendance in the country. After May Day, however, people of all ages started to come to church. The world seemed to be turned upside down and many looked to a higher power for comfort. A fair number of people started wondering if all that was happening was the end times described in Revelation. Was Jesus coming back very soon? Was this the Tribulation? The three churches were packed. A couple of people started holding home church services.

The churches were doing much more than just sermons. They used the big kitchens each one had to start providing meals for people. Church members would bring extra food, especially game meat and fish, and share it with fellow members, and anyone else in need. Churches became strong and cohesive groups of people. They were like all the other groups forming after the Collapse: gangs, just not the kind of gangs that hurt people. Churches were doing what they had always done—before the government moved in several decades ago and took over social services. Now, instead of taxes being collected and sent thousands of miles to Washington, D.C., passing through dozens of agencies, and finally trickling back to Forks, the charity stayed in Forks. As a result, much more of it got to the people who needed it.

One area that became disturbing very quickly was people getting cut off from their medications. Old people and others on life-sustaining medications were dying. It was sad, but everyone expected it. The other unsettling thing was all the people on mental illness medications. There were some people who started going crazy once their meds ran out.

One of them was Donnie Phillips, a guy Steve went to high school with. No one knew that Donnie was on anti-depressants. After about a week without his meds, he tried to kill his kids. A neighbor, Bob Francis, came over and had to shoot Donnie, as he was attacking his children who had locked themselves in the bathroom. That was especially hard on Steve; he knew both of them from high school, and one had to shoot the other.

There were many people who were helping family as they went off their medications. They would remove all the guns and knives in the house and stay with them all they could. It was sad. Families who had mental illness in the family and had been able to mask it with medication, were now ashamed when their secrets were coming out. Most people understood and tried to help.

Steve sat back at his desk in the auto parts store during a quiet moment. He thought about all that was going on and how the town was reacting. So far, so good. Better than he would have thought. But this was only the beginning of the Collapse. Would things hold together for months? What about winter?

Chapter 106

The Gray Man

(May 10)

Ed Oleo, a handsome man in his late fifties with a full head of grey hair, looked out his big living room window at the Pacific Ocean. He lived in West Seattle, a nice part of the city, but not one of the trendy parts. He was surrounded by good solid homes, many with nice views of the water. Ed owned a real estate company, so he always looked at neighborhoods like he was selling a house. When he looked at his neighborhood he thought: water view, established neighborhood. That described West Seattle.

A Seattle water view was still spectacular, even with all that was going on in the world. Things actually weren't too bad in Seattle, at least not in West Seattle. Ed had known the country was living in a false economy and the house of cards would come down, eventually. It sure did, though, it wasn't yet as bad as he expected it to be. He expected all the city people around him to go berserk with hunger and start killing each other. He thought Seattle would look like a scene from an apocalyptic movie.

Ed was wrong. At least so far. The first ten days of the "Crisis" were pretty rough. The shelves of the area Whole Foods, an overpriced organic grocery store, went bare about two days after May Day. There was only one gas station in the whole neighborhood because the city planners had determined that most cars would eventually be electric. The one gas station in West Seattle went dry one day after May Day.

But, to Ed's amazement, his neighborhood kept calm. There was some crime, but they were minor thefts. Mostly teenagers. To get to West Seattle, one must go over a bridge. The police, what was left of them, stopped cars on the bridge which kept the obvious riff-raff out. None of his neighbors started carrying guns. None of them owned guns as far as Ed could tell. He owned a shotgun and felt like the best armed guy in a one-mile radius. Except for the criminals.

Even though violent crime wasn't a day-to-day problem, at least in West Seattle, there were plenty of private security firms. They were everywhere. Lots of former soldiers and police were gainfully employed by these firms, most of which had "arrangements" with the police to essentially do whatever they wanted. The businessman in Ed wished he'd invested in these companies before the Collapse.

The people of West Seattle were a little too compliant for Ed's taste, but he had to admit that it worked out well that they followed the instructions they were given on TV: remain in your houses, help is on the way, America will bounce back, yada yada yada. If the bad stuff, like the stores being empty and gas stations being closed, had lasted more than ten days, they might not have remained so calm. Ed knew his neighbors couldn't have done much for themselves. Almost all of them were software developers, in the financial industry or, the biggest industry of all, government.

They were helpless. Ed shook his head and thought that if his neighbors couldn't take their Prius to Whole Foods every day to get fresh goat cheese or whatever they ate, they would curl up into a ball and die. Turns out they didn't die; they just complained like they were dying, but amazingly they actually made it ten days without goat cheese. Ed imagined that the withdrawals from the $7.00 lattes were pretty hard, but they lived.

After about ten days of failure after failure, the government actually started to get food and a little fuel into the city. Ed was amazed. One day, the rumor went around that a semi had arrived at Whole Foods, so people rushed out to get some food. It was true: a semi was there. But there were two disappointments.

First, people had to fill out an application for an "FCard," which was a government electronic ration card known as a "Freedom Card." The Freedom Corps people, wearing yellow hardhats, helped people fill out the applications and explained that the FCard could be used to get food and a limited amount of gasoline. It would draw on a person's bank account and investments. People were euphoric: the banks had been closed, so they could finally use their money. Ed knew that the government was basically stealing their money in exchange for a little bit of food, and he came up with another word that began with "F" to better explain the FCard. But people were so thankful their government had worked hard for them and come up with a solution. Ed just shook his head. It was so obvious what was happening, but the sheeple didn't care.

Everyone got an installment of food while their FCard application was being processed. Ed called it a "ration," but the FCorps person at the application table corrected him. "It's an installment, not a 'ration,'" she said to Ed in a snappy tone.

The second disappointment was the food in the truck. It was

"typical American" food or, as one of Ed's neighbors called it, "truck stop" food. Lots of processed grains like biscuit mix, cheap pasta, mashed potato mix. There was even gravy mix—no one in yuppie West Seattle had eaten gravy mix in decades. The truck even had beef jerky. "Who eats that?" One man in line asked, "Truck and tractor pull fans?"

One lady asked the FCorps person handing out "installments" how much sodium the jerky had. Sodium? That's a concern now? Ed shook his head again. What's wrong with these people? They should be glad they have some food. It only cost them their entire life savings. They should be thankful, Ed chuckled to himself.

Once the shock of having to eat "truck stop" food wore off—and with grumbling stomachs it wore off very quickly—people were glad to get their "installment." All across West Seattle, people were eating instant mashed potatoes for the first time ever. It was amazing how something like a few semis full of "truck stop" food could put everyone in a better mood. There was hope now. The semis would keep coming. They could use the FCards. The food would get slightly better and better with each truckload. Pretty soon, things would be back to normal, they kept telling themselves.

Not Ed. He knew what was going on. The government had finally taken over the last remaining parts of the economy. People were thanking the government for taking all their money in exchange for some instant mashed potatoes. Ed, the businessman, could see what was happening.

It was an inflationary depression. The worst of both worlds. Usually, inflation and a depression are opposites. The inflation is a sign of an overheated economy so prices go up. A boom. A depression is the opposite, the lack of economic activity. Prices fall because no one can buy things. The government wizards who created the Collapse managed to combine the two for an inflationary depression.

The inflation came from creating too many dollars out of thin air and international reluctance to keep financing America's absurd debt. As investors moved away from putting their money into dollars, they started buying up commodities, like food and oil. The ongoing war in the Middle East spiked the price of oil. The entire U.S. economy—all those semi-trucks and everything in them—was dependent on cheap oil. When oil got really expensive, the prices for everything else skyrocketed, too.

At the same time that everything cost more, no one had any money. Who could buy anything when gasoline alone cost $10 a gallon? The economy ground to a halt. Taxes were ridiculously high, too, leaving even less money in most people's pockets. Government regulators were in overdrive, so no rational person would invest in a business only to have a bureaucrat shut them down the next day for no particular reason. Small businesses closed temporarily or just went out of business.

Finally, it got so bad that government couldn't ignore it anymore. Immediately before the Collapse, government started laying off public employees. It was too little too late and it dumped millions of people into the unemployment line. They couldn't pay their mortgages, let alone buy anything. Plus, inflation raised the prices of all the necessities, especially food, so what little money people had went to food, and maybe a little gas. Everything else was dropped.

Especially buying homes. Ed saw that homes were listed for a quarter of what they were in the real estate boom that happened years ago and still weren't selling. Ed's real estate agency hadn't sold a home in six months, and they used to sell hundreds a month.

The economy was essentially dead. America turned into a nation of bankrupt convenience store customers. All the money they had went to Doritos and gas. It was pathetic.

In the few months right before the Collapse, one of the main ways Ed was surviving was by tax evasion. Like millions of other Americans, he pretty much quit paying taxes because everyone knew the IRS couldn't possibly put everyone in jail. The IRS only had enough agents to go after the vocal tax protestors. And they did. While most of the violent felons were released from prisons due to budget cuts, the government still had plenty of money to pay for jail space for tax protestors. It showed where their priorities were.

In the months leading up to the Collapse, the federal government was collecting less than half of what it was a year earlier, and tax rates had gone up substantially. Everyone evaded taxes, except the poor because they didn't pay any. They even collected the Earned Income Tax credit, which was a tax "refund" even though they didn't pay any taxes. It was a complete handout under the guise of a tax refund. Some of them cheated, too, by submitting multiple claims for their "refund." The whole system was corrupt.

And no one cared. The rich evaded taxes, the middle class quit paying them and the poor got their Earned Income Tax credits. No one had a stake in caring.

Ed's savings were gone. He still had plenty of money in the bank, but the banks were closed. His investments were now pretty much worthless with the stock market basically ceasing to function.

He had planned a glorious retirement. He was a Baby Boomer and that's all he and his friends had talked about when they hit their early sixties. Oh well. Just another thing that died when America finally collapsed.

Since his bank accounts and investments were worthless, Ed decided he'd get an FCard. Might as well get some mashed potatoes for he and his wife. He'd paid for them with his taxes and savings. Then he laughed to himself. A few years ago, he would spend hours on the computer obsessing over which fund to put his money in and the returns of this stock or that one. Now he was willing to trade it all in for some "truck stop" food.

Ed was trying to be positive. A dark sense of humor helped many people get through these times. "At least we won't have to worry about how to pay for health care," he said to his wife. "There isn't any health care anymore." He hated going to the doctor, anyway. Problem solved.

Most of the people living around Ed were smart business people. Their regular businesses had been destroyed, but they were still capitalists at heart, even if the government had slowly squeezed almost all the entrepreneurial spirit out of them. Within a week of May Day, some of his neighbors started figuring out things that people needed and how to make money by providing them. They weren't "gouging" people, just accepting much-needed things in exchange for providing much-needed things. Little businesses started to spring up. They were all illegal, of course, but the government was powerless to stop them.

Ed knew a lot about homes. Not just the real estate sales part of them, but also how they were built. He had been either a licensed home inspector or dealt with home inspectors for almost thirty years. So, he let people know that he could look at things in their houses and maybe repair them. Ed had a network of handymen he used on his properties. He would send the work to them, for a slice of it, of course. People would take cash, but in such high amounts that almost no one had that kind of money lying around after the banks closed. Payment would be in goods—food, gas, liquor, whatever—or FCards. There were no photos on FCards; it was all the government could do just to get them up and running without fancy do-dads like verifying people's identity, so FCards could be traded. Just like packs of cigarettes in prison.

Ed wondered if the government intentionally created FCards that could easily be traded and thereby created a new currency; one that didn't have anything of value to back it up. Just like the old dollar.

Plus, the more people with FCards, the more people were fed and not plotting to overthrow the government.

There was one other thing that got traded, but not with Ed. Attractive women seemed to have no trouble acquiring things. Not just women; Seattle had a very large gay population, so attractive men willing to do anything were also well taken care of. At first, most of the "escorts" involved in this would never have considered it. Especially all the cute yuppie soccer moms in West Seattle. Ed had assumed the soccer moms were doing it to feed their kids, but most houses had enough food, even if it was "truck stop" food. To Ed's surprise, most of the women didn't do it to feed their kids; they did it for luxury items. (Well, just day-to-day items taken for granted before the Collapse. But they were "luxuries" after the Collapse.) Not a majority of women did this, but a sizeable minority of them did. Some husbands and boyfriends were fine with it—morals seemed to decline even more after the Collapse—but many weren't. Most women did it secretly. It was survival.

The churches in Seattle did not slow down the rapid moral decline after the Collapse. The churches in Seattle had always been very weak. Church attendance was essentially nonexistent there before the Collapse. After the Collapse, many people in Seattle, as elsewhere, went to church to find some answers. However, the churches in Seattle, which were uniformly liberal or extremely liberal, became administrative arms of the government. The Freedom Corps used churches as distribution points. The government appealed to the people's religious sentiment (what was left of it) as a propaganda tool. "Jesus would share" and "Render unto Caesar" were the government messages aimed at church goers. The government even created the "Faith Corps" for clergy to join. A government religious agency to carry out the government's objectives? The Founders of the nation were spinning in their graves.

During the first few weeks of the Collapse, the government was clearly the strongest organization in the country. But, as the weeks wore on, criminal gangs got stronger and stronger. In the end, the gangs were stronger because they ran the government. Just like what happened in Mexico.

Criminal gangs were often organized along ethnic lines, like the Russians or Mexicans. The criminal gangs ran protection rackets and sold guns, drugs, prostitutes, and gasoline. "Gang gas," as their gasoline became known, was often diluted with water so it didn't run reliably in vehicles. "Gang gas" was useful for arson, but couldn't be counted on for running a car. The government still sold pure gasoline, called "government gas." It was usually reliable.

One of the biggest items gangs sold was guns. Every imaginable kind of gun was for sale. Some were law enforcement and military weapons sold by corrupt cops or soldiers. Guns were illegal, of course, but that law was rarely enforced. When a gun law was enforced, it was a tool to get rid of a government opponent or rival gang member.

Something interesting about guns happened during the Collapse. Guns, which were totally illegal, became a status symbol. People with political power or gangs who were above the law would openly display them. Displaying a gun meant, "I don't have to follow the law. You need to fear me. I can ruin you." The liberals in West Seattle, who hated guns, seemed to love it when powerful people displayed them. It was like the liberals loved the fact that people — *their* people — had power. It was reassuring to the liberals that their kind had so much power. It was hypocrisy, of course: no one can have guns except us, the powerful.

It reminded Ed of the liberals before the Collapse and how they revered rich liberals, like Michael Moore, who were multimillionaires but wanted to take away all the money from the "rich." Hypocrisy was power and the liberals loved the power.

In addition to the traditional criminal gangs, there were also white-collar gangs. They became known as the "Rotary Club gangs." These were the people who, for example, ran health care and sold black market medical services. If someone needed to see a dentist and have some anesthesia for a root canal, they paid the gang that was protecting the dentist's business. They paid the gang in whatever they had, like FCards, and they got dental work. Of course, with all the regulations, a law-abiding dentist must take their insurance and process that, which was impossible given the Collapse. So, when the legal way to operate became impossible, illegal ways sprang up. People needed dental work, after all.

White-collar gangs were interesting because of the people who were in them. Most were government bureaucrats like, in the example of a "gang dentist", the health care regulators who looked the other way when the dentist was accepting FCards. They no longer had government jobs, but they had connections that were extremely valuable. While they wore white collars, everyone knew that they could rent some muscle and hurt people. It was the natural progression of government power. At first, they were regulators using soft governmental force like regulations to get what they wanted. Now they weren't even trying to hide the fact that they were using very direct and brutal force to get what they wanted.

There was another category of gang that was neither a traditional ethnic gang nor a white-collar gang: cops. Some police, most of the ones still left in larger cities, were corrupt. They were either in a gang themselves or were paid by gangs to look the other way, arrest competitors, or use police force on whomever the paying gang wanted. Almost all of the good cops, which had been the majority, left the force during the budget cuts or because they couldn't stand the pre-Collapse corruption. The bad ones—the really bad ones—were what was left. And they were having a field day.

Ed heard rumors about another group to beware of: paras. They were non-government paramilitary groups. Vigilantes, essentially. Since the police were either incapable or bought off, paras would go out and fight crime and corruption. All Ed knew was that once in a while a white-collar or criminal gang member would wind up dead and the cops would just smile.

All of this—the criminal gangs, white-collar gangs, corrupt cops, paras, women selling themselves, everyone breaking the law and dealing in black or gray market, barter instead of cash, small businesses springing up, the economy totally halting—reminded Ed's neighbor, Dmitri, of life during the Russian collapse of the 1990s.

Dmitri was so calm about what was happening. He'd seen it before. Ed asked him what the main difference was between the Russian and American collapses.

"Guns," Dmitri said. "You Americans have so many guns in private hands. In Russia, only the government had guns. There was no way to stop them. But Americans have guns. This is how you will stop this. If you are not too fat and lazy, as I think you might be. Pardon me. I mean no offense. But this is what I see. Good news is your guns, bad news is you have become fat and lazy. We will see which part of America wins."

"How did you make it through the Russian collapse?" Ed asked Dmitri.

"I was the gray man," Dmitri said.

"The what?"

"A gray man," Dmitri said, "is one who lives in a dictatorship or corrupt society without being noticed. Instead of being a freedom fighter, the gray man just blends in, like he is gray; not black or white. He goes along with the authorities when he has to. But when the authorities are not looking, the gray man does all he can to bring them down. He cheats on his taxes, he might sabotage something small, he might even go out at night and hunt down government agents. He is an informant for the resistance, but he does it quietly, without advertising that he is a freedom fighter."

"In the former Soviet Union," Dmitri said, "most people were gray men and women. That is why the regime fell so quickly. Years of weakening the regime from within by the small bits of resistance from the gray men led to the fall of the authorities. And once it was clear that the authorities were losing power, millions of gray men and women sprang into action. This is why the Soviet Union fell apart so quickly. Most people were gray to some degree and they were ready to make life as miserable as possible for the government once they had a chance."

Dmitri thought for a moment. He was struggling with what he was about to say. "I would not have lived if I had been an open freedom fighter. I could only survive by being a gray man." He paused again. "It is not cowardice that leads a gray man to quietly resist instead of openly fighting. It is survival. I did all I could." He looked at Ed and said, "I did all I could." Dmitri obviously felt guilty that he hadn't done more.

"I'm sure you did plenty, Dmitri," Ed said. He thought about what Dmitri said about being a gray man. It made sense. It solved the problem Ed had been struggling with, which was how to resist, but not get killed in the process. Dying didn't accomplish much. Dying was a pretty bad survival plan.

Ed decided that he would be a gray man. But, could he pull it off? Or did the government already know about him? Before the Collapse, he had sued the corrupt state board of realtors and won. He had exposed them. Except no one had cared. With all the government had on its plate now, would they really be keeping track of people who had sued them a few years before? They were struggling to keep people fed. Ed hadn't talked too much about his case at the time because, as glad as he was to expose them, he was still scared of them, so he kept his tussle with the government relatively quiet.

He was doing his part to undermine the government's economy. He wasn't paying his taxes. He laughed at himself: He considered not paying his taxes as his patriotic duty to the cause of liberty. He didn't mind keeping the extra money, either. He was running a small illegal business and helping people fix their homes. That was something small to undermine the government. He owned a shotgun illegally. That was something. He would do more once he got the chance.

But, now the time wasn't right for bold actions ... like the shotgun. Ed knew he would end up doing more than his current tax cheating and small business. He didn't want a lifetime of regret for not doing enough, like Dmitri. Besides, he had seen these government bastards up close. They had tried to ruin him. It was payback time. Just not right at that second. When the time was right.

To be the most effective gray man possible, Ed decided to fool the government into thinking he was a loyal subject. He would quit talking about how he hated them. He would even put up one of those Freedom Corps signs in his yard. All the government suck-ups had them. They were like the "National Recovery Act" signs people had in their homes and businesses during the 1930s telling everyone that they were supporting the government's various economic controls. Yes, Ed would laugh every time he pretended to support the government while he was using that supposed support to blind them to what he was really doing.

He sat back and looked at Dmitri. Gray men like him had done a lot. Ed could do the same. In West Seattle he couldn't exactly hoist a Don't Tread on Me flag. His FCard would be taken away and he'd get arrested for something, probably for having that shotgun. What would that accomplish?

Instead, Ed would choose to survive. He would hollow out the government economy a tiny little bit by having a side business. He would slowly and quietly build up a network of fellow sympathizers. He wouldn't directly ask them if they opposed the government; he'd get to know them and decide whom he could trust when the time was right. Then they would do what Dmitri did.

Ed looked at Dmitri, who was still deep in thought about what more he could have done back in the Soviet Union. Ed smiled and said, "Dmitri, I have some vodka. It's Stolichnaya. Imported from Russia. Would you care to make a toast to the United States government and all they are doing to help us in this unfortunate time of need and how they can count on us to make whatever sacrifice is necessary to see them succeed?"

Dmitri smiled. Ed was talking like a gray man now.

Chapter 107

Professor Matson

(May 10)

Professor Carol Matson sat in her little house near the University of Washington in Seattle and stared at the clock. It was moving so slowly. She realized she was procrastinating. She had to force herself back to finishing the work she had in front of her.

Grading student papers. Yuck. She'd been grading them all day and now it was late. That was the part of teaching she hated. She loved the students, but hated grading papers. She also hated the petty backstabbing of faculty politics.

Oh well. It's what she needed to do to have the job she loved: teaching Latin literature influenced by Simon Bolivar. He was a Latin American revolutionary in the early 1800s. Carol was in a very specialized field of study. In fact, she was one of seven scholars in the world who studied this subject fulltime. She was kind of a big deal in the world of Bolivarian literature.

How had she gone from tiny little Forks, Washington to being a Bolivarian literature professor at the University of Washington? Like her brother Grant, she had gotten the hell out of Forks. She was brilliant, so she got a full scholarship to Columbia University. She took the opportunity to get away from the poverty and abuse there in Hickville in a heartbeat. She gravitated toward Latin studies because, although she was white, she felt the plight of the Latino. She understood being poor and trapped in a socioeconomic class where people were oppressed. Her dad was a total dick, but he was right about politics. She was a socialist like her dad. A stopped clock is right twice a day.

She got her master's degree in Latin Literature at Stanford and got her PhD in the same from Harvard. She loved the recognition she got in school. She was always at the top of her class and every paper she wrote was published in a scholarly journal. She was addicted to academic success. She did everything she could to keep achieving.

It took a toll on her personal life. Actually, what personal life? She moved around a lot, going from Columbia to Stanford to Harvard. She had no time whatsoever for dating. Men were mostly evil, anyway.

The oppressors. Most of the guys she met in her academic world were either gay or total wimps. In fact, looking back at it, she had never really met a normal guy. Most of her female friends and professors were lesbians and constantly told her how bad men were. She wasn't into the lesbian thing — not that she was judging.

After a series of short teaching jobs at various little colleges throughout the country, she finally landed back in Seattle at the University of Washington. She liked it there and she was on the tenure track. She loved living in Seattle. People there were ... well, progressive like her. No rednecks around. She loved walking her dog in the amazing parks in Seattle. She loved the food at the organic grocery stores. She loved the lattes. She loved the whole Seattle experience. It was the exact opposite of Middle America in Forks. That's where everyone was stupid and bigoted. She looked back at her life. She had accomplished everything she set out to. Life was good.

Then the Crisis started. All the conservative politicians, the rednecks who ran the country, even when Democrats were in charge, decided to get some votes by punishing public employees. That's how the Crisis started. The conservatives decided to slash the budgets and lay off public employees like ... university professors. The voters were so greedy. They wanted more money for their pork rinds and NASCAR. Idiots. They wouldn't pay their fair share of taxes so people could be educated. So shortsighted. If there aren't any Bolivarian literature professors, how can a society be truly educated?

It was no surprise that the people rose up during the Crisis. By the "people," she meant the public employees being unfairly targeted for the draconian cuts. She joined the unions in their protests, but she never got violent like some of them did.

Carol, as a proud socialist progressive, had never liked the government. It was so corporate and reactionary. But, she had to admit, during the Crisis, the government was doing the best it could. There were shortages at the stores, but that was to be expected. Fat greedy Americans shouldn't expect to get everything they wanted on demand, so shortages would actually teach them a lesson. She had been hungry for a while several days go, but it wasn't the government's fault. It was using its emergency powers to go get these teabagger "Patriot" militia whackos. Then the government finally did what it should have done years ago: nationalized most of the economy. What took so long? Carol was especially happy about the FCards. What a brilliant solution, converting bloated retirement accounts of the rich into food for the masses. Simon Bolivar would be proud.

She and her brother Grant weren't close. He was an okay guy and she wished him the best. He would probably say the same about her, but they were so different. She couldn't stand his politics. What a hillbilly knuckle dragger he was. All that conservative crap he was always talking about. And he was religious. He had fallen for every lie the capitalists had put out there. It was sad, really. But whatever. He wasn't hurting anyone.

Or was he? One of Carol's colleagues, a professor in the Latin Studies department, told Carol that a "Grant Matson" was on the POI list. Was it her brother? She was afraid for him. His crazy politics had gone too far.

Yep, it was him. Grant Matson of Olympia, Washington who worked for the Washington Association of Business. Oh no. Her own brother was a terrorist. Her first thought, she was embarrassed to admit, was whether she would lose her job because of it. Wait. She couldn't lose her job. She was tenured. The stores around the University were pretty well stocked. She was even starting to get her beloved lattes again with her FCard. She would be fine.

This would all be over soon, she said. She'd probably be teaching again in the fall. The government would solve the problems. They had all the smart people working for them. How hard could it be get rid of these right-wingers? The teabaggers were stupid. Not educated at all.

She hoped her brother wouldn't get hurt but, quite honestly, he had done this to himself. If he wanted to be a macho "Patriot" and that was against the law, then he needed to pay for his actions. It would all work out. She was confident that socialism would make people's lives better in America. Just like it had all over the world.